I0819426

THE SAPPHIRE SEA

Books by Davis Bunn

The Miramar Bay Series

Miramar Bay
Firefly Cove
Moondust Lake
Tranquility Falls
The Cottage on Lighthouse Lane
The Emerald Tide
Shell Beach
Midnight Harbor
The Christmas Hummingbird
The Christmas Cottage

The Outer Banks Series

Fortunate Harbor
A Sea Glass Christmas
The Sapphire Sea

THE SAPPHIRE SEA

DAVIS BUNN

kensingtonbooks.com

KENSINGTON BOOKS are published by

Kensington Publishing Corp.
900 Third Ave.
New York, NY 10022

All Kensington titles, imprints, and distributed lines are available at special quantity discounts for bulk purchases for sales promotion, premiums, fund-raising, educational, or institutional use. Special book excerpts or customized printings can also be created to fit specific needs. For details, write or phone the office of the Kensington Special Sales Manager: Attn. Special Sales Department, Kensington Publishing Corp., 900 Third Ave., New York, NY 10022. Phone: 1-800-221-2647.

Library of Congress Control Number: On file

KENSINGTON and the K with book logo Reg. US Pat. & TM Off.

ISBN: 978-1-4967-5424-0
First Kensington Hardcover Edition: May 2026

ISBN: 978-1-4967-5425-7 (ebook)

10 9 8 7 6 5 4 3 2 1

Printed in the United States of America

The authorized representative in the EU for product safety and compliance
is eucomply OU, Parnu mnt 139b-14, Apt 123
Tallinn, Berlin 11317, hello@eucompliancepartner.com

This Book Is Dedicated To:

WENDY MCCURDY

with heartfelt thanks

And very best wishes for success and happiness

As you turn the page

Chapter 1

Rocky Mount, NC
November, 2005

By the time he turned six, Colin spent a lot of time at the living room window. He watched the cars come and go, traced designs on the glass made by the mix of sunlight and dust, and waited for his father to return home. Those very first signs of his father's mood were crucial.

Soon after his mother's death when he was four, Colin started reading. His father had increasingly become silent and remote, and Colin found comfort in the mystery of letters. He learned mostly through watching education shows meant for children twice his age. By five he had read all the children's books available. By six he was reading everything he could get his hands on and was sneaking books on mathematics from the public library.

Their housekeeper was a heavyset woman named Adsila, whose mother was Cherokee and her father black. Adsila was as quiet as his father, who was sheriff of Edgecombe

County. Colin's father had done something to keep Adsila's son from going to prison. Her loyalty to Sheriff Roger Eames was total.

The summer before Colin entered school, Adsila began taking him to the public library four blocks from their home. The Braswell Memorial Library had opened three years earlier and still shone like a new penny. Colin loved those visits more than anything. Adsila would lead him into the children's section, then sit at a table in the Periodicals where she could keep an eye on him and read magazines for two hours. Adsila was fully aware of how Colin took books from the adult section. As long as he remained where she could see him, Adsila seemed unconcerned. Colin could have stayed there for years, surrounded by all these new friends.

His mother seemed very close to him then. Brenda Eames had often read her son to sleep, and occasionally Colin heard her now, whispering in that singsong manner she had used when he was still very young. Other times he sat and thought of their happiest moments together, days spent on the Outer Banks, Roger standing in the waves surf casting, his wife seated next to where Colin built sand castles. Brenda Eames could spend hours watching the ocean. She always came home smiling.

One day several weeks into June, Adsila told him, "I seen you in there, doing something on your daddy's computer when he's off working."

Colin had no idea how to respond. Two years after she entered their home, his relationship with Adsila remained a mystery. The midday sun turned the sidewalk into a brilliant mirror. He walked alongside her, and remained silent.

Adsila continued, "You need to ask his permission."

The words froze him. Colin stood in the heat and squinted up at her. "I can't."

Adsila was a handsome woman, in a strong and somber way. She inspected him for a time, then asked, "What is it you do online for all those hours on end?"

"I go to Davidson School."

"And do what, exactly?"

"It's called Plan Day."

"You mean, Play Day."

Colin saw no reason to correct her. "Will you tell him?"

Adsila studied him a moment longer, then started on, "Let's get out of the heat."

Over the past two years Colin's father had undergone a gradual transition that worried Adsila and terrified his son. Colin always took the same position when he heard the car pull into the garage. His father was a big man, well over six feet and heavy with hard muscle and a harder life. When he was sober, his father's tread held a dancer's grace, quick and natural.

On the bad days, Colin slipped up beside the opening where the parlor met the hall running the length of the house. Standing half in and half out of the kitchen. Waiting to see if his father headed for the cabinet beside the refrigerator where he always kept a half-gallon bottle of Maker's Mark. Something about those bad afternoons left Roger carrying a barely controlled fury.

On the worst days, Roger stopped at a bar frequented by off-duty police. Then he arrived late and stumbled his way through the normal motions of crossing the garage and locking away his weapons. He came in and ignored his dinner in the warming oven and took out the bottle and a glass. The first drink went down before he even seated himself at the table. He would sit there and glare at the opposite wall, muttering disconnected words about how the region was turning into a place he no longer recognized. Those nights, Colin scampered upstairs, often not venturing down for dinner. A night's hunger was far better than confronting his father in a rage.

As his father's drinking came to dominate most evenings, Adsila began staying longer. She was comfortable with wordless hours, drifting through her housework with scarcely a sound. His father seemed to find an odd solace in her silent presence. On occasion Roger talked politics with her—politics in their hometown, politics at the state level, or the awful government in Washington. Adsila often hummed a tuneless note, neither agreeing nor disagreeing, saying almost nothing.

Colin's entire world changed the year he entered school. It happened on the nineteenth of September, the hottest autumn day anyone could remember. When Colin thought back on it later, it seemed impossible that so much could have been compressed between one rising and setting of the sun.

The events began as soon as Colin entered the kitchen. He was still rubbing the sleep from his eyes when his father turned from spooning coffee into the machine and said, "I'm making us breakfast. Where is Adsila?" When Colin pointed to the washing machine running in the garage, Roger said, "Go tell her to join us. I've got something you both need to hear."

Colin remained where he was, watching this man who looked like his father and wore his father's uniform. But the words did not make sense. His father never did anything in the kitchen except eat and drink. He never spoke to anyone at the start of his day. Putting on his game face was how his father had once described it over a glass of Maker's Mark. Getting ready for whatever the streets threw his way.

"Did you hear what I said?" He used what Colin called his cop's voice. Hard and definite. "Tell her she needs to get in here on the double."

The laundry room was located in what once had served as a bathroom for workers. Their home was surrounded by almost two acres of lawn. Every day he wasn't on duty, right through the winter months, Roger Eames was out trimming and weeding and mowing. When Colin entered, he found Adsila standing by the ironing board, watching. He relayed the message and raced back into the kitchen. "She's coming."

"Make yourself useful, why don't you. Get out the butter. You want some eggs? Sure you do, you're a skinny little runt, you need to put on some weight."

Colin squeezed himself into the corner between the fridge and the sink and watched as his father used a fork to swish the eggs around the frying pan. Colin knew the Teflon coating might get scratched, but he didn't say a word. When his father was in a rage, going unnoticed was safest. Only his father didn't look angry. Colin decided he had no idea what his father's mood might be.

Soon as Adsila entered the kitchen, his father started talking. "Big things are happening for me. Big tidings I got to share. I want you both to pay careful attention. I don't have time to be repeating myself. Not today, and not for a lot of days to come." He turned and used the fork to point Colin into a dining table chair. He waited there, motionless, until they were both seated. Colin watched half-cooked egg drip from the fork, wondering what it all meant.

His father turned back to the stove and said, "Got a call from the mayor yesterday." His fork moved with blinding speed, whipping the eggs before he lifted the skillet and spilled the contents onto three plates. "The mayor himself. Seems the movers and shakers have been talking about me. They decided I should become county commissioner. The fellow they've backed for ten years has a family crisis. He's just been reelected, so he's waiting until the start of next year, then he's resigning. They'll back me, and the other commissioners have all agreed to do the same. Two years they want me in that job. One round. Then it's on to Raleigh. They want me to run for the state senate."

He carried over two plates and deposited them in front of Adsila and his son. Returned for forks and his own plate. He seated himself between them and began eating. His motions were jerky, like a dog used to fighting for scraps, that was how it seemed to Colin. Like a man who was so excited he was almost angry. He said between bites, "You and me, boy, we're going to be in the public light. That was the real reason why the mayor called me. To make sure I understood. *We* understood. That things are changing for the better. And to make it work, we have to be a team. You're going to be out there in the public light with me." He took aim with his fork. "Adsila, now, your job is to get my boy ready when it's time for him."

"I don't have nothing to do with any of that." Adsila rose to her feet. She stared down at Roger, her gaze as hard as her tone. "You want me to clean your house, that's fine. But what you got to understand is, this boy of yours is nobody's puppet."

Colin tried to remember another time when Adsila had stood up for him, and came up blank. Clearly his father was just as surprised. "Who said anything about that? I need him—"

"And I'm telling you this isn't just about what you need." She planted fists on hips. "You lost your wife, you been dealing with it best you can. But the truth is, you've had the heart ripped out of your chest. And that blindness means you don't have any idea how much that boy is hurting, same as you. His momma is gone and his daddy . . ." She stopped, huffed once, then quietly declared, "Your boy is special. It's high time you see that for yourself."

His father stared at the empty doorway as her gentle tread made the kitchen floor creak. Only when the garage door clicked shut did he jerk slightly. He examined Colin and asked, "You going to give me any trouble?"

Colin had no idea what his father was talking about. Even so, he knew it was safest to shake his head.

"Good." His father picked up Adsila's plate and shoveled the contents onto his own. The bullet head bent back over and he resumed eating. His father's hair was cropped so short the scalp was visible. "Eat your eggs."

On the school bus and in the hallway and as he entered class, Colin mulled over what had just happened. It was the first time Colin had ever heard Adsila mention his mother. Recalling the words made his eyes burn.

He was usually the first to sit down. School was an enormously confusing place, loud and rough, the children constantly doing things he didn't understand. The classroom was quiet, at least until the bell rang. He liked the smell of chalk and dust and the cleaner they used on the floor. The teacher was strange as well, how she exuded such delight over the simplest of things, shining down her special joy when a student got something right.

"Colin, good, I was hoping you would be here." She entered and smiled in her lovely, special way. "Will you come with me, please?"

He looked at the clock on the wall above the door. "It's almost nine."

"What do you know, you can tell time." She walked over and smiled down at him. "Those are the first words you have spoken in this classroom. Ever."

He had no idea how to respond except, "Class is about to start."

"It is. But there's someone I want you to meet, and she has time for you now. Her name is Celeste Talbot. She's a very special lady, and she's come a long way to meet you." She offered her hand. "We don't want to keep her waiting."

They walked like that, him holding the teacher's hand, through the crowd of noisy children, all of whom watched the two of them. The girls stared, the boys laughed out loud. Colin felt his face flame red, but for once he did not mind. He liked her closeness, the scent of lilacs in her clothes, the warmth in her hand as she guided him forward.

They entered the principal's outer office, where a dark, heavyset woman stood by the window, studying a file. She turned toward them and said, "Is this the man of the hour?"

"Colin Eames, can you say hello to Dr. Talbot?"

"How do you do, Colin?" She did not seem to expect a reply. Instead, she motioned to the principal's open door. "Why don't we go inside?"

Colin knew they probably expected him to be frightened, especially when his teacher remained in the outer office. But there was something about this big woman, a deep, penetrating force to her gaze, that left him feeling okay. He liked the way she studied him. Like she *saw* him. Like she *cared.*

The room was empty save for them. The lady pointed him into a straight-backed chair, then pulled another one in so close they almost sat with their knees touching. She looked even bigger from this angle, a dark mountain of a woman encased in a navy suit. "I want you to call me Celeste, all right? Adsila is my sister-in-law. She's married to my older brother. She's spoken about you a few times, and I've also heard some things from your teacher. I'm going to give it to you straight. Most of the time I'm called in when a child has troubles. Problems at home, in the street, maybe even problems inside themselves. I'm supposed to deliver a first assessment. That's a fancy word meaning I'm supposed to check you out. See if you need help. Are we clear so far, Colin? Are you paying attention?"

"Yes."

"That's good. Real good. Because the only way we can make this work is, first, you need to be paying careful attention. Second, you need to tell me what's on your mind. Will you do that?"

He nodded.

"There, see? I knew you were going to be a great one to work with. Do I scare you, Colin? Are you frightened?"

He shook his head.

"Can you say that out loud for me?"

"No, I'm not scared of you."

"And what a lovely voice you have. Okay, Colin. I want to ask you a question. And I want you to give it to me straight. Tell me the first thing that comes into your mind. Just let it out. Nobody else but us two here is going to hear what you have to say. What is it you're thinking?"

It just popped into his head. Like a tiny electric spark he had not even noticed until that moment. "What is a tempest in a teapot?"

She actually laughed out loud. "What on earth?"

Colin liked her then. She had a laugh like a big human bell. "It's something I read last night."

She lost her smile. "You *read* it."

"Just before I went to bed. The last thing."

"Where did you read this, Colin?"

"The Raleigh *News and Observer* editorial page." He was sorry to see her smile go away. "I know what a tempest is. And a teapot. But the two words together, they don't make sense. The editorial had it in there twice. Once, maybe it was a mistake. But not two times."

She reached for her purse and drew out her phone. "I think maybe I'd better record this conversation. Is that okay with you, Colin?"

"I guess."

"What do you think tempest means?"

"A big storm. Violent. Dangerous."

"That's exactly right." Her words came more slowly now. Careful. Precise. "A tempest in a teapot means someone or something is making a big fuss about nothing."

Colin rocked back and forth. "Wow."

"Okay, Colin, remember what I said at the beginning? I need you to be honest with me. I can almost see the gears in that beautiful little head of yours grinding away. Tell me what you're thinking. Let me share in what's happening here."

He loved how she watched him. Totally focused on *him.* There was nothing else in the world except her and him. Together. Talking with her was as easy as being silent most of the time. "I love having things become clear. What you said, it makes me understand the editorial. The person writing—his name was Doctor Arthur M. Bell—he's angry because the Supreme Court wants a university in Wisconsin to change its admission policy to promote affirmative action. He says a state university should be allowed to make its own mind up. Not follow rules laid down in Washington." He stumbled twice in explaining, over *affirmative* and *admission.* "Long words are hard."

"Yes, they most certainly are." She seemed to find a need to draw in closer still. "Do you like reading the editorial page?"

"I like how it shows the way people think."

"Why does that interest you, Colin?"

Suddenly he found himself wanting to cry. Since his father

had started drinking most nights, he'd come to hate it whenever Colin cried. Stop acting like a baby, he'd said, shouting at Colin. Stand up and be a *man*.

Colin swallowed hard and said, "People are so confusing."

She reached out and gripped his knee. Just for a moment. But in the touch Colin felt the same warm strength he saw in the woman's gaze. "Do you like numbers?"

He nodded. "A whole lot."

"I'm going to skip over the simple stuff and go straight to the gravy. Can you tell me what is seven times eight?"

"Fifty-six."

"Okay. Good. How about fifty-three times one hundred and six?"

"Five thousand six hundred and eighteen."

She studied him a moment, tapped on her phone, studied him some more. "Do you know what a square root is, Colin? No? Okay, the square of a number is when you multiply it by itself. So the square of seven is . . ."

"Forty-nine."

"Right on the money. So the square root is the opposite value. When you multiply it by itself, it gives you the original number. So the square root of seven, what do you think that is?"

"That's a hard one."

"Why is that?"

"Because the numbers just keep going on and on."

If anything, the fire in that dark gaze grew fiercer still. "Give me just the first five numbers."

"Two point six four five seven." His heart raced with the thrill of learning something new. *Square. Square root.* He was going to have fun with those.

She rose to her feet. "You just wait right there. I won't be a moment."

Celeste Talbot moved fast for a woman her size. Colin heard voices in the outer office, then Celeste returned holding a newspaper and a book. "Okay, now. Have you seen today's paper?"

"No. I only read it after school."

She handed him the front page. "So tell me what it says here . . . let's see, this article looks safe enough. What does this headline say?"

"'Deal with Iran's regime back on the table.'"

"Do you know what that means?"

"Not exactly." Colin saw her register a genuine disappointment. He suddenly found himself wanting her to be pleased. So he rushed, "I mean, I know they're negotiating"—another tough word—"and Iran is saying America has to lift sanctions. But I don't know what's happened since yesterday because I didn't read the paper yet."

"Iran has dropped their demands for us to take the first step, is what I think they're saying." She was flipping through pages of the book she held as she spoke. Then she handed it to him. "Can you read this?" She saw he was looking at the three people now crowded into the doorway. "Don't pay them any mind, Colin. Just read this text, please."

He leaned over the page and read where her finger pointed. "'All too often in childhood the fires of genius falter. There is a very great risk that unless proper care is given, the fire may become snuffed out.'"

"All right, that's enough." She took the book from him. "Do you understand that term, snuffed out?"

"Like when a candle stops burning."

"Exactly. And that's what I want to speak with your father about. Keeping your candle lit." She was intent upon him, laser focused. Which meant she saw his sudden flash of fear. She glanced at the trio in the doorway, then looked down at the file in her lap. She turned a page. Another. "Your father is the sheriff."

She had not asked a question, and Colin saw no need to respond.

"Your mother passed away when you were very young. I'm so sorry. You must miss her very much." She closed the file. "I think maybe you and I should have a talk with your father."

CHAPTER 2

The day took on a pristine quality, as if sunlight itself was transformed into a gift. On the one hand, everything remained the same. Colin returned to his boring classes. During recess and mealtime, he stayed on the periphery as usual, observing the other children, staying safe. Just the same, the hours passed in a steady flow of mystery and change. Colin could not identify precisely why he felt that way, except for how eyes followed him everywhere.

When school ended that afternoon, Adsila stood on the sidewalk beyond the playground. Another first. She took him to the neighborhood diner. They had been there once before, on his sixth birthday, when his father had spent the afternoon at what Adsila called the cop bar. Colin ordered the same meal, cheeseburger and fries and root beer. Once he finished, she walked him down to the library, pointed at the adult section, and told him, "You don't need to sneak around anymore. Just go read what you want."

If he had needed any indication that the day continued along an amazing course, it was here and now.

Colin spent a few minutes walking along several of the aisles. He had heard the librarians refer to them as the stacks, a name that he liked very much. All the rows of books rising up higher than he could reach, even if he stood on one of the little ladders on rollers. Now and then he touched a title imprinted on a book's spine. Gently saying hello to friends he had not met.

He selected a book he had browsed through briefly at the end of his last visit. He took it to an empty table and sat staring at the cover, relishing in the freedom this hour represented. Colin found himself thinking back over how this remarkable day had started, the way Adsila had stood up for him. He had no idea what that exchange had meant. Nor, just then, did it matter.

The book's cover might as well have been a mirror into the past, the way it drew him from the library and sent him back to his favorite memory of his mother. Seated in the sand, listening to the waves, feeling the soft crystalline mush drip through his fingers and form a castle where they might someday live.

His recollection shifted then, taking him to a place and time he rarely allowed himself to revisit. Nights after their visits to the Crystal Coast, Colin's mother always told him the same bedtime story. About a place called the Sapphire Sea, where everybody loves everyone, and happiness is a way of life. Mistakes are forgotten and forgiven. Songs are sung for a lifetime. And dreams are meant to be shared. It always made Colin's mother sad, talking about this place only she could see. Yet somehow it drew them closer together. As if she revealed to him her secret place, the one nestled deep in her heart.

Two and a half hours later, he looked up to find Adsila and Celeste standing over him. "What's that you have there?"

He closed the book and turned it around so they could see the cover: *The Art of Thinking.*

"Told you," Adsila said.

Celeste drove a nearly new Buick SUV. It was the nicest car Colin had ever been in. She watched him rub his hand along the seat. "Do you like cars, Colin?"

He nodded. "A lot."

"What else do you like? I know you like reading. It sounds like you enjoy math. And I know people confuse you. What makes you happy?"

So many of her questions left him feeling confused and unsettled. Even so, he was able to say, "I'm happy now."

She glanced over, then back to the road, then looked at him again. But she remained silent until she halted at a stop sign and could give him her full attention. "Why do you think that is? That you're happy."

"Because you see me."

The muscles of her jaw and neck bunched tight. A horn honked behind them. She returned her attention to the road and did not speak again until they pulled up in front of his home.

Adsila and two other people stood by cars parked on the street's opposite side. Celeste rose from her Buick and walked around to Colin's door, as if she intended to shield him. She asked her sister-in-law, "You're certain about what we'll find?"

"It's Friday," Adsila replied. She pointed to Roger Eames's car. "You take a good look there, you know what's going on inside that house."

It was the first time Colin realized Adsila knew why he waited by the front window. His father's car was parked with two wheels in the grass, like he had taken aim at the garage's open door but could not quite bring the vehicle into alignment. So he left it where it was, partly blocking the curved walk leading to their front door. On days when Roger Eames could not enter his own garage, Colin knew he would be missing another meal.

Celeste turned and waved to the people waiting across the street. "Let's get this over with."

Adsila locked her arms across her middle. "Who's that woman there?"

"She's from Child Services. I need a formal witness, in case there's trouble." She waved to the other person, a tall man in a police uniform. "Thanks so much, Jerry. I owe you one."

"No problem." He smirked at the car, asked, "How do you want to play this?"

"I'm hoping we won't need you. But if you could stay out here, you know."

"Got it."

Celeste turned to Adsila. "You should go."

"What for? The man is going to know I had a hand in this."

"Just the same." She hugged the larger woman. "You did the right thing, bringing me in."

Adsila remained as she was, her arms held tight to her ribs. "Sheriff Eames took care of my boy when he got in all that trouble. I owe him." She cast a single glance at Colin. "But his son is special. This boy deserves better than he's getting."

"It's why I'm here." Celeste stood by the curb and waited until Adsila drove away. She told the others, "Let's get this over with."

Colin used the key hanging from the strap he always carried around his neck, along with a tiny ID inside its plastic cover. His father had told him time and again never to lose it, never take it off outside the house. He never did.

Then he opened the door, and the smell hit him.

The odor was strong as a punch to his gut. The pungent stench formed part of his nighttime terrors.

"Stay right here, Colin. Angie, you best record this." She started inside the house, then turned back and waved to the police officer. "Jerry, do *not* let this child inside."

Even when she was so severe she sounded angry, Colin was not afraid of her. The heat was a harsh element, strong as the odor drifting through the front door. He heard Celeste call out, asking if anyone was home. He could see her move swiftly from room to room, followed by the nervous young woman who held her phone up like a shield. Colin felt the sweat begin to gather and bead on his face and back. The heat and pungent odor pressed on him, pushing him away from where he stood. His feet remained planted on the front step, but inside he shifted back. Farther and farther away.

He watched from a far distance as Celeste came rushing back outside, drawing the younger woman by a hand on her shoulder. The social services officer walked at an angle so as to keep her phone aimed behind them as . . .

Roger Eames stumbled into view. The beast from Colin's nightmares was revealed now, the sickly stain down the front of his disheveled uniform, the massive hands that grasped at nothing, the rage, the roar.

Celeste yelled, "*Jerry!*"

The police officer rushed forward and took an iron grip on Roger Eames, halting his forward momentum, shouting at the man to back up, take it easy, hold where he was or be cuffed and stuffed inside the police car. Colin doubted his father heard anything at all. Colin felt Celeste place a hand on his shoulder and guide him around. But all he could see was how his father raged. The beast. At him.

Celeste led him back to her Buick and restarted the engine. When the cool air struck his face, he began to tremble. But Celeste had already turned away, talking on her phone now. By the time a second police car arrived and they subdued his father, Colin was shivering from head to toe. The sight of three officers forcefully stopping his father from reaching Celeste's car only made his tremors worse. Almost like he was freezing. Even though he kept sweating the whole time.

CHAPTER 3

Celeste lived in a modest home on the outskirts of Mill Village, a historic neighborhood that had once held tenant houses rented to workers of the Tar River factories. The street was lined with older houses, mostly single story, and was crowded with old cars and workers' vans. The yards were mostly neat and the porches were lined with flowers in hanging pots. Many were fenced in, and most of those held children playing and shouting. All the faces Colin saw were black.

She carried his little case up the front walk and through the door and into a room at the very end of a long hallway. There was no window and very little furniture, just a wooden chair and child's desk and a pallet neatly made up on the floor. "You'll be safe here," Celeste declared, setting his case in the corner. "Now go wash up and come join me in the kitchen."

When he emerged from the bathroom, Colin found a girl standing by the next door. She was a good head taller and watched him pass with a hard gaze. As he entered the kitchen, he heard her say, "Mama's done brought home another stray. Skinny and white and scared like them others. At least this one don't look all beat up." And a boy's voice replied, "Huh."

It was just the four of them at dinner, Colin and the girl and her younger brother and Celeste. Her two children cast Colin unwelcoming looks, then ignored him entirely. The woman made no effort to break the silence. Colin did not mind. He had lived with silent meals all his life. The food was different from what he was used to, so spicy it made his mouth tingle. He realized the two kids were watching to see if he complained. He ate everything, then accepted a second portion. Her children seemed disappointed, but Celeste rewarded him with a pat on the head.

After dinner, when he started to help clear the table, Celeste gave her two children a very hard look. "Now isn't that nice." The sullen girl got the message and stood and carried her plate to the sink. The boy did a boneless slide off his chair, walked back down the hall, and slammed the door.

As the girl lifted the drying towel, Celeste pointed to the living room and told Colin, "There's a few books in there. Go see if you can find something to read, then come back and keep us company."

The room was spotless, the furniture old but well cared for. The entire rear wall was covered with shelves, and every shelf was crammed with books. Colin had never seen so many books outside the library. These were lined up like soldiers on parade, many of them hardbacks with titles he did not understand. He took one down at random and tried to make sense of the words: *Signs of Arrested Development in Pre-teen Adolescents.* He replaced it on the shelf and chose one from a line of leather-bound books, all of which held the same gold lettering. The titles shouted a silent symphony that made him shiver.

When he carried it back into the kitchen, Celeste turned from washing dishes and asked, "What you got there?" The question turned the girl around as well. Celeste's daughter looked at the book in his hands and her face grew harder still. It seemed everything he did made her angry. But Celeste merely turned back to her chore. "I bought all those books at a garage sale. 'Novels That Shaped the World.' Only made my way through half a dozen so far."

The girl spoke for the first time since entering the kitchen. "What you going on about? That boy's too little to know what he's holding."

Colin opened the cover. The title page was written in a script he had never seen before, with curling ends to the letters so that they flowed into each other. He thought it was the most beautiful thing he had ever seen. "What's a musketeer?"

Celeste watched her daughter turn around, this time her anger tinted with something new. Surprise, perhaps. Celeste smiled and pronounced the word correctly, then said, "A musketeer was an old-timey soldier. That was in France, back when there were kings fighting the church for power." She glanced at her daughter and continued, "The story is all about how love and honor can take you through the hardest of times."

The book had a musty smell, like it too belonged in some distant era. A time set apart from days when a drunken father raged at people who shielded his own son. He turned the page and started reading.

The next morning Colin woke to discover the book on the pallet beside him. He had fallen asleep reading, and the pages where he left off were crimped from having been folded wrong. He sat up and ran his hand over and over the paper until he could no longer see the creases.

He used the bathroom, then dressed and walked down the hall. The house held a calm air, and Colin sensed the two children had already left. Celeste was talking on her cell phone, a trio of files open on the table before her. Colin listened as she talked about several names, something about reassigning appointments. Then she noticed him standing in the doorway and said, “I have to go. You know where to find me.” She cut the connection and smiled. “I was just coming to wake you. Do you like pancakes?”

After she started breakfast and had deposited a glass of milk on the table in front of Colin, Celeste left the kitchen and returned with his book. “Show me how far you’ve gotten.”

Colin was frightened she would be upset over the creased pages. But if Celeste noticed, she gave no sign. She studied the number at the bottom of the page. One hundred and sixty-five. “Did you understand everything you read?”

“Not all the words. But I like the story.”

“Did you now.”

He nodded. “A lot.”

She patted his head and moved to the stove. “Child, you’re a wonder.”

The pancakes were served with butter and a bright splash of cherry jam on the side. Then she placed a small bowl of fruit by his left hand. Another glass of milk. “I need to go shower and dress. Are you going to be all right here on your own?”

Colin slid the book over beside his plate and began eating. The pancakes stayed crisp and moist because there wasn’t syrup to make them soggy. He alternated bites, one with jam and the next with a bit of fruit. There was apple and blueberry and watermelon. He didn’t like the watermelon very much, but having something that wasn’t a favorite made all the other flavors taste better. The antics of the musketeers kept him company through the entire meal. It was the best breakfast he had ever eaten.

Celeste made him go shower, and when he entered his little room he found fresh underwear and socks and shirt and long trousers laid out on his pallet. He didn't like how the trousers felt on his legs, especially in the heat. But Colin dressed in them anyway. When he emerged, Celeste gave him a quick inspection and ordered, "Tuck in your shirt. Good." She took a brush from her purse and passed it through his hair. He had never much cared for how it looked, half brown and half yellow with a hint of red stuck in as well. But Celeste said, "Your hair reminds me of autumn." He liked anything that made this woman smile.

Celeste drove in silence for almost an hour, then turned in by what to Colin looked like a big-city hospital. It reminded Colin of where his father had taken him to see his own mother, Colin's last remaining grandparent. The woman had been very old and very sick. She had examined him for a long moment, her eyes the only part of her that seemed alive. Then she had turned her face away. As if she had accomplished a bothersome chore. His father's grip on Colin's shoulder tightened momentarily, then he had steered his son out the door and down the hall and out to the car. His father had driven Colin home, as silent and expressionless as his own mother.

Celeste pulled into a parking space marked "Administration" and cut the motor. She took her phone from the cup holder between the seats and pressed a number. She said, "We're here." Celeste listened a moment, then, "No, Arnold. Have I ever wasted your time before? Don't tell me—I know perfectly well how old he is." Another pause, then, "We'll give him another five minutes. If he doesn't show up by then . . . Wait, I think I see him. And he's got the lady from Sojourn with him, what's her name, Fitzgerald."

A car passed their spot and pulled into a visitor's space farther down the line. A man with unkempt white hair rose from the car. He appeared to be in a great rush. Colin thought the woman who accompanied him looked angry. The man pulled a briefcase and jacket from the back seat, then made a mess of putting on his coat as together they rushed for the entrance.

Celeste said, "They're heading in now. Try to smooth their ruffled feathers, will you? Yes, I'm coming."

She stowed her phone in her purse, then said to Colin, "You remember what I told you yesterday?"

"I remember every word."

Something in the way he spoke seemed to calm her down. The irritated glint vanished from her gaze, and she smiled at him. "Child, you don't know what a breath of fresh air you are."

Colin replied, "I like you very much."

"Well, that's something we have in common, then." She pointed to the entrance. "I know there's a dozen different reasons in there for you to get scared. But you can't be frightened, you hear what I'm telling you? Don't you go quiet on me either."

"I won't," Colin said. "I promise."

But she wasn't done. "It's all going to seem very confusing. These people, they might not even seem nice to you. But none of that matters. You have to show them the very best that you are. How smart you are, how perceptive, how aware."

He felt that final word echo through his brain. *Aware.* He liked the power she gave it. The intensity of her gaze, the fierce protective nature that he could almost taste.

"Will you do that for me, child?"

"Yes." He wanted to say he would do anything to make her pleased with him. But she was already up and exiting the car.

The lettering over the entrance read, "UNC-Greenville Child Care and Development Center." The lobby was very big and the walls were covered with photographs of happy children and paintings of rainbows and animals and trees and lakes and sunlight. Even so, Colin felt a vague unease, as if a secret whispered in the cold air-conditioning, something dark and hidden behind a hall of closed doors.

Celeste must have noticed his unease because she took a firmer hold of his hand and said, "Remember what I told you."

They took the elevator to the fourth floor. A man in a white doctor's coat stood in the hallway, his arms crossed around a bulky file. He looked askance at Colin, as if he could not bring him into focus. "Really, Celeste? Really?"

The woman released Colin's hand, but only so she could move in close to the doctor. She kept moving forward until she would have collided with him had he not stepped back. Whatever he saw in Celeste's gaze brought him to a state of rigid uncertainty. She remained there, glaring at him, as she said, "Colin, say hello to Dr. Arnold."

"Hello."

"Hi . . . Colin, right?" He cleared his throat and stepped around the big woman. "Why don't we get started?"

But she wasn't done. She slapped his chest with the file she had brought, a sharp sound like hands clapping. "The only reason I put up with your attitude is because you're working part-time at the academy."

"Celeste . . ."

"Yes, I know your focus is adolescents. Yes, I know he is *six years old*. And I'm telling you, look closely and tell me whether his *age* matters even *one little bit.*"

Celeste locked him with her gaze. When she finally turned around, she knelt in front of Colin. "You won't see me. But I'll be right there."

Colin wished he could hug her. "Okay."

She must have found what she sought in his gaze. Because she rose and turned back to the doctor. "This is as serious as serious can be."

"Sure, Celeste. Okay."

"If you don't think you can *handle* this, if you can't take this *seriously,* you just let me know. I'll inform the director, see if we can't— "

"Celeste, I'm telling you I've got this."

"All right, then."

He watched the big woman walk down the hall, knock on a door, and enter. Then he turned to Colin. "Come with me."

The room was almost completely featureless. The walls and table and chairs were all a vague off-white. The ceiling was tiled in white blocks that were perforated with little holes. The lighting came from long white fluorescent bulbs with metal strips forming a checkerboard pattern. The wall to Colin's right held a long mirror, tall and framed in wood painted the same color as the walls. Each corner of the room held a small black bulb. Colin thought they were probably cameras.

Dr. Arnold seated himself across the table from Colin and set the two files unopened on the surface between them. "Do you have any questions before we begin?"

He could hear a tight undercurrent to the man's voice. Colin had learned early and well to detect such elements. At home, this hidden rage could be very dangerous. It usually marked the time when he did his best to melt away. Even if it meant missing a meal. But Colin remembered everything Celeste had said, and did his best to erase the fear.

Colin asked, "Is Arnold your first name or your last?"

The man in his white coat was younger than Celeste and had tanned skin. He looked very fit. Not strong like Colin's father. But athletic just the same. "Arnold is my first name. My last name is Weinbrandt. Can you spell that, Colin?"

He could because he had seen it before. A deputy sheriff on his father's force had the same name. Colin had seen the badge when the deputy drove Roger Eames back from the cop bar and helped him up the home's front steps. Colin spelled it, making sure to put the *d* before the *t*.

As he opened one of the files, Arnold Weinbrandt watched Colin. "How old are you precisely?"

The way he emphasized that last word, *precisely*, seemed important. "What time is it?"

Arnold glanced at his watch. "Eleven-seventeen."

"Six years and four weeks and seven hours and twelve minutes."

Arnold studied Colin as he shifted pages. "Six years and four weeks and seven hours and twelve minutes. How many seconds does that make?"

Colin found it easy to look at the man while he calculated. Arnold Weinbrandt seemed so impersonal. So disconnected. There was no danger here. He knew Celeste was worried about something. Something that had to do with him. But he also knew he was safe here. "Sixty thousand nine hundred and fifteen."

Arnold drew out his phone, tapped swiftly, glanced at Colin, then took a pen from his shirt pocket and made swift notes. Then he opened the second file and took out a sheaf of papers inside a smaller plastic sleeve. "I want to give you a test of logic. Do you know that word?"

"Yes."

"Define it, please."

"The computer logic or the other, I don't know what that one is called."

Something in the way he answered eased the hard glint in Arnold's eyes. "It's called the philosophical definition."

"'Reasoning conducted or assessed according to strict principles of validity.'"

"Where did you read that?"

"The Webster dictionary. We have one at home."

"Do you know what those words mean?"

He nodded. He had looked them all up. "It means figuring out the solution of a problem based on evidence. Nothing else. Not how much you want it to be one way or another. Not the way you hope things will be. Just evidence. Lining it all up in the right order and then accepting the answer. The only answer."

Arnold turned and stared at the mirror for a long moment. Then, "Tell me why that interests you."

"It's a way to test everything. Look away from the confusion. Find what is really there. Find the real answer." He didn't know if he had said what he should, but he thought he found a hint of something new in Arnold's gaze. Almost a smile. But one that came nowhere close to his mouth.

"There are three basic kinds of logical reasoning. You understand those two words together, yes? Good. These are deductive, inductive, and abductive. Have you heard these before? No? Can you say them back to me?"

"Deductive, inductive, abductive."

"Good. Deductive reasoning is where the conclusion is guaranteed. A general rule combined with solid evidence leads to one specific conclusion. Inductive is where the conclusion is probable, not certain. Abductive reasoning begins with an incomplete set of observations and proposes a set of likely solutions." As he spoke, Arnold lay out a series of pages. Each one held drawings. "We are going to apply inductive reasoning to geometric designs. I want you to study each of these. Take as long as you need. When you are ready, I want you to tell me what is the one aspect that all of these designs share."

Colin knew the answer before Arnold finished speaking. "I'm ready."

"Don't speak until you're absolutely certain—"

"They all share something that's not there."

This time, the doctor rocked all the way back in his seat. The chair squeaked softly as the legs shifted on the cement floor. He looked at the mirror again. "What is the missing aspect?"

"An isosceles triangle." He took his time and said the hard word as best he could. Isosceles.

Arnold kept his gaze on the mirror and said, "You were right and I was wrong."

Colin figured he was speaking to whoever was on the other side of the glass, so he did not reply.

Arnold turned back to him, studied Colin a long moment, and then said, "Okay. We're going to shift gears. Ready?"

"Yes."

"All right. From this point on, my aim is to identify your boundaries. There is nothing bad about giving me a wrong answer, or saying you don't know something. That is actually my goal here. I want to see how far you can take these elements of reasoning and deduction. Nothing more. Do you understand?"

"Yes."

"You mustn't be frightened or worried if you don't know the answer. Just tell me, and I'll explain things, and we'll move on."

"I'm not scared," Colin replied. And he wasn't. He was so excited it was hard to stay in his chair.

This time, the smile touched his entire face. "Then let's begin."

CHAPTER 4

They stayed at it for another hour and a half. It would probably have lasted much longer. Colin didn't care. It could have gone on for days. Weeks, in fact. When the chair could no longer hold him, he slipped around the table and stood beside Arnold, who shifted his chair over to make room for him. They chattered with an increasing sense of shared energy, flying through the lessons, spilling papers everywhere. Colin couldn't say which he liked more, getting the answer right, or the sudden electric illuminations that came when Arnold explained something that he could not figure out on his own.

But the door finally opened and Celeste came in, smiling larger than Colin had ever seen. She was followed by the man who had passed them in the parking lot and the other woman, grey haired and precise, but in her own tight way Colin thought she looked as pleased as Celeste.

Arnold said, "We're not done."

The woman said, "I for one have seen enough."

"More than enough," the grey-haired man agreed. "Young man, you are an astonishment."

They all left together. Arnold joined the two other strangers, walking ahead and talking all at once. Celeste led him down the hall and asked, "Are you hungry?"

He realized, "I'm starving."

She found that humorous. "So let's go see if they've got anything here worth eating."

They descended two flights of stairs, then walked a long hall, passing several conference rooms and a classroom and then a cafeteria filled with noisy children. Colin was immensely pleased when they passed those doors.

They entered a smaller cafeteria filled with adults in soft conversations. The windows were tall and frosted with sweat from the AC. Green plants grew from large ceramic planters. The walls held beautiful photographs. Celeste said, "What do you feel like?"

"I could eat anything."

"Well, you're the man of the hour, which means you can have anything you want." As they walked down the line and he settled on beef brisket and mashed potatoes, she asked, "You want some vegetables with that?"

He shrugged. "If I have to."

"Not today, you don't. You want a Coke?"

"Lemonade."

"Lemonade it is." She filled up a glass and set it on his tray, then said, "Some days it is just so good to be me."

Colin liked that enough to laugh out loud.

"Child, you should do that more often." She gestured to the line of desserts. "Anything suit your fancy?"

As they started toward a table, the silver-haired gentleman called over, "Celeste, the attorneys are here."

She settled him at a table by himself. "You going to be all right, sitting here alone?"

"Sure."

"That's my little man." She pointed to where the adults gathered. "You need something, I'll be right over there."

He ate slowly, relishing every bite. The brisket had been cooked until it flaked on his fork. There was a lake of gravy covering his plate, so much it had spilled onto the tray. Colin started to use his only napkin to mop it up, but nobody was watching, so he ate and reviewed some of the more challenging exercises Arnold had shown him. He did not mind the solitude at all. In fact, he almost felt as though it was important. He was so used to making himself small. Finding the tight corner, the little area behind his bedroom door, any place that left him feeling momentarily safe. Here was different in every way. The light was different, even though it came from the same sun. The food, the quiet conversation, the solitude . . . Glorious. When he finished eating, Colin took a long breath, so long he wondered if he could just keep on breathing in, growing bigger and bigger until he actually filled all this beautiful space.

Abruptly the silver-haired man answered his phone, spoke briefly, and all the adults rose as one. Colin stood and started to pick up his tray, but Celeste halted him with, "No, leave it there." She hurried over and pulled out a chair next to where he stood.

The older woman with the severe face said, "Celeste, they're waiting."

"You go ahead, I'll be right up." Her gaze never left his face. "Do you trust me, Colin?"

"Yes."

"They want you to be present for what's going to happen. I don't like the idea, but . . ." She shrugged. "I'm just one voice. Never mind. I want you to listen carefully. Your father is coming with . . . No, Colin. Look at me. There is no reason to be afraid. You're not going to be alone with him. I'm there, and all these other people, they're all on your side. Now I want you to take a deep breath and *calm down.*"

He tried. He really did. But the fear of losing everything this day had held left his muscles jerking slightly. Like they were being pulled by tight electric strings.

She rose to her feet. "All right. Let's get this over with."

They were the last to enter the conference room. This place was completely different from where Arnold had examined him. The table was polished wood and so large sixteen leather chairs on swivel bases could fit around the gleaming surface.

Roger Eames was seated with his back to the windows. When Colin entered, just his eyes shifted. Two grey gun barrels that held nothing. No love, no recognition, no rage. Cop's eyes. Colin would have stopped and run away, but Celeste was there behind him, her hand on his back, guiding him down the long line of adults seated across from his father. Past the silver-haired man and Arnold and the other woman and now two more, a man and woman, both young and wearing similar charcoal-grey suits. The adults watched as he slipped into the chair and Celeste pushed him up close to the table. Some of those on his side of the table had to lean over to see him. Once he was settled, the young woman seated next to him said, "You were saying?"

A slender black man with angry eyes was seated to his father's right. To his left was the mayor of Rocky Mount, a man with silver-grey hair and a heavily pockmarked face. They had once attended a barbecue cookout at the mayor's house. The mayor had two teenage boys who looked like they would have happily bullied Colin had their father not been keeping a close watch. Colin thought the mayor held the same bullying manner as his sons.

The black man said, "We wish to register an official complaint against Dr. Celeste Talbot."

The woman seated next to Colin was very attractive, but

her voice matched the black attorney's for harsh edges. "On what grounds?"

"She forcibly restrained Sheriff Eames, a highly decorated police officer, from approaching his own son."

"I fail to see how the lady seated to my left could *forcibly* keep the sheriff from doing much of anything."

"You know very well what I mean. She ordered a local police officer to stop Sheriff Eames from approaching his son in what was undoubtedly a highly charged and emotionally distressing situation for them both."

"Aren't you forgetting something?"

"No," the lawyer replied. "I am not."

"There is the matter of why everyone had gathered in the first place."

"That has nothing whatsoever to do with my complaint!"

The woman seated next to Colin smiled tightly. "I'm fairly certain the judge in family court will disagree with you on that point."

The two attorneys acted as though they were the only people in the room. Colin felt the breath catch in his throat. They *acted.* They were *performing.* This confused him, like so much of adults' behavior. He felt a gradual slipping away of all the wondrous events and the feelings that had carried him through the day.

In desperation, he tried to look at the people and their words from the perspective of what he and Arnold had been discussing. From logic. Deductive logic was impossible. There were too many unknowns to draw a straight-line conclusion. That was the term Arnold had returned to time and again. A straight-line calculation resulted in only one possible outcome. Abductive reasoning was needed here. Working with incomplete knowledge, searching for . . .

His father's attorney said, "That you would even suggest taking this matter to court indicates you are far from possessing all the relevant materials."

It was the silver-haired gentleman who said, "Enlighten us. Please. We're all ears."

Colin thought the attorney's expression was theatrical. "I'm sorry, who exactly are you?"

The woman began, "Dr. Saunders is head of a trust. . . ."

"A trust."

"Correct."

"And his role here is . . ."

"An interested third party."

"What possible interest could a private family matter be to you?"

"The child."

"Colin Eames."

The gentleman nodded. "Yes. The child's . . ."

Celeste offered, "Status."

"Excellent. Yes. The child's status is of great potential interest to my trust."

"Meaning what, exactly?" The dark gaze swiveled back to the woman next to Colin. "Do you intend to level some sort of scurrilous charge against Sheriff Eames?"

The female attorney made a process of lining up her pad and file and pen. "We were addressing the matter of missing evidentiary elements that would explain why we don't wish this to go to court."

"Answer my question, Counselor."

She lifted her gaze. "Why ever would we want to level charges against a highly decorated officer? What could possibly have placed such a notion in your head?"

"You were the one who mentioned family court."

Throughout the exchange, his father's gaze never wavered. Hard and tight and fastened in unblinking coldness. On his son. For the first time ever, Colin was able to look *beyond* the gaze. There was the sense of being placed at a mental distance, safe behind the wall of these adults lined up beside him. That was the one element his search for abductive solutions made clear. He was not alone in this. They were here because they sought to protect him.

As if in reward for having arrived at this deduction, Celeste reached over and placed a hand on his.

The attorney seated across from them said, "Sheriff Eames's wife died exactly three years ago yesterday. I could think of no more tragic a reason for my client having consumed more than might be considered either sound or reasonable."

Colin withdrew his hand. The moment seemed frozen in time. His father's attorney noticed Colin's reaction. "I suppose that element was not included in whatever the boy said."

"I'm sorry. Were you suggesting the child has reason to accuse the father of something?"

The attorney chose to ignore her question. "My client recognizes his consumption of alcohol reaches unhealthy levels at times. As a result, he is voluntarily entering supervised counseling, which will permit him to maintain his vital position on the force." He opened a file and passed documents across the table. "I don't have enough copies, so you'll have to share. I mention this to emphasize how vital, how absolutely crucial Sheriff Eames considers the care and support he lends to Colin's upbringing. . . ."

The attorney droned on. But there was a muffled vagueness to the words now. As if Colin was trying to understand them through a filter of running water.

He was back in that time again, a period he carefully kept locked away. Only now among all these people, the memories stabbed him. The hospital, the endless days, the fear, the loneliness. Her death. All of it. Colin felt like his entire world was being shaken apart, then reknit into a different form. Everything that had come before, it needed to be reexamined in the light of being utterly alone. What his father's lawyer said was a lie. Nothing about the past three years suggested his father had ever cared. Or supported. Or loved.

He opened his mouth. He wanted to ask if there was something in him that made his father sad. If he reminded his father of what they both had lost. If that was the reason why the only emotion Colin had ever witnessed from his father was the unbridled rage during his drunkenness.

Celeste gripped his hand more tightly, silencing him as firmly as if she had clamped his mouth shut.

The silver-haired gentleman broke into Colin's thoughts with, "I think perhaps it's time we moved to the primary reason for this meeting."

His father's attorney scanned the faces seated across from him. "What is going on here?"

"This meeting has nothing whatsoever to do with the issue of Sheriff Eames's behavior on or off the force," the young woman seated next to Colin declared. "Unless you wish to include it yourself."

"In family court," the gentleman added. He motioned down the table to where Celeste was seated. "Where Dr. Talbot serves as official adviser."

"To all the family courts in eastern North Carolina," the woman attorney added. "On matters related to child welfare."

"Again, that is not why we asked you here today," the gentleman said. He turned to Arnold. "Dr. Weinbrandt has spent the entire morning making a thorough evaluation of Colin Eames. Arnold?"

Arnold Weinbrandt said, "Colin Eames is, quite simply, a genius. I do not mean his IQ is above the threshold. I am speaking about something else entirely. Young Eames shows a potential that appears only a few times in every generation."

For once, his father turned his attention away as the

lawyer seated opposite them said, "Where are we going with this?"

The silver-haired clinician replied, "I am here representing the board of Outer Banks Academy for the Gifted. The lady next to me, Mrs. Fitzgerald, runs the academy's department known as Sojourn House. We want to offer Colin Eames a place. Effective immediately."

Colin's father laughed out loud. "This is a joke."

"I assure you, sir, it is anything but."

"I know that place. The tuition is what . . ."

"Thirty-five thousand dollars per annum. Room and board for live-in students, which we would like Colin to become, are an additional— "

His father laughed a second time. "This is nuts. Do I look like a moneybags to you?"

"No, sir, you do not. Which is why we are happy to announce that so long as your son proves his abilities are genuine, and he is willing to put in the required work, his costs will be fully covered."

The mayor spoke for the first time. "I know for a fact the Outer Banks Academy doesn't offer scholarships."

"Officially, Commissioner, that is correct. But the majority shareholder and chairwoman of a Fortune One Hundred company is a graduate of OBA. She established a very special, and highly confidential, annuity. This trust is the reason why I and Mrs. Fitzgerald are present. A limited number of students from financially depressed circumstances have all their fees and expenses covered. They are also housed at the special campus facility that Mrs. Fitzgerald runs." The gentleman showed a remarkable ability to smile with cold rage. "Isn't that wonderful news, Sheriff Eames?"

"We require specifics in order to assess this revised situation," his father's lawyer replied. His former ire was gone now. The man's features looked washed out.

"Which we are happy to provide." The gentleman looked

down the table at Colin. "Perhaps now would be a good time for the young man to leave us to settle the details of his transfer."

Celeste rose and guided him back down the line of seated adults. He felt his father's cold fury track him, and he knew why. Colin's father lived by dominating. It was a cop's method of staying alive. Colin had heard him use the words often enough. They were part of the danger chant, spoken every time the Maker's Mark landed on the kitchen table. And here he was. Colin Eames. Stripping away his father's control.

Only when the door clicked shut behind him did Colin allow his tremors to surface.

Celeste guided him across the hall, over to a hard wooden bench. She seated herself next to him and said, "Take as long as you need."

Her comforting presence helped pull him back. "What does it all mean?"

"I'm going to speak with you like I would an adult. The answer is, your father came into that meeting with one thought in that cop's mind of his. Attack first to protect himself." Something in those words made Celeste so angry her entire body clenched. "And that is just like a cop. Bringing out his weapon and taking aim before he even understands what is going down. Only this time the person who got shot was the man himself."

"I don't understand."

Celeste looked at him, her gaze burning with the coals of old pain. "Your father thought you'd been telling tales about him and what it's like inside your home. And I expect there's a lot of things you could tell us, if you had a mind."

Colin had no idea how to respond.

"We all suspected that might have been the situation, what with the way you've acted and what we found there yesterday. But making a case is tough, especially against a decorated officer of the law. And you're not abused in any way we can see or show a judge." She turned to the closed conference room door. "So there we were, all concerned over how we were going to get your father to grant us the right to house you in a place where you could grow. Discover what your gifts truly mean."

Colin recalled the words she had made him read from the book in the principal's office. He recited from memory, "'All too often in childhood the fires of genius falter. There is a very great risk that unless proper care is given, the fire may become snuffed out.'"

"There you go." She pointed to the closed conference room door. "So now we know there was abuse. There are problems your father wants to keep secret."

"He's going to be appointed a county commissioner."

Celeste rounded on him. "Is that a fact."

"He told us yesterday. At breakfast. And they want him to run for state legislature."

"That explains why the mayor drove all this way down here." She rose to her feet. "Don't you move a muscle. This is news that can't wait."

But as she started across the hall, Colin asked, "Why doesn't he love me?"

"What that man feels is anyone's guess. You can't allow—"

"Did I kill my mama?" The words burned his mouth, his throat, his heart. Three years of nightmare fears pushed out. "Did I do something? Is that why Daddy is that way?"

Celeste squatted down beside him. "Listen to me, Colin. The medical records claim your mother died from what is known as an embolism. We can talk about the specifics another time, if you want. We can also discuss what it means for a child to carry the sort of guilt that you're feeling just now. How important it is to release this, let it out, and heal."

She rose back to full height, and stayed there long enough to add, "You are alive, Colin. You have *gifts.* Your job is to *live* and do the absolute most you can with what you've been given."

Colin remained seated on the bench and felt the thought resonate through him. Like the hall and the air and the light all shook with him, trembling from the power of the words that rose like a great, silent explosion.

Chapter 5

The days passed, then weeks, months, years, until finally it seemed to Colin that the only home he had ever known was his narrow room in the Outer Banks Academy.

The original structure had been built in the fifties, in a style that befitted an institution with lofty ambitions. Carolina brick was buttressed with Appalachian granite, and more of that precious stone framed the tall windows and formed an archway over the entrance. Sojourn House, the residential hall for all the academy's scholarship students, was a throwback to that very same era. The interior had been remodeled so as to quadruple the number of bedrooms, sixteen over the upper two floors. They were all single, all slightly larger than the small chamber he had known in Celeste's home all those many nights ago. Every four rooms shared one bath. The downstairs held a computer room and television lounge and dining room and kitchen and office and Mrs. Fitzgerald's apartment.

Edwina Fitzgerald was British and lived by the clock. And because she held the power to dismiss any student who did not live up to her expectations, the children who resided in Sojourn House did likewise. They rose at seven, ate breakfast at seven-thirty, spent twenty minutes on morning chores, followed by studies, class, afternoon chores, study hall, then precisely ninety minutes of what Mrs. Fitzgerald called "downtime." Dinner was followed by chores and a half hour of television, then study until lights out precisely at nine. She was a fearsome lady, given to precise diction and commands she would only utter once. The year Colin turned twelve, fourteen students lived in Sojourn House. He had never known a student to be kicked out. Just the same, they all lived in fear of it happening.

Though he actively despised the rules that encased and defined his daily life, he understood the reason. Most of the kids were from families too poor to ever consider granting their child a chance to study here. Many arrived with no sense of discipline whatsoever. The very concept of obeying rules astonished them.

Then there were the others.

They drifted through their days in a fog of their own making. And some had come from situations far worse than his own. Their nightmares and their screams woke Colin at least once a week. There was a night counselor who dozed in the office. His name was Grant, and he wore a pristine white shirt and trousers. He always took the stairs three at a time, reaching the frightened child in seconds. Colin would lie in his bed staring at the dark ceiling, listening to the man's deep rumble as he calmed away the shadows. The next morning, no mention was ever made of nightmares or stained bedsheets or a child with deep purple bruises under their eyes. Mrs. Fitzgerald did not allow it.

That morning Colin was scheduled to miss his first class so as to meet his adviser. As usual he left the house by way of the kitchen door. Camila, the cook, was a small woman with knotted strength and a knowing gaze. She silently watched him cross the kitchen and depart.

Colin stopped at the edge of the house, where the building melded with trees separating the campus from US Highway 17. The rumbling of traffic had been part of his life for so long, he no longer even heard it. When no one was passing along the sidewalk, he stepped forward.

Outer Banks Academy resembled a small college campus. Behind the older buildings fronting Sir Tyler Drive was an oval green space, beyond which stood a trio of ultra-modern structures bearing the names of wealthy patrons.

He entered the middle building and climbed to the top floor. His adviser's office was the third down on the left, facing back over the central gardens. Dr. Arnold Weinbrandt was a full-time faculty member now, handling tutorials and counseling. He shared a narrow antechamber with one of the teachers, but that door was closed, which meant Colin could sit and prepare himself for the meeting. Normally he let Arnold guide them through whatever process the school required. Their meetings had become almost perfunctory in that regard. Arnold reviewed the series of positive checks from his teachers, then offered a few words about where Colin was going next. Then they chatted about news events Colin didn't understand. Sometimes they just played chess. But Arnold had specifically requested this meeting and indicated there were issues that needed to be resolved.

And then there was the other matter.

Over the past four months, Colin had been making secret plans. Elements that had nothing to do with the academy and everything to do with his own personal future. He wanted something that would mean breaking a lot of rules. He *needed* this. And he could not tell anyone why.

For the first time in years, he was frightened of what this meeting might hold.

The wall dividing the antechamber from Arnold's office was paper thin, and the voices inside were very loud. Colin heard Arnold say, "This is the third time in a month you've left campus—"

"This isn't a campus! It's a *prison*!"

Colin instantly recognized the student's voice. She was one of the school's unofficial elite, the daughter of a local business tycoon and the glamorous former second wife. She was now being raised by mom number four. The man's name adorned the wall above this building's entryway. The girl was beautiful, spoiled, and . . .

Colin heard another woman's voice say, "If this behavior continues, we will have no choice but—"

"But what? Expel me?" Her laugh held a distinctly musical tone. Everything about her was both confident and unpredictable. She had most of the older guys and some of the teachers watching her every move. She was fifteen years old. "Do that and see what happens to your *building fund*!"

The woman said, "We have no choice but to send you to detention—"

"*No!* I'm not staying a *second* longer in this *awful place* than I have to!"

"Kimberly, this situation is critical to your future—"

"The name is *Kimmie*! And this meeting is *over*!"

The door slammed back and out she came. Blond hair and big-city bling and a too-short skirt and eyes that flashed on him with cold fury. "Hi there, Superfreak. Enjoy the show?"

When Colin entered the office, the woman seated beside Arnold said, "From the ridiculous to the sublime."

"Hi, Colin." Arnold Weinbrandt did his best to smile. "Come sit down. You know Sandrine, of course."

Dr. Sandrine Powers, the new head of Outer Banks Academy, was a very attractive woman in her midthirties. Her own smile did not diminish the anger in her gaze. "How are you, Colin?"

"Fine." But having her here was not good. So bad, in fact, he had to say, "I need to speak with Dr. Weinbrandt alone."

She pretended to laugh. "I seem to be everybody's favorite person today."

Arnold said, "We have matters to discuss that require Sandrine's presence."

Colin remained standing by the doorway. "This is supposed to be our private time."

Sandrine said, "Perhaps I should go."

"No." Arnold's voice hardened. "Dr. Powers has guided your education and your life here for almost a year. She is taking time from an extremely busy day to help me with an important issue related to your future. Now close the door and come sit down."

Resigned, Colin walked over and seated himself across from them.

Arnold's office was shaped for conferences like this. His desk was actually pushed over against the side wall. The center of the room was dominated by a small oval table, just large enough for five chairs to fit around it: Arnold's office chair and four others. Two of these chairs were now pressed against the wall by the door. The chair where Colin sat still felt warm from the girl.

Sandrine asked, "The word that Kimmie used when she saw you . . ."

"Superfreak," Arnold said. He appeared to share Colin's surprise that the school director did not know. "They use that a lot."

"Who is 'they'?"

Colin replied, "Almost everybody."

Arnold said, "It's how the other students refer to those living in Sojourn House."

Sandrine's cheeks flamed red. "Why am I only hearing about this now?"

"There's nothing anyone can do about it." Arnold's irritation was evaporating. He looked more weary than anything. Almost resigned. "Anything we say would only make matters worse."

Sandrine drew a file from her purse and slapped it down on the table. "They'd better not use that in my presence."

Colin remembered other times when a sudden shift in his world's axis had come because strangers had declared themselves to be on his side. He found himself relaxing as Sandrine opened the file and said, "I've been speaking with Dr. Braxos about you."

Braxos was head of the math department. He wore rimless reading glasses, grey wool ties and jackets that looked scratchy. "He doesn't like me."

Sandrine actually smiled. "Dr. Braxos doesn't like a lot of people."

Arnold said, "Braxos probably feels threatened."

"There is no 'probably' about it." Sandrine turned the page. "An eleven-year-old who knows more about math than he does? The man would be happy to see a knife sticking out of Colin's back."

"That might be taking things a bit far."

Colin watched the two adults, talking back and forth about his own personal nemesis on the faculty. Like he was one of them. "Braxos came here to teach gifted kids."

"There are gifted, and then there are gifted." Sandrine lifted her purse and fished around. "Where are my glasses?"

"Jacket pocket." When Arnold reached over and retrieved them, Colin had the sudden impression that these two were more than simply colleagues. There was a casual intimacy to the gesture. "Here."

"Thank you." To Colin, "You know perfectly well we accept a number of students because of who their families are. 'Gifted' is a term that has to be flexible, as far as the school is concerned. It's the only way we survive as an institution."

Colin felt the last bit of tension ease away. "That makes sense."

"Of course it does. The simple fact is, Braxos is a dinosaur. But he is a dinosaur with tenure. Do you understand what that means?"

"You can't fire him."

"I suppose we could. Given a valid enough reason." She bent over the file and mused quietly, "If, say, he ran off for a dirty weekend with a certain student we certainly won't name. And if we could catch them red-handed."

"And I think we've taken that matter just about as far as we legally can in this student's presence." Arnold smiled at her as he spoke.

Colin sensed it was at least partly an act. A subterfuge meant to put him at ease. "I asked him if I could study something new. He said not yet. I don't want to wait."

Sandrine lifted her gaze. "So that's what it was."

Arnold asked, "What is it, exactly, that you want to do?"

Colin took a long breath. The prospect of his next step left Colin feeling physically ill. But there was no choice. None. Another breath, and then he lied to his friend for the first time ever. "I want to study Boolean logic."

The two adults exchanged glances, and then Arnold said, "Unpack that a little bit."

"Boolean logic is a form of algebra. It's a formal notation for describing logical relations. It's centered on three words known as operators: *or, and,* and *not.* All values are noted as either true or false. . . ."

He stopped because Arnold held up his hand. "I know what Boolean refers to." Arnold's voice had resumed its normal soft intensity. "I want to know why this is important to you."

Another breath. Another lie. "I want to study artificial intelligence. This is a good place to start."

"The mathematical foundations of AI," Sandrine said. "At eleven, no less."

"I just turned twelve."

"I'm surprised poor Braxos didn't run screaming from the room."

Colin inspected himself. Wondering if some great rift might open up in his body, exposing the terrible deed. Instead, he felt nothing. A faint whiff of some vague disorder, like smoke from a distant fire. Otherwise, nothing except a resolve to see this through to the end. Because there was no other way out.

The academy's director said to her colleague, "Which brings us to the point."

"Sandrine and I have had a word with UNC Wilmington," Arnold said. "They are willing to have you attend classes. Term starts the week after next."

"You'll need to meet with their head of department," Sandrine said.

"And the dean of admissions," Arnold added. "Both those meetings are set for Sunday afternoon."

"They are putting you down provisionally as a visiting student," Sandrine said. "But if you prove yourself, as I'm sure you will, they'll matriculate you with next autumn's incoming class."

Arnold asked, "Do they even offer Boolean algebra to undergrads?"

"I'll check." She made a note. "If not, I'm sure they'll make adjustments."

Colin felt like the news held such force it literally pushed his lies from the room. Like their words had taken on solid form and were cascading all around him, bombarding him with pulses of silver energy, cleaning away the dark elements he had introduced. He wanted to shout, to leap from his chair and go racing around the room. He could scarcely draw a breath, he was so excited.

"You will officially remain a student here at Outer Banks Academy. And continue to live at Sojourn House." Arnold smiled at his expression. "But Sandrine will have a word with Mrs. Fitzgerald on your behalf."

"Not on your life," Sandrine said. "As academy director, I hereby assign you that particular job."

"I am happy to decline," Arnold replied.

"You can't. I'm your boss. I'm giving you a direct order." She turned to Colin and continued, "The house schedule obviously will require changes to fit your classes."

"How do I get there?" He hated to mention it, especially now. But there was no choice. "I don't have any money."

"Ah. Of course. I almost forgot." Sandrine seemed to be enjoying herself now. "I have had a word with the head of our secret benefactor's trust. Actually, it was her attorney."

"You met him, sort of," Arnold said. "He was there at your preliminary examination."

"The trust has taken a personal interest in you and your development. They will cover the cost of your university studies. You can arrange for a car service to take you to and from the UNC Wilmington campus three times each week. You'll still attend other classes here, of course."

"Look at that face, will you."

"I think he's happy."

"Happy doesn't come close," Arnold said. "Our Colin has left happy and entered the stratosphere."

Sandrine asked, "You mentioned something you needed to discuss?"

Colin wondered if this was what it felt like to become an adult. Having the confidence to speak openly in front of someone who, just ten minutes ago, had been a stranger. "I want to learn how to swim. Outer Banks Academy doesn't have a pool. I need . . ."

"You need help." Sandrine turned to Arnold. "Ideas?"

Colin said, "There's a public pool two miles from here."

"Not on your life. I know that pool. The complex is not in a safe area. Which means the pool represents a risk we don't need to take." Arnold thought a moment, then said, "What about Landfall?"

"Now there's a thought." To Colin, "Your adviser has become seriously addicted to golf."

"Everybody needs an outlet. Right, Colin?"

"I personally can't see the point," Sandrine continued. "Whacking a little white ball over and over and over—"

"Walking the emerald course, doing my absolute best at an impossible game, talking with friends, putting the rest of the world on hold. What's not to love?"

Colin liked how they were involved in each other now. Being open in front of him in a way that was intensely private. And yet they included him. "But I want to swim."

"Landfall is a country club. It's located just over a mile from here. They have a great pool." Arnold took a page from Sandrine's file and made a note. "I'll have a word and see what we can arrange."

CHAPTER 6

The next day was Saturday. At nine that morning Arnold drove him to the club. Faculty were not generally allowed to visit with students off campus. Colin had learned that his first year in Sojourn House. Though Arnold was a counselor and taught no classes, the rules of fraternization were still very strict.

Colin had been off campus a few times each semester, more often in the slower summer season. Each month there would be a sheet listing the scheduled trips for Sojourn House residents. A couple of days in advance, Mrs. Fitzgerald would make an announcement. She tried to make it sound like a treat. But the strictly regimented way she arranged things, starting with the announcement itself, made most trips feel more like a chore to Colin. A duty. He could tell that most of the other students felt the same way.

Once they traveled by ferry to the Bald Head Island nature preserve, the southernmost bastion of the Outer Banks. At least once a semester they attended films at the local

Cineplex. But Mrs. Fitzgerald chose the films and then deflated the enjoyment afterward with question times. They visited museums. They always stopped somewhere for lunch, the other patrons staring at them like they were on display. He liked it better when Celeste arranged to pick him up, though it usually meant spending time in her children's company. Then last year the older girl went off to college, but her son's sullen attitude never changed. Troublesome was the word Celeste most often used when she spoke about him. Colin could see she was worried, but had no idea what he could do to make things better. They remained close through all those times, and it was Celeste who had given him the idea about swimming.

The week before Colin was scheduled to meet with Arnold, he told Celeste, "I hate how I look."

"Not liking your appearance is part of growing up. This is when you start learning to see yourself as an individual, which means examining every wart and wayward hair through a microscope."

"This is different."

"Oh, is that so. Tell me how I am supposed to believe that because you're a genius and everybody is oohing and aahing over you, you're not going to think and feel like a teenager every now and then."

There was a phone in the little hallway off the kitchen that the students were allowed to use. Cell phones were off limits, as were personal computers. Mrs. Fitzgerald did not allow any device that she could not personally monitor. The cook, Camila, was supposed to observe and report on every phone conversation. But apparently few of the Sojourn House students had anyone they wanted to talk to. And none of them had funds to buy their own equipment. Colin had seen the hall phone being used only a few times. Camila seemed to like him, which he found very strange, since the only time they spoke was when he was assigned kitchen chores. But whenever he phoned Celeste, the cook seemed to go out of her way to be elsewhere.

"That's not what I mean," Colin said. "I'm fat."

Celeste gave that a moment. "I will admit that you're a tad overweight. It comes with finally getting fed like a growing boy should."

"I'm fat and I hate how I look. Not just that. All the other people in the house, they're strange looking."

"Those day students, they're still calling you that name? Superfreak?"

"Yes, but that's not . . . I want to do something about how I look. I can't buy clothes. I don't have money. The stuff Mrs. Fitzgerald gives me to wear, it's like a uniform. That's what the others call it. The superfreaks in their Walmart supergear."

"I could wring their necks."

"I can't do anything about how I dress. But maybe I can do something about being a fatty. I want to try."

"Don't call yourself names." But she had taken on a thoughtful air. "I don't recall Outer Banks Academy having a gym."

"They have one. It's small, but I guess it's okay. I went there. They made fun of me."

Celeste was silent, then suggested, "What about swimming?"

"I don't know how." Even so, the idea sparked something in him. Photos he had seen rose behind his eyes. "Outer Banks Academy doesn't have a pool."

"You're always going on about how you want to get out of that place. Ask them if you can go to a pool. Check it out online, see what you can find. When do you next meet with Arnold?"

"He's set up an appointment in five days."

"Find out where there's a pool before you see them."

"Go in prepared," he said. But now he was thinking about that other thing.

"There you go. Speaking of which, didn't you tell me you're having dinner—"

"I don't want to go."

"—With your father. And his new wife. Colin, wanting doesn't matter. If your daddy were to raise a stink, there's a chance he might be able to take you home. You want that?"

"No. Not ever again."

"He's remarried, he's a state senator up in Raleigh, he's in the process of adopting his new wife's two kids. If he had half a mind, he could show a court just how great—"

"No." The hand holding the phone felt so hot he thought he might melt the device. "All right. I'll go."

"Of course you will. Be polite to his new wife. It should go just like all the other visits."

Thankfully Roger Eames's wedding had taken place in Jessica's hometown of Asheville, a nine-hour drive from Wilmington. Colin's father had only given him seventy-two hours' notice of the event. So Celeste had guided him through a nice, polite, meaningless letter apologizing for how the academy wouldn't let him travel up on his own and wishing them every happiness. The newlyweds had stopped by for a visit three weeks later, when his father was down on some business. The new wife had shown Colin the sort of empty cheeriness that probably made her a great politician's wife. Nothing could possibly touch this woman. She was Teflon through and through.

Colin was tempted to tell Celeste what he knew was coming. Not suspected. The fact that his father had remarried made the next moves a near certainty. Only the timing was not yet set. But Colin couldn't risk it. Celeste was an adult. She saw things from an adult's perspective. She would wait until it happened before bringing her strength to bear. And by then it would be too late. They weren't dealing with a simple cop and union chief any longer. The danger was real, and it was happening. Soon.

Celeste said, "You be sure and let me know how things go."

CHAPTER 7

Arnold Weinbrandt drove with one elbow propped on the open window, the other draped over the wheel. He took it slow, carefully describing the mile and a half distance from the school to the club. The way could not have been more straightforward. Walk down South Mooring, left on Deer Island Lane, take the Arboretum bridge over the lake, then right onto Landfall Drive. A strong wind blew from the east, rippling surface waves on the Cape Fear River. Every now and then Colin thought he could smell the ocean's faint fragrance. A quarter mile before the club's entrance, the golf course came into view.

Arnold drove a small Lexus SUV, the NX. Colin liked the luxury, and the way they sat fairly close together, and how Arnold's golf clubs rattled softly in the rear hold. As if they too were excited over the journey. Arnold noticed Colin studying the rolling emerald fairway and smiled. "Say the word and I might know someone willing to introduce you to a lifelong addiction."

"I want to learn how to swim."

"Then swim it is." He hesitated, then asked, "You understand why I didn't want you going to the public pool?"

"Yes."

"I don't want you to feel like I'm being overprotective."

Colin said what he thought Arnold wanted to hear. "Before he entered politics my father was sheriff of Edgecombe County. You knew that."

"Of course."

"Rocky Mount and Wilmington are a lot alike. Money is coming in, many new companies, high-tech jobs, housing developments, shopping centers." Colin kept his gaze on the road ahead, even when Arnold slowed so as to study him. "And then there's the bad side. The people left behind. Rocky Mount and Greenville and Wilmington all lead the nation in per-capita opioid addiction."

Arnold said quietly, "I'm from Greenville."

"I know."

"It's a great place."

"So is Rocky Mount. And Wilmington. I like it here a lot." Colin faced his adviser. "I know I need to be careful."

The club was Carolina in style, whitewashed stone with a pillared front portico and tall windows. Arnold opened the car's rear door, shouldered his clubs, picked up his golf shoes, and waited until Colin had taken out the plastic shopping bag holding his new swim trunks, sandals, goggles, and towel. "Why do I need flip-flops?"

Arnold led him around the main house, over to where a sidewalk met a high metal fence. "Wear them when you're in the changing rooms and the showers. This is a public place."

Colin had no idea what he was talking about, but just then the pool came into view. The club sat on a promontory overlooking the lake, and the pool was down one step. Beyond that were tennis courts, and farther out spread the golf course.

The pool sparkled impossibly blue and green and clear. The laughter of children drifted in the hot, still air. He thought it looked like a liquid jewel.

Arnold pointed to a smaller building beyond the tennis courts. "That's the pro shop. When you're done, go and sit there. If you need me, speak to anybody and they'll come find me. We'll drive back together. Unless you'd rather walk back— "

"No. I'll wait."

"Fine. Good." Arnold studied Colin a long moment, then said, "Something's bothering you."

Colin saw the concern in those dark eyes. He thought back on the first time they had met, the cold hostility, the way Arnold wanted to dismiss him as a waste of time. "Thank you. For everything."

"You're worried about tonight's dinner with your father and his new family."

He nodded. The day dimmed slightly. But not because of the visit. Not really. Because he had lied to his friend. It was wrong. He knew it was. But he didn't know any other way to move forward. What he was planning, he knew Arnold and all the other adults would think him crazy. They would insert themselves into the process. But Colin had spent the last four months analyzing. Observing. Knowing what his father intended. His only hope, small as it was, came from . . .

"Colin, do you want me to go with you?"

"No."

"Or Celeste. She could— "

"No." He said it overloud, the word forced out with his fear and tension. He said it softer. "No. I'll be okay."

The pool enclosure was full of conflicting impressions. The negative was so intense it almost drove him away. If he had not felt such a strong draw to enter the crystal waters, he would never have made it past the dressing rooms. The other children shouted and laughed, the words so strange it sounded to him like a foreign language. He was amazed at how easy they felt, how they formed a tight unit that constantly exploded in noise and movement. He undressed very slowly, marking how the others fit everything into small lockers and took the key and pinned it to their trunks. He waited until most of the others left, then finished undressing and slipped on the swimming trunks. The cloth was stiff and strange feeling. The sandals were very odd as well, with a single thong inserted between his big and second toes. None of it was unpleasant. Just new.

He took his towel and goggles and entered the light.

A trio of clocks stood on tall metal poles. The swim class was not scheduled to begin for another fifteen minutes. All the other children raced to the pool's edge and jumped into the shallow end. Colin seated himself on the edge of a chaise lounge and studied the situation. He knew a large part of his discomfort came from how he hated the way his body looked. His skin was pasty white. The excess flab created ugly little dimples and folds, which he could see just by dropping his chin. The skin on his legs looked like Camila's bread dough before she slid the rack into the baking oven.

But it was more than that.

Colin was used to being the outsider. The superfreak. But this was different. He was entering the outside world. On his own. For the very first time. Without the protection of people he could trust. And what he felt was the same distance that had always separated him. In his family. At the school. In Sojourn House. Which meant . . . what? That he was carrying this distance with him? That he was going to stay alone and isolated all his life?

"Hi there. Are you Colin?"

He turned and looked up, but it wasn't possible to see more than her silhouette because she stood with the sun directly behind her. He nodded.

She lowered herself onto the chaise lounge beside him. "Hi, Colin. I'm Mira Brooks."

She was beautiful.

Colin had seen attractive girls before. Any number of the Outer Banks Academy students were attractive. And rich. But this girl was . . .

"I understand this is your first time at a pool, which is wild. How old are you?"

"Twelve."

"Amazing." She was sixteen or seventeen and tanned a uniform bronze, almost toffee colored. She wore a red one-piece bathing suit with a white cross by her left shoulder. Encircling the cross was the lettering, "Landfall Country Club Certified Lifeguard." Her hair was bundled up tight under a red swim cap, but one dark strand had escaped and fell by her right ear. "I can't remember my first time in a pool. My mom says I was born with flippers. Are you scared, Colin?"

"No."

"Because if you are, I'm here to tell you, you'll be totally safe. That's my job. To teach you how to swim, and keep you safe. And I am very very good at my job."

"I'm not scared."

She had eyes almost as dark as her hair, only the sunlight revealed a deep coloring, like a second shade hidden beneath the black surface. He had never seen eyes like hers. "Then how is it you've made it all the way to twelve and you've never been at a swimming pool?"

"I've lived at Outer Banks Academy since I was six. They don't have a pool."

"Outer Banks Academy, that school over by Market? Wow, so you're like super smart?"

He tested the air and found no hint of scorn. "I guess."

She linked both hands around a knee and leaned back. "So

tell me something about how smart you are. I've never met a genius before."

He had no idea why the words came out as they did. Only that it was incredibly easy to talk with her. "I start at UNC Wilmington next week."

She dropped her foot to the concrete. "Get out of town."

"I'll still be living in Outer Banks Academy. Sojourn House, that's my dorm."

"For real? You're going to UNC?"

"I want to study things and the academy can't teach me."

"Like what? Give me a for instance here."

He released a portion of his hidden aims. Easy as drawing breath. "Advanced calculus. Statistics. Algorithms applied to predicting trends."

"I don't even know what half those things are." She remained like that, studying him, until a whistle blew. Mira rose to her feet in one fluid motion. "Come on, genius. Let's introduce you to my world."

The class was exhilarating and exhausting in equal measure. Colin had very little experience with anything to do with physical exertion. The academy had gym classes, but he had seen them as just another opportunity for the day students to ridicule him. Plus they were easy to avoid. None of the Sojourn House students took gym.

This was different. The other children were mostly younger, which made them less willing to mock a bigger kid. And Mira kept a careful eye on him. Which Colin found oddly thrilling. It was far more than just being smiled at by a beautiful older girl. There was something to their connection, a spark that he could not define. He felt an odd mixture of pleasure and excitement when she slipped into the water and showed him how to move his arms and legs together, fashioning the stroke she called freestyle. She looked so graceful, the water seemed to part willingly and then slip back together after her passage. Colin fought the water, exhausting himself in the process. Even so, the struggle gave him an odd sense of accomplishment. As if just by being here, just by trying, he was doing something important.

Then it was over, and the class was dismissed, and the pool was opened to all the other children who had gathered and waited impatiently for their chance to jump in and scream and splash around. Colin sat on the edge with his feet dangling in the water, as tired as he had ever been in his entire life. Mira was still there, standing by the lifeguard's high chair with four other teenagers in their red swimsuits and caps, all of them with whistles either slung around their necks or dangling from one hand. She stood with her back to Colin, but he knew from the way the others glanced over that she was talking about him. Normally he hated being the center of attention. But something about this day and this place left him feeling safe.

When the strength returned to his limbs, he fit the goggles back over his eyes and slipped off the edge. The water no longer fought him, because he was not moving. He kept one hand on the ledge, but not for safety. He pushed himself down so his head was fully submerged. He wanted to feel again what it was like to be surrounded by the crystal blue. The water created an entirely new environment. Colin felt as if he had departed one world and entered another. One where sounds and light and sensations were all dominated by this new medium. All around him, kids played and splashed, their noise transformed by the translucent blue. But he was untouched, even when one of the kids jostled him. Colin felt it, but the momentary contact meant nothing. He stayed there until his lungs were burning, then popped up and breathed and breathed and breathed, like it was the first time he had ever tasted air.

Then he realized Mira was standing on the edge. Next to her was Kevin, the other instructor for their class. She smiled down at him. "Having a good time?"

"This is wonderful."

"Look at this kid," she said to Kevin. "Have you ever seen a smile that big?"

"The guy is hooked," Kevin agreed. "Maybe you should rest a while. Swimming really tires you out."

"One more time," he said, taking another breath, then levering himself down into the crystal depths. When his lungs forced him back up again, they were gone.

CHAPTER 8

Five thirty that afternoon, Colin was seated on the bench to the left of the academy's main entrance. His father was always late arriving. But Colin remained punctual, mostly because he didn't want his father to show up and go wandering around. The academy was Colin's haven, the place where he felt safe. Now that he had mostly moved beyond the reach of his teachers, this safety was why he put up with Sojourn House and Mrs. Fitzgerald and all her rules.

The year before, Colin's father had been made president of the North Carolina Sheriff's Association. This besides now serving as a state senator.

Every few weeks, Roger Eames's growing list of responsibilities brought him down to Wilmington. A few days in advance, he or one of several assistants texted or e-mailed to say when he would arrive for a dinner with his son. The messages from his father's aides were always more polite and personal than those coming directly from Roger Eames.

Earlier that week, a seismic event had struck North Carolina's political landscape. The Republican congressman representing the state's first congressional district suffered another heart attack, his third. Soon as he was released from the hospital he announced his retirement, effective immediately. Colin paid little attention to politics, but his daily search of news services for information of a different sort had alerted him. Over the coming days, he grew certain this was the event he had been dreading—not that particular occurrence, but something that marked the start of his ticking clock.

The state's Republican Party was now led by the former mayor of Rocky Mount. When it came time for the governor to name a temporary replacement, it was only natural that they select State Senator Roger Eames. This was largely a symbolic gesture, as the national elections were in less than six months. The appointment was intended to pave Roger Eames's way into national politics.

Colin was mentally reviewing the implications of these developments when a black Cadillac Escalade pulled into the forecourt. Colin did not realize it was his father until the face leaned toward the windshield and waved him over. His father had always driven four-door sedans, Fords mostly. This massive black beast signaled a change. When it came to dealing with his father, change was never good.

His father was talking on the phone when Colin climbed on board. Soon as Colin shut his door, his father slapped the SUV into drive and punched the gas. His voice held the edgy growl that took Colin straight back. It was the warning sound, time for his son to go find the safe alcove. Being trapped in this huge vehicle, seated high off the road, left him swallowing against the acrid taste of old fear.

His father said, "I don't understand why you're bringing this up at all."

The woman who responded spoke with a strong southern accent, yet her words held as sharp an edge as his father's. Colin flinched as her voice struck at him from all sides. The car's speakers were embedded in doors, footwells, under his seat, behind him, everywhere. "Because we need your support on this, Senator."

"Well, you're not going to get it."

"I'm afraid that's not an acceptable answer, sir."

"Tough. I'm a law and order guy. You're asking me to back away from the pledges I made, the reason I got elected in the first place."

"Only temporarily. Only for this term."

"It's not happening. Not for a single solitary *second* will I give you or this cockamamie resolution my support."

"Senator, after all the donations we've made—"

"I didn't ask for a penny of your money. Not once."

"Even so, if this is indeed your stance we will have no choice but to withdraw our support. If that happens, you risk losing what may be your only chance to enter national politics—"

"You do what you've got to do. And don't ever call me again." He stabbed the button on his steering wheel. Then stabbed it again. "The nerve of those people. I'd like to wring their collective necks."

The SUV went quiet after that, his father fuming and Colin scarcely breathing. His father wore what had become his standard attire, a dress shirt with a white collar, this one with grey stripes that matched the color of his trousers and silk tie. The jacket to his suit was set out carefully on the rear seat. The fancy clothes only magnified his father's bullish strength, like the veneer of oil applied to a loaded gun.

Traffic on US 74 was rush-hour heavy. Abruptly his father swung the wheel, raising a trio of honks from cars behind and to his right, and powered down a side street. Going was easier then, and the open, shaded avenue seemed to ease his rage.

Abruptly his father demanded, "What were you thinking about?"

Colin looked over. "What?"

"When I showed up. You were staring into the distance, I don't know, like you were in some sort of trance." He showed his son that familiar gun-barrel grey gaze. "They don't go in for that kind of stuff at that school of yours, do they?"

"No."

He turned back to the road ahead. "Because I've heard things. Crazy, liberal notions that don't have any part of my son's life."

Colin felt a distinct buzz at gut level. It was as if his father had finally given voice to all the suspicions Colin had been carrying around for four months. Ever since he learned his father had become engaged. To a divorced woman with two young boys of her own. "They don't teach anything like that."

"So what is it you were thinking?"

He knew he shouldn't say it. Even before the words emerged, he knew it was wrong. Dangerous. But the words just seemed to punch out of him, like they had been waiting for this precise moment, and would not be denied. "Do you ever go back to the beach?"

His father flushed beet red. "What kind of question is that?"

Colin had no idea why he spoke as he did. Even so, the words could not be denied. "You asked what I was thinking. I was remembering how Mom sat on the sand and watched the ocean—"

"Today of all days, you can't give that a rest?" A tremor shook his body and partially shredded the words. "I'm taking you to meet your new family and this is . . ."

Colin could almost see the rage taking hold, the struggle his father went through to keep it under control. His own response surprised him. His heart raced, he crammed himself tight against the side door, his body felt frigid and clammy at the same time. And yet the fear seemed to belong to someone else. He heard himself say, "Did she have family? Where was she— "

His father's voice took on the same rough edge as when he spoke to the woman. "Here we are, eight years later, and *you won't let it go.*"

The questions that woke him in the night pressed out, struggling against his desire to smash them back inside. "Why don't I remember her funeral? I remember going to the hospital with you— "

Roger Eames slammed on the brakes so hard Colin would have shot against the windshield were it not for his seat belt. "Brenda is *dead.* All that has *no place* in our future."

They drove the final mile and a half in silence. When they pulled into the restaurant's parking lot, Roger Eames cut the motor and just sat there. Gripping the wheel with such force his knuckles were bone white. "Brenda's family is from Jacksonville. Downeasters, they're called. Been there for two hundred years. Not a penny to their names, house falling down around their ears, the biggest snobs on earth. They were furious when she agreed to marry a sheriff's deputy. They cut her off."

He kneaded the wheel, the leather squeaking in protest. "Your mother asked me to contact them when she got ill that last time. They hung up on me before I was finished. Two days later, her old man showed up. Offered to pay thirty thousand dollars toward her hospital bill if I'd let them take the body back home. The medical expenses had me drowning in debt. Where that vile, bitter old man got the money is a mystery. Once I agreed, he said everyone would be better off if I didn't attend the funeral. Not one question about you, their own kin. Not a word."

Roger Eames rose from the car, slammed his door, and strode away. Leaving his son still seated in the new Escalade, wishing he had never come. As usual.

* * *

The Port Land Grille was his father's regular hangout in Wilmington, with its dark wood and heavy leather furniture and huge steaks. When Colin entered, his father stood talking with his new wife while her two sons glared in Colin's direction. Everything about Jessica Eames was precise, measured, cautious. Her two boys were ten and thirteen, and both were much bigger than Colin. As they took their seats, Roger's new wife eyed Colin with frigid displeasure. He had angered her husband, her gaze seemed to say. He deserved whatever punishment Roger wanted to give him. Her two boys eyed Colin across the dining table with predatory gazes.

Following a nearly silent dinner, once the table was cleared, his father told his new wife, "Why don't you show him?"

She extracted an envelope from her purse, pulled out a group of photos, and spoke directly to Colin for the first time that evening. "These are pictures of our new home."

His father took the photos, sorted through them, and slid one over in front of Colin. "This is your room."

The words chilled him to the point where his tremors could not be fully suppressed. Colin sat with his head bowed over the picture, clenched tight with the effort required to remain as still as possible. The pale ivory room contained a caramel-colored carpet, a small desk, empty bookshelves, a narrow bed. Lifeless and deadly.

He endured an endless parade of pictures, each one marked by his father's description. Front yard, living room, kitchen, den, office, on and on the parade of images continued. Each one hammering the same message with massive force. Colin was almost out of time.

His father directed Colin into the front passenger seat for the drive back to the academy. His new wife took up a place between her sons. When they pulled into the academy forecourt, Roger Eames broke the silence with, "When school is out, we'll start making some changes. Jessica is home schooling her two boys. We'll just add you to the mix." He watched Colin open his door. "You've been involved with these liberal nutjobs long enough."

Colin stood by the academy entrance and watched his father drive away. As the Escalade pulled into traffic, the two boys leaned toward the side window and shot Colin a warning look.

He had to get this right.

Chapter 9

Sundays meant most of the Sojourn House rules were relaxed. Their breakfast was half an hour later than the rest of the week, and many of the students did not attend at all. Their rare shopping expeditions took place Sunday afternoons. Clothes came from Walmart. Their hair was cut by a barber who stopped in once every month. They waited in either the television lounge or the computer room for their turn. The barber was a woman whose fingers stank of cigarettes. She had a way of twisting her wrist slightly that painfully pulled Colin's hair. She started every trim by warning them, boys and girls alike, not to fidget, else she might take off an ear. Allowances were handed out by Mrs. Fitzgerald, along with any admonitions or warnings. They were then free to do whatever. When it was Colin's turn, Mrs. Fitzgerald greeted him with, "Come in and shut the door."

She pointed him into the chair opposite her desk. "Well, Mr. Eames, it seems that your studies are about to undergo a significant change."

He had no idea how to respond. The chair was solid oak

and uncomfortable where the hard wood touched the bare skin below his shorts. Colin refused to let himself fidget and sat perfectly still.

"You are not the first student who has been granted the opportunity to attend college classes. Ah, I see that surprises you. It's been a while, but there are precedents." She lifted a page from the file open on her desk and slid it across to him. "As far as the other students are concerned, you are now in transition. Which means some of the regulations that frame the other students' lives here are, well, I suppose relaxed is the best term to use. But there are still rules, and you must closely adhere to each and every one of them. Tell me you understand."

He had heard some of this from Arnold on the way to and from the swimming pool. He had spent much of the previous night preparing his own list. "I need to be allowed to study later at night."

"Do you, now."

"And I need a personal computer. And permission to keep it in my room. I can't have other people using it."

Her expression tightened. "It is not customary for a student—"

"I'll be missing meals. I need money for food. At the university. And books."

She inspected him with a distinctly frosty gaze. "It would be advisable not to use your newfound duties as an excuse to overreach."

"A laptop would be best," he persisted. "Something I can carry with me to class. And a backpack. And a key for my room. I can't allow other people to mess with my work."

He knew he was taking a big risk, making the woman angry. But he could feel Arnold and Sandrine standing behind him now. Allies on his side. And something more. The conversation with his father stayed with him, the pressure of the ticking clock. There was so little time to get this right.

Colin slid from the uncomfortable chair and picked up the sheet of new instructions.

She was still sitting there, studying him intently, when he left the office. Colin glanced over the page as he climbed the stairs to his room. The heading read "Colin Eames: New Daily Schedule." He shut the door, crumpled the page, and threw it in the trash.

When he returned back downstairs, Mrs. Fitzgerald's office door was closed and the ground floor was quiet. One young girl played a game on a computer. Colin walked to his favorite machine, set in the inner corner so that light from the front window fell over his right shoulder. He dropped the bag with his swimming gear and towel to the floor. He had almost an hour before he needed to leave for his Sunday lesson.

He worked on his secret project. He rarely used the Sojourn House computers for this anymore. Virtually all his computer time was spent in the school library. He had no evidence that Mrs. Fitzgerald monitored the in-house computer files, but he had learned to take great caution.

What initially had been a few vague ideas had grown and developed and hardened until it occupied virtually all his waking hours. His classwork required no time whatsoever. The instructors were supposed to set challenges for him in monthly tutorials. But they had no idea how far ahead he had become. He told them what he thought they wanted to hear, at the level they counted as accelerated. He accepted their accolades, agreed to whatever new assignment they selected, and pretended he was kept fully occupied. The subterfuge had grown and expanded until he had spent months living a myth. All so he could hide from everyone his true work.

He had hacked the academy's mainframe and set up private files that only he could access. He would have preferred a cloud account, but those firewalls were impenetrable and he didn't have any money. So he employed a double-blind system to hide his presence from anyone who might go hunting. The school's computer geeks were good. But their primary focus was on protecting the financial accounts and academic grading and student files.

The school was big on teaching current affairs, which Colin found increasingly bizarre, since so much of its structure was designed to keep the world *out*. But it served his purpose now, since the library system had subscriptions to the major online news feeds. Colin focused on the sources he had come to trust: the *New York Times* business section, the *Wall Street Journal*, the *Financial Times*, the *Fortune* daily feed, and the online zines he had decided were mostly reliable. He had been doing this twice daily for four and a half months, building his system in the process. The result was an ability to scan the articles and see not news but data that he would then translate into numbers and input into his newly developed algorithmic system. After that, he began the real hunt.

As he checked the latest updates on the house computer, he occasionally lifted his head and scanned the room. But it was just him and the girl. Mrs. Fitzgerald was gone for the day. When he finished, he still had fifteen minutes left. He switched over to his favorite pastime. Cartoons. They had taught him to read, and held him still. Only now he was rarely interested in the cartoon itself. What fascinated him was the changing landscape. CGI work was driven increasingly by new software designed to insert ever-higher degrees of reality into the story. Colin switched to the websites catering to software designers and was scanning for the latest development and news about upcoming films . . .

When he saw it.

The rumor was couched in geekspeak, little snippets about a major change to the gaming landscape.

Colin's heart rate surged.

He switched to another site, a third, a fourth, angry now that his fingers could not keep up with either his eyes or his brain. Then, in all places, he discovered a tight little paragraph hidden deep in the bowels of an online Hollywood rumor mill.

He cut off the computer. Bounced a few times in his chair. Running through everything imbedded in his design and how this news fit into his system.

No question. This was it.

He rose from the chair and hefted his bag and left the house. It was impossible to feel so excited, and so burdened. Incredible to have finally identified the compass heading, only to be saddled with the hardest task of all.

As he crossed the bridge and started along Sun Runner Place, the image of his father drawing him into the whitewashed prison of a Raleigh bedroom flashed before his eyes.

He had to make this work.

Chapter 10

Swim class was much harder today, even though he knew what was expected of him. Colin's muscles felt spongy and stubborn, as if they were reluctant to do what he told them. Even the exercises that had been easy the previous day came with difficulty. Just the same, it felt good to lose himself in the tasks. He loved being in the pool, even more than the day before. As if the experience was magnified, now that he knew what to expect. He relished how total it was, how easy to set aside his project and his thoughts and even his father. All of it washed away in the joy of being surrounded by the crystal blue.

Sometimes when he submerged himself and stayed under, Colin found himself thinking about his mother. What surrounded him here, the light-filled water, the weightless joy, held a whisper of what she had found so special about the sea. He had not been back to the beach since her death. He wondered if he ever would again.

When class was over, he took up the same position as the

previous day, seated on the pool's boundary, ignoring the shrill noise as all the other children were released for their Sunday swims. He swished his feet back and forth and thought on what it would be like to swim in the sea. Moving along the border of thousands and thousands of miles of blue. The depths going down into blackness . . .

He was startled from his reverie by Mira leaning down beside him. "You were looking good out there today."

"It felt a lot harder."

"Sure, I get that. Your muscles are learning new rhythms. How do you feel?"

He liked that. Thinking of the swim strokes as rhythms. "I'm really tired now. But it's a good tired."

"Next week we start the breaststroke." She crooked her arms, extended them fully at a forty-five-degree angle, then brought them together. "You'll feel even worse after that, learning to push forward with your leg strokes."

"I can't wait."

She slipped down beside him. "So how are things for the new UNC brain?"

"I meet with the dean of admissions and the head of math in a couple of hours."

"That's just wild. I mean, here I am sitting next to . . . How old are you?"

"I just turned twelve."

"Wild." She had the most beautiful smile he had ever seen. "Happy birthday."

"Thanks."

"What did you do to celebrate?"

The question made him uncomfortable. "Nothing. I mean, it's just a day."

She lost her smile. But the sense of ease did not diminish. "My folks would like to meet you. Is that okay?"

"Sure, I guess."

"They're over by the kiddie pool with my brother and baby sister." She rose to her feet. "Come on, I'll introduce you. Then I've got to get back to work."

Colin had no clear idea what he expected, meeting Mira's parents. He had assumed she was South American, Brazilian perhaps, with her tall, languid shape, already fully a woman. He did not know much about girls of her age. Mira was nothing like the older academy students. She possessed a singular poise and grace.

"Mom, Daddy, this is the boy I was telling you about. Colin . . . I'm sorry, I forgot your last name."

"Eames. Colin Eames." The mother held the hands of a young girl who danced waist deep in the kiddie pool. A boy of perhaps four or five played by the knees of his father, pushing a sailboat around. Both parents were blond, tall, with ready smiles and clear gazes. "Hi."

The father rose from his seated position and offered Colin his hand. Like he was meeting an adult. "Very nice to meet you, Colin. I'm Ethan and this is my wife, Alexi. And that's Noah. Can you say hello to the young man, Noah?"

The boy kept pushing his sailboat and did not glance up. "No."

"And my little squealer there is Gracie."

"I'm not a squealer. I'm a princess."

"Hi." Colin had no idea how old Mira's parents might be. His judgment of adults' ages was basically limited to nearly old, old, very old. But Mira didn't fit with the rest of the family picture, the two blond kids, both with their mother's crystal blue eyes.

Alexi patted the stone next to where her husband had sat. "Come join us, Colin. Can you stay with us, Mira?"

"For a few minutes, I guess."

The mother didn't even wait for him to seat himself before

asking, "So Mira tells us you're studying at Outer Banks Academy. Is it nice?"

He felt Mira's warm presence settle on the pavement behind him. "It's been really good to me."

Alexi continued to hold her daughter's hands, but her attention was now fully on him. "How long have you been there?"

"Going on six years."

Her father wore a faded surfer's T-shirt that partly hid vivid lines of old scars on his neck and right arm. The skin was deeply puckered, the indentations very pale against the man's tan. Ethan said, "Mira says you live in one of their dorms."

"It's just the one house for scholarship students. They call it Sojourn. There are fourteen of us in there now."

"How many students does Outer Banks Academy have?"

"A little over four hundred."

He did not mind their questions, or how they kept looking at each other over his head. They shared an easy comfort with each other, the same open familiarity he had found in Mira. There was no danger here. Nothing to run from.

Ethan said, "Mira told us something about UNC Wilmington?"

He nodded. "I start there next week."

Mira said, "He's meeting the dean of admissions this afternoon."

Colin said, "My adviser at the academy thinks it will all go okay."

Ethan asked, "What do you want to study?"

Colin felt himself begin to rock in place. It was not like him to trust people. Especially a family he just met. But there was something about them, not the individuals, but the *unit.* Plus there was the simple, unassailable fact . . .

He needed help. And he didn't have much time.

Colin built on the partial confession he had started with Mira. "Integral and multivariable calculus. Real analysis. Statistical logic and probability."

The news was greeted with silence, finally broken by Mira saying, "Told you."

Alexi said, "Your parents must be very proud." When Colin did not respond, she asked, "Do you have family?"

He thought back over the previous night's dinner and quietly replied, "Not really."

Another silence, then Mira said, "Daddy probably knows some of the stuff you'll be studying."

"Not like he's talking about. I'm a CPA. An accountant."

Colin felt another electric surge, strong as hope. "I love numbers."

Ethan laughed out loud. "A man after my own heart."

Alexi said, "Why don't you come have dinner with us tonight?"

"Say yes, Colin." Mira stood. "The chief is giving me the stink eye. Tell them yes, then I have to split."

Chapter 11

Precisely at eleven-fifteen that morning, Arnold's little Lexus SUV pulled into the academy's forecourt. When Colin opened the passenger door, his adviser greeted him with, "You've cost me nine holes of golf. You owe me big-time."

But the man's cheerfulness was in direct contrast to his words. That was one of the things that had endeared him to Colin. How he was both open and honest with his emotions.

"Not to mention the conferences you've forced me to attend," Arnold went on. He turned north on Highway 74 and accelerated into traffic. "And all the complaints from the fearsome Fitzgerald. My God, that woman can talk."

Colin watched the sunlight and the cars and the buildings along the highway. He had traveled this same road any number of times. Only today was different. He was entering a new phase. One defined by liberties he had never known before. It was like he had grown a new set of eyes, one that saw the world in a completely different manner.

"Not like my old buddy Colin," Arnold said. He was dressed in Saturday casual, yellow knit shirt and khakis and loafers. "The man here can go hours without speaking a word. You'd better not do the silent thing with the dean. Or the professor. You open that big mouth of yours and you make sounds. It's called talking. You should try it more often." He lifted one tanned arm from the wheel and waved a fist in the air between them. "You go quiet on the dean, I'll make you caddy for me every weekend until you turn thirty."

Colin felt a burning urge to tell him what he had planned. He had shared everything else of importance with Arnold. Through six long years, Arnold had been the person Colin had trusted with his life. Celeste remained there in the distance, a strong presence hovering just beyond the academy's reach. The two of them had taught him so much, starting with what it meant to trust. And here he was, repaying their gifts with lies.

Arnold glanced over and instantly lost his smile. "What's wrong?"

Colin swallowed hard, forcing down all the words he dared not speak. "Do you remember the first time we met?"

"Of course I remember. With Celeste ready to beat me to a pulp if I misbehaved. How could I forget." Another glance. "Why does that make you sad?"

"I never thanked you. I wish I knew the right way to say that. How much . . ."

Arnold's gaze softened to a pair of dark wells. He reached over and ruffled Colin's hair. "You're my guy. And you always will be."

Colin took a long breath, easing himself away from the guilt and the sorrow. "I've met some nice people at the club. A family. Their daughter teaches my swim class. They want me to come to dinner tonight."

Arnold's laugh carried an easy, weekend languor. "So I guess I'm not the only one charmed by your silent ways."

* * *

They didn't speak again until they entered the vast parking lot adjacent to the Mayfaire Plaza. Arnold pulled up next to a small square building across from the shopping center and led Colin into the bank. Colin tried to mimic Arnold's calm attitude, taking things in stride. But he had never been in a bank before. The entire episode was thrilling. Signing the account card, accepting his book of blank checks, then the teller handing him a hundred dollars inside a little envelope stamped with the bank's logo. "Your debit card should arrive within a week."

He waited until they were back in the car and circling around to the shopping center's far side to ask, "I have a thousand dollars?"

"Counting the hundred in your pocket. I know, it's crazy. I told them they were nuts, trusting you with that much money." Arnold's grin was infectious. "But would they listen to me, your adviser? No, they would not."

As they crossed the vast parking lot, Colin felt it all begin to release him from the chains of childhood. "Wow."

"Don't go running off to Tijuana."

"I won't."

"There is no way I'm going to chase you south of the border."

"I'm not running anywhere." As they approached the open-air shopping center he asked, "Will I ever get to meet her?"

"Who?"

"The CEO. My sponsor."

"Probably not. Your benefactor is a very private person. There's the lady who runs a major corporation, and there's the lady who lives a very private life. All this time, I've never even spoken with her."

"How did you get this money?"

"Simple. After you met with Sandrine and me, followed

by an hour of listening to the fearsome Fitzgerald moan, I called the woman's attorney. You saw him at that first hearing. I said, 'There's this guy, you might remember him from six years ago. He's a little nuts, but other than that not a bad egg.' And the lawyer said, 'I'll get back to you.' An hour later, he calls back with the cash."

Colin followed him across the lot. "I'd like to thank her."

"Write her a letter. I'll give it to the attorney."

"Will she get it?"

Arnold reached for the door. "Your guess is as good as mine."

First stop was a barbershop, where the people treated Colin in the same manner they showed Arnold in the next chair. He took careful note of how Arnold spoke, telling them it was Colin's big day, he needed to look respectful, and heard the man standing behind Colin's chair reply that respect was big on their list of styles. The barber's hands smelled of nothing. Incredibly beautiful music played in the background. Midway through the cut, Colin asked about what he was hearing.

The man was grey-haired and small and very fit looking. "That's Benny Goodman. You never heard of the great man?"

"He's wonderful."

"Wonderful is the right word. You and I are going to get along just fine." The barber spent the rest of the trim on a running commentary of the clarinetist and his orchestra. His work with Gene Krupa. The famous 1938 concert at Carnegie Hall. When the melody "Sing, Sing, Sing" came on, the barber revealed an amazing tenor, humming the melody and then switching to a harmonic second. All the other barbers were smiling by the time he whipped the cloth from around Colin's neck. He even brushed him down to the song's tempo.

Colin stepped from the chair and said, "That was the best haircut of my entire life."

The barber offered him a hand. "Little man, you come back here any time you like. We've got a whole world of music to explore, you and me."

As Arnold led him from the shop, he said, "The kid makes friends everywhere he goes."

They stopped in the food court for lunch, then headed into Next. Arnold insisted he buy multiples of shirts, trousers, shorts, underwear, socks. New sneakers, dark brown loafers, canvas-and-leather belt, gym shorts, and Next T-shirts. When Colin protested he would soon grow out of everything, Arnold waved it away. "That's the fuming Fitzgerald talking. She's not here. Hurry up and choose. I'm bored out of my mind." He stared over the racks, seeking the exit. "I forgot how much I hate shopping."

But Colin loved every minute of it. Each choice was another fragment of liberty set into this new definition of his life. The fabric felt exquisite against his skin and fit better than anything he had ever owned. And every moment was spiced by the music that still bounced around in his head. Jazz. He loved the mathematical precision of how the instruments fit together. Flying high, but always in control.

After Next they entered Circuit City, where Arnold bought him a phone with a thousand minutes and a Dell laptop. It was a modest system with an AMD processor, a thirteen-inch screen, and not enough memory. Not great, but great just the same. Everything went on Arnold's card, the clothes and lunch and haircuts and phone. The hundred dollars made a reassuring lump in Colin's front pocket. Not having to spend his own money made the day sweeter still. As they left the shop, Arnold told him, "Load your phone and get comfortable using it. Take it with you everywhere. There's no traveling around Wilmington without a lifeline."

He left the mall dressed in one set of his new clothes, and carrying so many bags they bumped against his legs with every step. Arnold carried more than he did, including a new backpack. Another first.

When they returned to Highway 74, Arnold reached for the radio and said, “You want music?”

“Jazz.”

“A man after my own heart. Jazz it is.” He hit the second button. “And away we go.”

The UNC Wilmington admission dean’s office was in Kenan Hall. Arnold pulled into a visitor’s slot and led him up the front stairs, through the main entrance, down a long hall. “I taught here while I did my graduate work at Chapel Hill. Back before the last ice age. It’s a great place, and getting better. Wilmington started off as a training school for local companies requiring skilled workers. It’s grown into a very solid university, and the graduate programs are coming up by leaps and bounds.” Arnold looked down at him, seemed to find what he sought. “They need a star on the rise. You may just fit that bill.”

Colin had no idea what he meant, but liked the feeling it gave him.

They entered the dean’s office together. Arnold positioned his chair slightly behind Colin’s, a reassuring presence who was not entirely connected to the meeting but there just the same. Dean Sykes was a pleasant enough woman, precisely trimmed silver hair, sweater and skirt of a pearlescent grey, gold watch, keen arctic gaze. She spoke softly, asked a number of questions, but Colin had the impression it was all perfunctory. As if the decisions had all been made long before he arrived. She took no notes. Twenty minutes later it was over. As he stood, the dean said, “You are far from the first young person to study here. Your age is a curiosity, nothing more. You must show yourself to be worthy of this opportunity. In your studies and in your behavior. Do I make myself clear?”

His meeting with the professor responsible for the UNCW Department of Mathematics and Statistics was something else entirely.

For one thing, Arnold seated himself on a bench that faced onto Lions Gate Drive. "Your meeting is with Professor Fremdt. Room 202."

"You're not coming?"

"The dean is one thing. You'll be meeting this man every week. You need to start like it will continue." Arnold stretched out his legs and turned his face to the sun, catlike in his relaxed state. "You'll be fine."

A Sunday torpor had settled upon the building. Even so, Colin felt eyes on him, heard comments trailing along behind. He tried to tell himself that it was simply more of the same, only coming from older students.

Fremdt was a big man who exuded a restless, almost fierce energy. His office was large enough to hold a long table with a dozen chairs slid around so as to all face the blackboard covering the side wall. Fremdt watched him enter and barked, "Eames, right?"

"Yes, Professor."

Fremdt had a round face made even bigger by a shock of unruly dark hair, beard, and black oversized glasses. He spoke with a distinct accent, but clipped off each word, as if he had spent years making sure his students understood him clearly. "So. This academy, I have heard of it. Every student is gifted, no?"

Colin found himself thinking of the attractive daughter of the major benefactor. "Some are. Others definitely not so much."

"Who teaches you the math there? Is it Braxos? I know him. Not a bad brain. Not so gifted, though. He teaches you what?" Fremdt directed that last question at the paper he took from a file on his desk. "So. Advanced algebra. Good, good, maybe you can come teach my first years how to count. Limits, binomial theorem, complex numbers, integrals, you cover all this, yes?"

"I've been going a lot further on my own."

Fremdt flipped to the file's next page, ignoring the sheets that fell onto the floor. "Nothing is said of this."

"I didn't tell him. I haven't told anyone."

Fremdt shifted his head up, down, to the left, as if trying to fit Colin into his field of vision. "And why is this?"

"Last year I showed him an equation I didn't understand. It made him mad."

"What was this equation?"

"Using algorithms to calculate statistical trends."

"Yes, I can see Braxos now. Not liking how an almost child is showing what he doesn't know. And now? Where has this secret brain of yours taken you?"

"Linear and nonlinear differential equations."

Fremdt fumbled for the chair behind his desk, seated himself while watching Colin. "The equation on the board there to your left. Do you know what it is?"

"Yes."

"So swift he answers. All right, my young brain. Speak. The professor listens."

"It shows limits and continuity in a multivariable equation." Fremdt had become very still, like the energy inside was being compressed further and further. Tight and powerful, but not dangerous. Colin decided he liked this man. "There are scalar functions of two variables with points in their domain that give different limits when approached along different paths."

He nodded. Once. An almost violent up-and-down motion. "You read this, yes? Which book?"

"John Hubbard. *Vector Calculus*."

"An old work. Not up to date on many things."

"It's all the school had in its library."

"And what are the variable limits?"

"Approaching zero through *y* equals *kx*. But with the origin approached along the parabola, the function value has a limit of plus or minus point five."

Another birdlike adjustment of his head's position, then, "There on the shelf to your right. Shifrin's book, *Multivariable Mathematics*. Yes, that one. You take and you read. Term starts next week. Advanced calculus meets Monday, Wednesday, and Friday, eight o'clock. All the students who are asleep when they arrive, I wake them up fast. Be on time." He waved at the door, almost punching the air with his stubby fingers. "Now go. I must grade papers of these ones still learning how to count."

CHAPTER 12

Six thirty that evening, Colin was seated on the same bench by the academy's entrance where he had waited for his father. The other Sojourn students had been eating dinner when he slipped out. Mrs. Fitzgerald had left for the weekend, and Camila had merely looked at him when he said he was having dinner off campus. He left a note on the battered desk used by Grant, the night counselor, giving the Brooks's address and saying he didn't know when he would be back.

A solitary bird perched in the Carolina pine to his right, peeping softly as the twilight glowed against the streetlights. The highway's noise was a faint whisper in the background. There was no wind, and the early spring heat still radiated from the earth at his feet. He wore the same outfit he had worn for his interviews. The feeling of weightless liberation that had propelled him through the afternoon meetings was with him still. Every blade of grass, every needle on the branches overhead, gleamed with a special light. Not even the memory of the dinner with his father's new family could reach him. Nor the ticking clock. He knew what had to happen. Either he could find a way to move forward as he wanted, or he would confess everything to Arnold and Sandrine and Celeste. Even though that way carried a far greater risk of defeat. Just knowing the die was cast left him feeling calm. He would give it another three days, then go to the academy leaders and lay it out. Try to convince them that their natural reaction would lead to failure . . .

A horn beeped once as a Honda Pilot pulled through the entrance. Before it had fully stopped the passenger door opened. Then Mira popped out, shielding her eyes and pretending to gape at the arched entryway. "Where are all the other geniuses?"

"It's Sunday. Genius gets the day off." He waved through the open door. "Hi, Mr. Brooks."

"Climb in, sport."

"Sorry we're late," Mira said. She pointed him into the front passenger seat, slid open the side door, slipped inside, then leaned in close enough for Colin to smell the floral scent to her hair. "Daddy almost caught the house on fire."

He pulled into traffic and replied, "Not even close."

"He made an Everest of coals, then forgot he'd already put on the lighter fluid, did it again, and when he dropped in the match"—she made as large a circle with her arms as the car allowed—"boom."

"Colin doesn't need to be hearing this."

"Mom says Daddy is a born pyromaniac. She says it comes from four years in Afghanistan. That's where I'm from. Kabul."

Mira's father slowed and shot his daughter a look. Not angry, not worried. Just surprised. He opened his mouth, but no sound came out.

If Mira noticed her father's reaction, she gave no sign.

"I'm adopted. I guess you got that already. Daddy saved me. Which means I guess I have to excuse him for wanting to blow things up."

Ethan Brooks lifted one hand from the wheel and adjusted the rearview mirror. As if he needed to keep a closer watch on his daughter. Passing headlights illuminated the scars around his collar and disappearing into the shirt's sleeve. The shadows were deeper now, the scars more pronounced. Ethan noticed Colin's eyes on him. "Maybe Colin doesn't need to know our entire life history just yet."

Her natural effervescence filled the car with a joy as strong as light. "What kind of music do you like?"

"Jazz."

She bounced back in her seat. "Boring."

"Benny Goodman," he said. "Big band. Swing."

"My father likes Goodman," Ethan said.

"Yeah, Daddy. My *grandfather* likes that stuff. It's ancient history."

"I love the precision," Colin said. "It's like calculus. Variations according to very precise input. It results in different outcomes, but all holding to the same foundational structure."

The two of them were silent. Then Mira asked, "Do you understand what he just said?"

"Not even close." But Ethan was smiling now. "I like hearing it just the same."

The Brooks family home was in an older neighborhood of nice houses in Carolina Heights. The street was partially covered by live oaks and yellow poplar, like they quietly sought to shelter the people who dwelled there. Their home had a ground floor of Carolina brick and a smaller second floor framed in weathered cedar. Their large backyard was lined with a wooden fence that matched the upper floor. The young boy played with a Monster Truck while Mira's baby sister sat in her mother's arms.

A second family was present when Colin arrived, Roland and Regina Perez and their son, Lucas. The introductions were easy, casual, and led to a far-ranging conversation. Colin sat on a lawn chair near Alexi and Gracie and mostly observed. Lucas was a student at UNC Wilmington, studying history and political science. He planned to study law. Which was also what Mira hoped to do, then according to her the two of them were going to create their own law firm and fight the good fight. Which Lucas thought was a terrible idea, since they would do nothing but fight each other all day long. But in their jesting exchange Colin heard the distinct undertones of love. They had known each other since kindergarten, they went to the same church, they fought constantly. All this he learned from the adults who sauntered over from time to time, explaining things as Ethan tended the grill and Regina set the table with Mira. Lucas was tall and slender and as silent as his mother. The Perez family were remarkably similar, very quick and alert, yet calmly content for others to dominate the conversation. Colin thought Lucas and Mira were perfect for each other.

When the burgers were ready they gathered around a long trestle table and held hands while Mira prayed. Colin watched the others bow their heads, and wondered at everything. The easy manner, the accepted ways, the strangeness. He felt like he was participating in some alien ritual. One where he heard the words, but their meaning completely escaped him. As they started eating, Colin recalled a book he had once read about explorers searching for the Nile's headwaters. How understanding the tribes they met became as great a challenge, and threat, as the journey itself.

How adapting swiftly made a daily difference between life and death.

The adults included Colin in their conversation by explaining things, mostly about themselves and what they were saying. But they did not press him to reply. Colin found that one of the most remarkable elements of an incredible evening. The food was excellent, burgers and a potato salad with pickles and boiled eggs and mayonnaise, cole slaw, grilled asparagus. Iced tea and sodas to drink. Colin ate until his belly felt stretched to painful dimensions.

Alexi took the two little ones in for bed. He joined the others in clearing the table while Regina made coffee and Mira set out cups and unwrapped two plates of cookies. Colin refused both, asking instead for a glass of water. The remaining adults jousted with old humor over politics. Colin learned that Ethan and Alexi and Mira were staunch Republicans, Roland and Regina and Lucas vocal Democrats. And how this defined so much of their lives. And yet they were friends. Which they all pretended to think was impossible. The good-natured jibes covered a great deal of passion and tension, none of which Colin understood. Even so, he felt like this was a rare gift, being able to observe families who clearly cared for each other, despite the differences, despite everything.

By the time Alexi returned downstairs, he knew this was it. He was going to take the next step. The prospect made him feel queasy, as if the food had congealed in his stomach. His mouth was dry, but he didn't want to raise the glass of water because it would have revealed the tremors in his hands.

He waited.

It was Alexi who offered him the opening. She took a sip from her cup, then used a pause in the conversation to look down the table at him. "Will you tell us something about yourself, Colin? I don't mean to press— "

"Yes she does," Mira said.

"My wife has a gentle hand with the scalpel," Ethan said. "Sooner or later she's going to pry you open."

"You might as well get it over with," Mira agreed. "Mom will only get worse, the longer you stay quiet."

"Whatever you would like us to know," Alexi persisted. "We're fascinated with what little you've told us. Really."

Colin took a long breath, then said, "I need to borrow ten thousand dollars."

CHAPTER 13

Lucas Perez spoke for the first time since starting dinner. "Get in line."

"I need you to promise to keep this secret," Colin said. He knew he was not saying it as well as he had in his many mental practice runs. Yet just taking this first step calmed him immensely. The tension was still there, but it had shifted from clenching him tightly to serving as a shield. Even if they said no, he was committed. "It's very important."

Alexi asked, "If we agree not to tell anyone, will you explain what you mean?"

"We won't say anything to anyone," Mira promised.

"Roland is an attorney and I am an auditor," Ethan said. "Confidentiality is the rule we live by."

"All of us agree," Regina said.

Roland asked, "Why do you need the money, Colin?"

"I want to take a long position on a stock."

The table went so quiet Colin could hear the sputtering tiki torches used to keep away the night insects. Finally, Alexi said, "Can you decode that a little for us?"

"I've developed an algorithmic method for tracking stock trends in the entertainment industry. There's a big opportunity coming. I want to invest before it happens."

Roland said, "There are any number of funds based on market trends. What makes you think—"

"This isn't about the *market*. I don't think a single *market* actually exists. This is about one industry. Actually, a number of different segments within the one."

Roland actually seemed pleased by his response. "Why entertainment?"

"Two reasons. There are more semihidden sources of advance news than any other industry. Most are unofficial websites."

"You're talking about the LA rumor mill," Roland said.

"A lot of dirt," Ethan said. "A lot of nonsense about stars who sell their souls for fame."

Colin heard the negative, the refusal, in Ethan's tone. But Roland looked across the table at his friend. A brief glance from those dark eyes. A silent communication that cleared the frown from Ethan's features. Roland said, "You've been tracking the online communication about the entertainment industry."

"Yes. And the major news sources."

"Which ones?"

"*Wall Street Journal. Fortune. Financial Times. LA Times. Variety. Hollywood Reporter. Deadline.*"

They were all watching him now. All sharing the same open expression. Beyond curious. Fascinated. Regina asked, "How often do you read these papers and magazines?"

"Every day. And a lot of other online sites."

"How long does all this take you?"

"Not long." He shrugged. "Half an hour, maybe a little more. It takes longer to input the data into my system. Two hours altogether."

"What about your schoolwork?"

"I lied to my teachers."

"You . . ."

"I told them I was having trouble with things I finished studying months ago." It felt better than good to reveal his secret world. Colin felt the weight lift balloon-like from his mind. "They don't know. They can't. I'm so far ahead they check my work and assign the next thing and leave me alone. Half the time my math teacher can't even explain what I claim I need help with."

"Let's back up a second," Roland said. "I want to know a little more about your sources. There must be a hundred analysts searching social media and news feeds for the latest opportunity."

"If it hits the public sites, it's too late for the first curve."

Alexi asked, "Do you understand what he just said?"

"Not really. What do you mean, curve?"

"You ride it. That's how it feels." Colin made a swooping gesture with his hands. "My analysis shows there are almost always two rises and falls before the news becomes official. Sometimes three."

"So the newspapers and journals . . ."

"They show trends. Patterns in each of the industry sectors. They form the foundation."

"And the event?"

"That comes mostly from specialist chat rooms. Sometimes the online industry sources. Not often."

"These chat rooms . . ."

"They are specific to the job. Professionals talking to professionals."

Lucas asked, "Aren't they like, super protected?"

"Most use the same firewall system." He was about to reveal how he had created a fake persona, then decided it could wait.

Roland asked, "You've found rumors about a what, a merger?"

"Acquisition," Colin said. "Yes. And no."

"Explain that."

"Entertainment stocks follow a set pattern. When the rumors grow to a certain point, the market buys in."

"And you predict this point with your . . ."

"Algorithms. Right. Then the rumors fade, something else captures attention, or a trend suggests the initial rumors weren't so great after all. The stock dips. Then the rumors start up again, this or next time including the real news sources. And the market rises a second time."

"So you're trying to get out in front of a new . . ."

"Product. It might lead to an acquisition. Whether or not that happens doesn't matter in this first rise."

"How many rumors, how many sources . . ."

"I only input the data once I've found the news in six different sites. At least a couple of these have to claim it came from different sources."

Roland made a process of realigning his cup and saucer and dessert plate. He folded his napkin, pressed it flat, set his fork on top. Pressed again. "You said two factors."

"There's a growing merger wave in the media sector. It's driven by deregulation and technological development. The E&M industry—"

Alexi asked, "E&M?"

"Entertainment and media," Roland said, almost impatient. "What this young man is saying jibes with information we're receiving through my firm's clients." To Colin, "You do know Wilmington has become one of the fastest growing offshoots of the LA entertainment groups."

"Yes."

He nodded. "Please proceed."

"All the industry sectors are transitioning to mobile access. New content offerings are being designed for the new environment. The industry is changing in the biggest ways since sound was introduced. There's a strategic shift to digital. Plus the big companies have strong cash reserves. And there's a growing number of private equity firms looking to invest."

Roland was nodding softly in time to Colin's words. "Which means any new potential acquisition . . ."

"It's not an acquisition," Colin said. His heart was racing now. Almost like Roland's quiet words were adding fuel to his own excitement. "Not yet."

"It's the rumors."

"The *potential.*"

Roland picked up his fork. Drummed the table. Once. Twice. A third time, then, "How sure are you that this works?"

"I've been doing it. For three and a half months."

"Using a sham account."

"Right."

"You started with a theoretical . . ."

"Ten thousand dollar investment."

"And you've made . . ."

"Two hundred and nineteen thousand dollars."

"In a hundred days."

"After paying out standard stock commissions. Right."

There were soft gasps from some of the others. But Colin couldn't be bothered to see who. Nor, did it seem, could Roland. "You have records of all this?"

"I kept dated notations of every move."

"How often did you lose money?"

"Twice," Colin replied.

"Out of . . ."

"Eleven," Colin replied. "Eleven investments."

The night and the silence settled in comfortably around him. Colin felt exhausted from the telling. So drained he wasn't even certain he could stand. He used both hands to lift his glass. His throat was so dry it was hard to swallow the water.

Alexi asked, "Why are you doing this, Colin?"

"Did you hear what he just said?" This from Mira. "Two hundred and nineteen thousand dollars in three months?"

Colin nodded agreement. "I'm through being poor."

CHAPTER 14

Mira and her father drove him back to the academy, only this time the journey was made in silence. No one spoke until Ethan pulled the Honda into the academy's semicircular drive. He cut the motor and sat there. Staring at the night like Colin's own father had done. Only there was no rancor here. No sense of fear. None.

When Ethan finally spoke, it was to say, "My daughter never speaks about her beginnings." He looked at Mira in the rearview mirror. "When you started in about Kabul, you shocked me right out of my skin."

"I don't know why I did. It just seemed . . ."

She let it trail off in a way that left Colin sensing a vulnerability. As if she had exposed a secret part of herself on a whim. And now was what? Afraid? Of him? He couldn't let the evening end on such a note. No matter what happened next. He knew there was every likelihood they would turn him down, and he would have no choice but to go to the people who would hear him out, then make all the wrong and dangerous moves. But that was not the issue here. He pushed the concerns aside and said what came first into his head. "My mother died when I was four. I don't know anything about her. I don't even know her maiden name. Her family basically disowned her when she married my father. It feels, I don't know . . ."

He stopped because he realized Ethan was staring at him. Mouth slightly open. The streetlights revealed a man in a state of utter astonishment.

Softly, so quietly it was little more than a whisper, Mira said, "Oh. My. God."

"Mira."

"Did you just hear what he said, Daddy?" She leaned forward. "What did it make you feel like, Colin?"

"Like this is the reason why I never felt complete." And suddenly he was glad for the dark, because he was overwhelmed by a sudden need to weep.

"Like you're missing a part of yourself," Mira said. "Like you'll never be whole."

Ethan noticed how Colin made two rapid swipes of his face. "Mira."

"I want to tell him, Daddy."

He did not reply. Instead, Ethan started the engine and rolled down all the windows. Then he cut the motor. And sat there. Staring at the empty street and the night.

"I'm a twin," Mira said. "Half of a broken whole. One that will never, ever be complete."

Ethan breathed deep.

Colin turned in his seat and watched as Mira tucked her feet up under her. Sitting cross-legged. Her eyes glowed warm and soft in the streetlights. "What happened?"

"I was sixteen months old. My brother hadn't been healthy since we were born. His name . . ." She stopped and wiped her eyes.

"Bacha," Ethan said softly. "It's the Pashto word for king."

“My parents took us to a clinic run by the Americans. It was next to the main air base. My aunt and uncle were there as well, and my grandparents. Everybody with something they wanted the American doctor to check out.”

“It was often like that,” Ethan said. “One person comes, everybody who can walk tags along. Some of the things they’d been living with, you wouldn’t believe.”

Mira went on, “We were standing in line to be seen by the doctor. The medic who took our details was a wonderful, beautiful man named Ethan.” She unfurled her legs and slid forward to drape her hand over her father’s shoulder. “And that was when the world exploded.”

“You don’t remember that.” He reached up to grasp her hand.

“I remember the light. The sound. The way I went flying from my father’s arms.”

“You remember what I told you.”

“I remember, Daddy.”

Ethan shrugged. “It was a car bomb. Planted outside the main gates. But they meant to take out the clinic as well. We were winning the minds and hearts of the locals. They couldn’t let that happen.”

“We were the only two people who survived. My entire family, gone. Ethan was injured, but just the same he went looking through the rubble. Searching to see if anyone else was still living.”

“And there you were,” Ethan said. “Your eyes shining like two dark jewels. Your body coated in dust. And still you didn’t cry. You just reached for me.”

“And you never let me go. Did you, Daddy.”

“I couldn’t. You were already my little girl.” To Colin, “The base chaplain was a good friend. He and his wife took her in. I finished my tour and came home and got busy with the paperwork.”

“First, you had to convince Momma.”

"My bride of six weeks before I shipped out." Ethan was smiling now. "Surprise, surprise. Alexi claims she already loved you long before I got home."

"From the first time she saw my photograph, that's what she says." To Colin, "That's how Daddy and Roland became friends. He's a family lawyer. He fought everybody until they let me be adopted."

"And we've stayed friends," Ethan said. "Despite him and Regina being seriously afflicted with the Democrat bug."

"Daddy keeps hoping they'll come around. He's the eternal optimist in our family," Mira said. "Dear sweet Lucas is the worst of the lot."

Colin was still coming to terms with everything he had just learned. "This is . . ."

"Amazing. I know."

He could see they were ready to go. The intimate moment was fading now. Colin opened his door. "Whatever happens about, you know, my investment, I just want to say, this was maybe the nicest evening I've ever had."

CHAPTER 15

Colin lay in his bed, listening to Sojourn House's quiet night sounds. Somewhere above a toilet flushed. From the bedroom next to his, the child murmured in his sleep. The floor creaked softly. Wind rustled the trees outside his window. Colin felt as though he was hearing it all for the first time. As though he had left for the dinner one person and came back another. So much had happened. If someone had asked him earlier, he would have said nothing could top the experience he had known at the dinner table, revealing the secrets he had prepared over a hundred hard and lonely days. And yet here he was, the words spoken in the car outside the academy's entrance echoing through his dark room. There was no room left over for anything else.

Through losing a twin, Mira had been brought to the same hollow experience that shaped him. Despite the love her adopted family showed, despite everything. The bond he had sensed that very first moment, when she had sat down beside him at the pool, the feeling so strong it seemed as though he had known her for years and years. It all had a reason now.

The logic that Colin normally prized as the paramount element in his world, it meant nothing in the face of this incredible fact.

Colin assumed he was too excited to sleep, too filled with a day crammed with incredible events. But it felt as though one moment he breathed in, and the next, the sun shone through his window.

Then he realized someone was knocking at his door. "Just a moment!"

He picked up the previous night's shirt and trousers from his floor, pulled them on, fumbled with the buttons, then opened the door. Mrs. Fitzgerald stood in the doorway, tall and formidable. "You have a telephone call."

"Okay. Thanks."

She did not move. "It is almost nine o'clock, Mr. Eames. Is this the sort of behavior I am to expect from you?"

He dry scrubbed his face. "I don't understand. Nine o'clock?"

She inspected him a moment longer, then wheeled about. "My office, sir. The instant your call is complete."

An hour and a half later, Ethan pulled into the academy forecourt. Mira was seated up front. Ethan used the electric controls to slide open the rear door and greeted Colin with, "Did we get you in trouble, making you miss school?"

He climbed in, set his backpack holding the laptop on the floor by his feet, and was still looking for the door's controls when it slid shut. "I start classes at UNCW next week. Everything is changing."

"You can say that again. Hi, Colin."

"Hi."

"Did you sleep okay?"

"Until nine. I don't think I've ever done that before."

"Not me, baby. I could sleep all day."

"Mira is our Energizer Bunny. She goes and goes, then collapses."

Colin asked, "Don't you have school?"

"Spring break. And no guard duty until three." She reached back and poked his leg. "You cost me a sleep-in."

"Ow."

"I'll give you ow." She poked him again.

"Stop, Mira. No bruising the boy genius."

And just like that, it was another easy day. They might be heading into a meeting that would decide his fate for years to come. But in that moment, it was Mira and her father and him. Together.

They drove downtown and entered the Murchinson Building's parking garage. Mira acted like a female balloon, bouncing about with them for an instant and then dancing away and then bouncing back again. They took the parking elevator to the lobby, signed in, and took another elevator to the ninth floor. Roland stood just inside the glass doors fronting the elevator lobby. He shut his phone and smiled as he pushed the door open. "How's my special girl?"

"Excited."

"That makes two of us. Good morning, Colin. Ready for round two?"

They entered the nicest conference room Colin had ever seen. One wall was floor-to-ceiling glass and overlooked the Cape Fear River. Another was lined with bookshelves holding hundreds of books. Half had two-tone leather bindings with gold lettering. The others were a deep rich blue. Roland watched Colin walk over and trace his finger down the ribbed back of one. "North Carolina statutes and case law. Federal is to your right. Are you interested in the law, Colin?"

"No." He liked how Roland spoke the word. With weight and respect. The *law.* "But I love books."

"Do you have a photographic memory?"

"Not exactly."

"Were you tested?"

"Yes. I made mistakes."

Roland told the others, "The proper term is eidetic. The tests are said to be awful. Right, Colin?"

"They were okay, I guess." Colin pulled down a book at random. He loved the heft, the onionskin pages, the dense text.

"The subject is given a sheet of paper with computer-generated dots. The page is taken away, and a second sheet is given. How long were you allowed to study each, Colin?"

"Twenty seconds."

"Then the subject is given a third sheet, this one blank. And told to list all the dots that were in the first page but not the second. In their proper places."

Mira asked, "How do you know about this?"

"Eidetic is often connected to serious development problems. It's been an issue in a couple of cases. And here comes Aaron."

Colin fit the book back into place as a small man entered. He was a head shorter than Mira and very skinny. But from that very first instant, Colin discounted the man's size. He carried a quiet intensity with him, a focus as tight as a laser. He shook Ethan's hand, smiled at Mira, then looked at Colin and said, "This young man must be the purpose for our gathering."

"None other." Roland said to Colin, "Aaron handles all our clients within the entertainment industry."

Aaron gestured to the chairs. "Why don't we all find seats and let this young man explain what has everyone so excited."

Colin talked for ninety-seven minutes straight. At some point they brought him a water, which he drank, and then someone filled his glass, and he drank that also. Describing the same concept, answering many of the same questions, did not change his feeling of being supercharged with the exposure of his dreams. And the pressure. All they knew of course was the opportunity's timeline. But that was enough.

Aaron asked far more probing questions. He insisted on seeing Colin's algorithms and then ordered him to do a step-by-step overview of how his fake investments had worked. Colin thought he had entered the meeting fully prepared, but Aaron's questions had him searching files and restructuring things from memory. Then he had to show how he had broken into the chat rooms, and where the current project's rumors had first surfaced, then how they reached crescendo. All the while, Aaron tracked the timeline of his fake acquisitions on Colin's computer. The only time he moved was to strip off his suit jacket and loosen his tie. He was the stillest man Colin had ever met.

Finally, the diminutive attorney said, "All right, I've seen enough."

Roland demanded, "Is this for real?"

"I can't follow the math. Which actually is somewhat reassuring. But the pattern of trends he has outlined is nothing short of astonishing."

Mira bounced in her chair. "This is just so totally wild."

Ethan said, "You guys left me in your dust about an hour ago. And I'm thrilled to bits."

Roland said, "So we are agreed? Aaron?"

"I'm in. Definitely."

"Ethan?"

"Green light."

Roland turned to Colin. Somber and official. And yet clearly pleased. "Here's what we propose. We establish a limited partnership. We supply you with the capital. You instruct us on the investments. In return, you receive twenty percent of all profits."

"Which is more than fair," Aaron offered. "On the high side of the going rate. The financial risk is all ours."

Colin looked from one to the other. "Capital?"

Aaron was the one to ask, "How many other potential investments have you targeted?"

"One more that might develop in a month or so. I'm watching six others. But ten thousand dollars, that can't be spread on so many longs."

"Hold on to your hat," Mira said, bouncing again.

"We are going to make an initial investment of ninety-six thousand dollars," Aaron said. "Thirty from each of us, and . . ."

"Three from me and three from Lucas," Mira said.

Ethan said, "You sure about this?"

"Absolutely, Daddy. No way you're doing this without us." She smiled across the table. "Anybody got a feather? We could knock Colin into next week."

Aaron went on, "We serve as legal conduits for several clients who do offshore investments. My aide's name is Lucretia Vaughan. She'll set up your accounts and handle the trades. Roland . . ."

"I'll handle it." To Colin, "There are some hoops we'll need to jump through before we can form the LLC. I suppose someone at the academy serves as your legal guardian— "

"No." He said it overloud. "Nobody there can know."

There was a moment's silence; then Ethan asked, "Why not, Colin?"

"It's complicated. But this has to remain secret."

Aaron looked at his partner. "Roland?"

The family lawyer studied the table in front of him for a long moment. Despite the silence, Colin found his sudden flame of fear subsiding. They were treating him as one of them. What he said mattered.

Roland looked up. "I can work this out."

"Then it's settled." Aaron rose from the table. "Sorry, I'm late for my lunch."

Colin asked, "When can I start?"

"The funds will be available to you this afternoon," Roland said.

"We don't need to wait for the paperwork," Aaron said. "Your timing issue is clear enough." He offered Colin his hand. "Young man, this has been remarkable. I look forward to hearing good news."

CHAPTER 16

Colin's target was Legend Inc., a publicly traded maker of electronic games based in North Carolina's Research Triangle Park. Industry analysts had long classed it as a one-hit wonder. Their first major release, a syfy adventure called *Barsoom*, had been a global hit. But they had rushed the sequel and relied too heavily on their ongoing success. The second game had bombed.

For the past four years, Legend had been developing a new game. During this same period, however, the industry had undergone seismic shifts. The user platforms, from laptops to Nintendo, had all seen major upgrades. The industry analysts working for the major banks and investment funds downgraded the company. As Colin worked his calculations, he visualized a flock of vultures in fancy suits and ties circling far overhead.

For a month and eleven days following his investment, nothing happened.

Colin's biggest relief to that nerve-wracking wait came

from meeting Mira. She texted once or twice each week, suggesting a time when she could swing by. Usually they frequented a café in the Mayfaire outdoor mall. Occasionally her lifeguard schedule meant they'd meet at the club's coffee shop. Lucas was usually with her at the club. Colin liked her boyfriend but vastly preferred being alone with Mira, listening to her talk. Once she took him to a favorite bistro for a meal after she finished school, just the two of them. That was the most special time of all. Mira drove a bright yellow VW convertible, a perfect vehicle for a beautiful young woman. Colin never said how nervous he was when she drove too fast and was too quick to use the horn. Not to mention how she spent as much time looking at him as the road. They never spoke about the investment. She never asked why he was skipping so many swim lessons. Mira talked about her life, her work with the Young Republicans, her relationship with Lucas, her application to the University of Virginia. The topic did not matter. For those brief interludes, Colin was able to set aside the pressures and the fears. She talked, he absorbed.

He wondered if her relationship with Lucas filled the void from the loss of her twin. After that first conversation, Mira never again brought the topic up. He did not want to risk the pleasure of those hours by touching on a sensitive issue. But for Colin, every meeting reinforced the sense that theirs was a bond that went far beyond two new friends.

The remainder of that interminable period, Colin barely slept. He skipped meals. He paced. He ran his calculations six, seven, eight times a day. Each new shred of information was a reason to panic.

Every Monday, Wednesday, and Friday, the Uber driver was waiting out front when he emerged at seven o'clock. The morning and afternoon commutes to and from UNCW took around twenty minutes, depending on traffic. He was signed up for three classes: calculus two and three, and advanced problem solving. Fremdt taught both the calculus classes. APS was handled by a postdoc.

Those first weeks at UNC Wilmington passed in a featureless blur. The classes were challenging, but despite his serrated schedule he found himself able to follow everything. When his professors called on him, Colin managed to respond. He got several things wrong, but if either professor noticed his superficial study habits they did not mention it aloud. Outside of classes Colin was stared at, but no one bothered him. Or at least if they did, he couldn't be bothered to notice.

He stopped attending academy classes altogether.

Six weeks after the funds had been invested, Arnold stopped by the house. "Where have you been?"

"I don't understand the question."

"You don't . . ." He took a long look at Colin. "What's the matter with you?"

"Nothing's the matter. I'm tired, is all."

"Your teachers are raising a stink."

"I can't go to class anymore. I just can't."

"And you missed our last appointment."

"I didn't. . . . We had an appointment?"

They were seated in the computer room. Colin hated using the house equipment, with the sticky keyboards and the hostile looks that tracked him. He was an oddity now, even among the Sojourn House residents. The place that once had been his refuge had become just another cage. The confines of his room were growing ever tighter. He came down occasionally when the other students were in class. Wandering from room to room, returning now and then to the screens. Whenever he was working downstairs, he used three computers. This allowed him to run the calculations from two different directions and follow the market graphs on a third. He saw Arnold studying the minute-to-minute updates in stock prices, and started to swipe the screen clean. But then he decided it didn't matter.

"What is this, Colin?"

"A project. For school." It had not grown any easier to lie. Despite how almost all his life was centered upon the secrets he dared not share. Not yet. But soon.

Arnold insisted they go for a walk. "Maybe we were in error, letting you start university so soon."

The daylight hurt his eyes. He went because at least he could breathe clean air. "No. It's great."

"It doesn't look great. It looks like the pressure is about to crush you."

"Everything is new, that's all."

"Braxos came to see me. He wants to know if you're still registered as a student here. He says he's about to give you a failing grade." When Colin responded by laughing out loud, Arnold's tone hardened. "This is serious, Colin. I've explained the situation. But you need to show up."

"I'll sit his exams. All of them. But no classes."

"You don't have the right—"

"I can't attend them anymore. I just can't."

Thankfully, Arnold responded by changing the subject. "Professor Fremdt says he is going to recommend you be matriculated in the fall."

Colin knew he had to respond. "That's great."

"You don't sound happy."

"It's a lot right now."

"I can see that." Arnold stopped beneath a vast cypress. "Will you try to get some sleep? And look at your clothes. They're falling off you."

"I'll take better care. I promise." He watched Arnold walk away, the man bowed beneath new worries. Colin wanted to race after him, confess. Instead, he forced himself to turn away. Walk back to the house. Climb the front stairs.

Draw up his calculations once more. Reenter the electronic hurricane of his own making.

Fifty-three days after Lucretia Vaughan followed his instructions and took a long position on their stock, the gaming industry's two major journals both broke the story. Their specialists had been invited to take part in beta testing the new project. Legend's new game was, in their mutual opinion, nothing short of sensational.

In the eighteen days that followed their online announcements, the stock went from a dollar and eleven cents per share to six and change.

When his ongoing calculations raised the first red flag, Colin was almost glad to call Lucretia and order her to sell. Sell everything.

Twelve minutes later, Roland called him back. "Are you sure this is the right move?"

"I am. Yes."

"I'm only asking because the *Journal*'s online news feed is singing Legend's praises. I have it up on my screen as we speak."

Colin was hunched over the straight-back chair in his bedroom. He could hear the other students moving back and forth along the downstairs corridor, carrying their evening meal to the dining table. Colin had not realized another day had almost ended until he noticed the smells. They made him nauseous. He knew he needed to eat, but he wasn't certain he could keep anything down. "That's why we're selling."

"Expand on that for us."

"Who is with you?"

"Aaron's here in my office. Lucas is on his way over. Ethan and Mira are on the other line."

"The news is out," Colin replied. "My calculations show the crest is either now, or happening soon."

"Hang on, let me tell Ethan." He waited as Roland relayed the message. Then, "Aaron says we should stop jiggling your elbow and trust you."

There was no reason why the words should make him want to weep. "I have to go."

"Wait. What do we do now?"

"Nothing. For the moment, we watch."

He cut the connection, descended the stairs, and joined the others in the dining room. The chamber held one larger table for eight, two for four, and two others for three. It was an odd situation, but it worked. The atmosphere was more casual and intimate than if everyone was forced to sit together. There were always a few empty chairs, which also helped. Colin filled his plate from the chafing dishes lining the sideboard. He chose the one empty table and ate alone. He had no idea whether he had been assigned kitchen duty. He had not glanced at the board holding the weekly list of chores since all this began. He helped bus the tables, then accepted the two dish towels from Camila, one damp and one dry, and cleaned all the dining room surfaces. He felt like a robot with its battery almost flat. Unfeeling, uncaring. Just going through the motions.

When he reentered the kitchen, Camila accepted the two towels and pointed him to the drying rack. Wiping down the dishes and putting them away meant he was the last student to finish.

As he closed the side cupboard, Camila said, "You been skipping meals. You sleeping okay?"

It was their first real conversation in six years. "Some. Not a lot."

"You're losing weight. If you're sick, you need to tell the lady."

"I'm not sick."

"You sure about that, are you?" Dark eyes surveyed his

form. "I guess you look all right, except for those plum bruises you got under your eyes."

"I want to stop being so fat."

She turned back to scrubbing the stove with a wire brush. "Well, you're going about it all wrong. What you want is to get yourself in shape. Eat right. Sleep. Exercise. That's how you lose weight and keep it off."

"I like to swim."

"When was the last time you got in the pool?"

"I don't . . ." He had trouble figuring out it was Friday. Which was when he realized he had missed several lessons. "I went last Sunday. No, wait. That was . . . four Sundays ago." He felt vaguely ashamed. That so much time, so many weekends could pass unnoticed. But it was all he could do just to hold himself together.

"You should be doing something every day." She used a soiled towel to go over the stove top. "You head off for your classes so early, you eating any breakfast?"

"I get a glass of juice sometimes."

"That ain't enough." She pointed at the three refrigerators lining the side wall. "Look in that middle one. Down there at the bottom. Those yogurts are meant for Grant, but I'll tell him. He won't mind you sharing. You take one, you mix it with fruit from the bowl. Apple, banana, something. Then you put some of them bran flakes on top."

"That sounds awful."

"Don't matter how it sounds. You got to eat a balanced diet, you want to lose weight and get in shape. That starts with breakfast. Else you'll just put the weight back on faster than you lost it." She went back to scrubbing. "I imagine you just ate yourself some meat and a pile of potatoes. With gravy, I bet. How many vegetables did you put on your plate?"

"I don't like them."

"Now you're sounding like a child. You want me to treat you like a little boy, or a man?"

Colin had no idea how to respond, and remained silent.

"Balanced diet," she repeated. "Cut down on the fat and the carbs. You're a smart boy, check out what I'm telling you online."

"No," he said. "I don't need to. I'll do what you say."

"Three meals each day. Stop skipping. Don't matter how busy you are. And eat smarter." She pointed at the exit. "Now you go get yourself some rest. And remember what I told you."

CHAPTER 17

Colin slept well enough, almost ten hours. For the first time in months, he also ate breakfast. The other house residents were busy with their morning routines, and Colin was tempted to have a glass of apple juice and depart. But Camila was there in the kitchen, and watched him prepare the bowl as she had instructed. She resumed her customary silence and merely pointed him to a chair at the kitchen's central table. The flavors were strange, but not unpleasant. In fact, he liked how the different textures blended together. When he finished he carried his bowl and spoon and knife to the sink and washed them carefully. After he had dried them and replaced them in the cabinet, he started to leave, then turned back and said, "Thank you."

"You see you hold to good habits now, you hear?" Camila addressed the wall by the stove. "Just because you've got yourself a good mind don't mean you can ignore what your body is saying."

He returned to his room, gathered his trunks and goggles and sandals and towel, then stood looking down at his laptop. The fact that he wasn't tied to the calculations left him weightless. He zipped his backpack closed and departed.

The walk to the pool for his Saturday morning class seemed to take forever. At some point during the previous weeks, the season had changed. North Carolina's version of spring had ended. The day was already summertime hot. The flavors of magnolia and pine and dogwood were made stronger by the stillness and humidity. Colin's legs felt leaden. His every step required conscious thought. When the club's golf course finally came into view, he stopped and stared. Reveling in the sense of having taken a major step into his own future.

Before class started, Colin sat on the pool's edge with his feet in the water. He felt utterly disconnected from the noise and laughter and people; it seemed almost natural for his mind to wander back to those early days. Colin wondered if this was what his mother felt, sitting by the ocean, staring out at what she had called the sapphire sea. Disconnected from everything that weighed down her life, able to breathe easy and find pleasure in this simple moment. She felt closer to Colin than she had in a long while. He could not actually see her smile. But he felt it.

Colin made it to the end of class, but barely. During his absence, the other children had spent the past weeks learning things his body simply could not handle. Thankfully, Mira was not working that day. The two instructors were new to him. They treated him like he was an invalid. They used a gentle voice. They were patient. They put him in his own lane. Colin spent much of the hour burning with shame.

Afterward he stretched out on the paving stones lining the pool's side, his feet dangling in the water. He was exhausted, but the sun and the hot concrete felt good on his skin.

He heard Mira say, "Well, hey, stranger."

Colin found it a struggle just to sit up. "I was terrible today."

"Yeah, I heard your backstroke wouldn't win any prizes."

"I let the days slip past. I'm sorry."

"Don't apologize. Not ever." She was dressed in a relatively modest two-piece suit, just another teen coming to the pool for a day off. She looked wonderful. "My folks are doing backflips over how the investment has turned out."

He waved feebly, swatting away any thoughts about the world beyond the pool. "I'm going to start swimming every day."

"Try and get here early. The pool has lap time from seven to nine. After that we're into the summer invasion." She pointed to the kiddie pool. "We're all over there, if you want to join us."

He followed her across the patio area, greeted the two families, accepted their congratulations. Ethan pulled a chair under the umbrella where Gracie was playing and told Colin, "You need to be careful in this sun."

"Come over here," Alexi said, rummaging in her large case. "Let me put some cream on your shoulders."

He did as he was instructed. Colin accepted their offer of raspberry tea served in a plastic cup, then took a slice of homemade egg salad on whole wheat. Discovered he was famished. Ate a second portion. And leaned back.

The peace and clarity that came from being here with these people was exactly what he needed. The fact that he had succeeded with the investment was very nice. But it did not define the feelings they had for him. At some level far deeper than his body's fatigue, Colin felt replenished.

When he returned from the pool, Colin called Celeste and asked if they could meet. She was attending a weekend conference at the university's college of health and human services and arranged to meet Sunday morning in the Child Services Department's lobby. The questions were there in her tone, but she did not ask why he felt such an urgent need, and he did not volunteer anything. When he cut the connection he discovered his heart was racing.

He went to bed straight after dinner. The events were about to start unfolding. Everything he had kept so carefully hidden away. It was all happening. But this was not the same as during the interminable wait for the stock to begin its climb, or the endless hours searching for the time to pull out. This was all part of a situation and plans he had been working toward. He could see that now. As he undressed and brushed his teeth and climbed into bed, he felt as if he stood at the edge of a river. All the events that had shaped his recent years, all the people who had impacted him, they and their lives were joined in this twisting, tumbling series of events. When he lay down, he had the impression that he had settled onto a raft and pushed himself into the endless, powerful flow. The instant his head hit the pillow, he was gone.

Sunday Colin took an Uber straight from the pool to the university. He arrived an hour early for his appointment with Celeste, but there was a coffee shop on the ground floor, where he had lunch. When it was time, he followed the signs and the sound of voices up the central stairs. The paintings and murals lining the UNCW Child Services lobby and corridor walls were different, but similar. He sensed the same dark shadows lurking just out of view. Only now he was old enough to name at least some of them.

Celeste caught sight of him and stepped away from an animated conversation. She greeted him with an almost formal air. "I've arranged for us to have a quiet space." As she led him down the central corridor, she observed, "You've lost weight."

Colin followed her into an empty office with two narrow windows. "I've been busy."

"With university classes." She smiled at his surprise. "Of

course I keep tabs on you. What do you think, now that you're all grown up I'd just drop you like a bent penny?"

The warm concern in that big dark face, the strength, the woman's solidity, it left him suddenly ready to weep with joy.

"Child, what's the matter?"

"I'm glad we can talk."

"Well, of course we can. If you've got a problem, why didn't you contact me sooner?"

"I couldn't."

"Well, we're here now. The door's closed. The world is out there. It's just you and me in here. Tell me what's wrong."

He had planned it all out. What to say and how. Instead, now that he was with her, he started at the end. "I've been making investments."

She listened with a wide-eyed astonishment as he described it. She made no comment as he stopped in midsentence, backed up, and talked about how he had lied to Arnold and Sandrine and his academy teachers. How he had held back. Created a myth that they accepted as truth. Not just Braxos. All the others. Which brought him back to the investments. He described creating the algorithms and the mock investments that followed. Honing his investment instrument in the process. He had read that term in the *Journal* and liked how it suited his work. His investment instrument creating the melody of money.

When he was done, Celeste touched the tip of her tongue to her lips. Hesitating. Then, "How much have you made? I mean, since all this went real and you started investing those people's money."

"Three hundred and ninety-seven thousand dollars. A fifth is mine."

"Child . . ." She seemed to find it difficult to shape the words. "Colin, honey, why haven't you told anyone before now?"

He found himself clenching down. Walking forward at

the level of thought and bone and sinew. Gathering himself. "Because the money isn't important. Well, it is. But that's not the secret."

"Seems to me that's all you've been doing for months on end. Manufacturing secrets."

Another step. Close enough now to peer over the edge. "I had to."

"I don't see why." When he remained tightly clenched and quiet, she showed a genuine irritation. "I don't even understand why you *think* you needed—"

"That's not why we're meeting. That's not the reason I'm here."

Something in the way he spoke pushed her back a notch. "Well, now."

"I've been preparing."

"For what?"

"For something that had to stay a secret. Until today."

"You're going to tell me the big reason behind you living a lie?"

"Yes." He took a long breath and . . .

Released.

He told her everything.

CHAPTER 18

Celeste insisted upon both spending another night in Wilmington and making the appointment with Roland herself. She said that way the attorney would view Colin's situation as separate from their investments. Colin gave her Roland's home number from memory, then listened as she talked. She began by apologizing for calling on a Sunday afternoon, her voice very different from anything he had heard before. She was very formal, her diction almost mechanical in its precision. And something more. Celeste spoke with solemn authority. There was no question in Colin's mind that she was the individual in control.

That night he ate dinner with the other Sojourn House students, only he filled his plate according to Camila's instructions. The taste of vegetables and meat without gravy was not bad, just different. He sat at the large table and pretended to follow the easygoing Sunday conversation. But most of his attention was given over to analyzing his eating habits. He realized he had been lazy, making choices that suited. It shamed him that he could be so intensely focused on his mind and his algorithms and his investment instruments, and at the same time deny his body its requirements. It wasn't just the food, or the missed swimming lessons. He had to learn a greater sense of balance.

For the first time in weeks, the path of his thoughts led him to his internal state. Colin had been so intensely focused that the absence that defined his internal world had become little more than a whispered longing. Now as he ate a silent meal, Colin wondered if this was how his entire life would unfold. Never knowing a time when the absence did not define him.

As if in response, a series of mental images took hold. Mira and Lucas. For the first time, Colin viewed them as a beacon for his own tomorrow. Perhaps.

He was drawn from the hopeful reverie by a voice asking, "Is it true what they're saying, you're going to the university?"

The boy who spoke was a newcomer named Lenny, an African American youth of eight. Colin had heard snippets of conversation about him. Lenny was the new amazement. His near eidetic ability was capable of vacuuming up whatever text or information was put before him. He was studying languages. All six offered at the academy. And linguistics, the root foundations of human speech.

Colin replied, "I started this term."

"What's it like, being there with all those big people?"

"They mostly leave me alone."

"They watch you, though, don't they. Give you the eye. Make you feel smaller than you already are."

He was a strange little fellow, with slightly mottled skin, like caramel and chocolate had not been fully blended. His eyes held a brilliant cast, an intensity that Colin liked. "I try not to let it bother me."

"I hear you." Lenny stirred his remaining beans and mashed potatoes with his fork. "That pretty much describes how it's always been for me. Trying to ignore all the looks and the talk."

Colin watched the boy form designs on his plate. Lenny's arm was tiny, his wrist and fingers fragile, bird-like. "Do you plan on going there?"

"I expect I won't be having that chance."

Colin realized all the room's other conversations had gone silent. "Why not?"

"They don't see me living that long."

The boy's casual reply shocked him. "Who is 'they'?"

"Pretty much everybody, near as I can figure. I've had fits since I was a baby. All the talk I'm not supposed to be hearing is about what it's done to my head. You know. The cumulative effect."

Colin sensed there was a purpose to the boy's confession. Lenny was not making idle conversation. He was after something. "If you could, you know, go there, what would you want to study?"

He looked up from his plate, the feverish gleam hungry now. Desperate. "The metalanguage of linguistics. The maths of language structure. I'd like that a lot."

"And Braxos . . ."

The boy went back to stirring the remnants of his meal into a series of geometric designs. "Braxos. Hunh."

Colin felt the link strengthen. "What are you doing this summer?"

"I expect I'll be staying right here. My momma's gone. I heard my daddy tell the school he doesn't know what to do with me."

"We could study together, if you like. I don't know the first thing about linguistics. But I do know maths."

The boy looked ready to weep. "I'd like that better than just about anything."

Colin rose from the table, carried his plate into the kitchen, and fell in with the others, doing his share of the Sunday evening chores. That done, he climbed the stairs to his room.

He slept and did not dream.

CHAPTER 19

The next morning, Colin rose before the house. He was downstairs at six, the air through the open kitchen window surprisingly chilly. He ate another bowl of fruit and yogurt and bran flakes, then left the academy and walked along empty streets. The club held to a sleepy morning rhythm, the only fast activity coming from other early swimmers. The pool was shockingly cold, but Colin found that after half a lap he actually liked it. He took his time, carefully studying his motions, trying to move through the water like Mira. He failed, of course. But it felt better than good to use that as his goal.

Afterward he sat in one of the pool chairs facing the sun. He stayed there just half an hour, long enough to feel his skin begin to crinkle. He used his cell phone to call for an Uber, then went inside to shower and dress. The car was waiting in the club's parking lot when he emerged.

As he traveled to the same shopping center where Arnold had taken him, Colin made a mental note to tell his adviser about using the car service for a personal matter. He knew it was ridiculous, worrying about an unapproved Uber charge when he had lived behind so many half-truths. But this was different. He could not explain it any better than that. Nor, that particular morning, did he feel any need.

He was the barbershop's first customer. The lone hairdresser on early duty was a young Latino who clearly disliked jazz. But when Colin asked, he grudgingly agreed to put on an album by Billie Holiday. "I don't like what she sings, you know, with the orchestra and stuff. But the lady has got a voice that can make even that old music sound good."

When the cut was finished, the barber asked Colin what he thought of the lady. He replied, "I never knew anyone could sing like that."

"She knows her notes, that's the truth."

"She doesn't just sing," Colin replied. "She speaks to your heart."

The young man chuckled as he brushed Colin down. "When the old man talked about you, I thought he was just blowing smoke. You're okay, little man. You come back any time you like."

As he paid, he said, "I need to buy a suit. Where is the best place for kids?"

The barber thought it over while Colin signed the debit-card slip. "Hugo Boss is probably your best bet. But they're expensive. Else go on down to Nordstrom, the big store right at the other end."

Colin walked the mall's sunlit avenue, feeling the current gathering pace. There was no distance to the day, no protective element, no choice except traveling with the force, allowing himself to become part of everything he had put in place. The tension so real, so vivid, he wondered if he would ever step back from it again.

The saleslady at Hugo Boss was reluctant to serve him at first. Colin felt a vague sense of shame over needing to assure her that he could pay. It was nothing like the embarrassment that had so plagued him in the early days. But still it tarnished the moment. His discomfort grew far worse when he stood in front of the triple mirrors and viewed his body from three sides. The clothes he had bought with Arnold hung on him like a partly deflated balloon. The weight loss was shocking when seen like this. The woman appeared touched by his dismay, for she took on a professional tone and guided him through the process of selection. At her advice, he went for a jacket and two pairs of pants, two dress shirts, and a tie. Two packs of underwear. A pair of shorts and new swim trunks that fit properly. The process was both exhausting and satisfying.

He emerged wearing the jacket of silk and cotton weave, two shades of blue and one of grey. Slate grey gabardine trousers. White shirt with matching grey stripes. Navy tie with grey diamond designs. The saleslady had packed his old clothes in a second bag. He carried those and his other purchases to the Starbucks and treated himself to a hot chocolate and melted cheese sandwich. When it was time, he ordered an Uber and was outside the main entrance when it pulled up.

Celeste was already seated in the waiting room when he entered Roland's law offices. She was dressed in a rich amber-colored suit of rough silk. She watched him set his shopping bags by the receptionist's desk and gave him a careful up and down. Then she said merely, "Well now."

"I've lost so much weight." Colin took the seat next to her. He knew the receptionist was watching them and pitched his voice low. "I never really saw it until just now, buying these clothes."

"You did good," Celeste said. "I started to say something yesterday, then decided not to add to your worries." She leaned back so as to survey him again. "This look, it's right for you."

The compliment warmed him. "You look pretty."

She huffed a quick laugh. "A lady of my size and years, pretty don't cut it."

"I don't know a better word."

"Well, it's nice that you said it just the same." She seemed ready to speak, then stopped herself.

"What is it?"

"Nothing that can't wait."

"We're here, we're waiting, when could be better than now?"

"Thing is, I've got a girl in college and a boy . . ." She shook her head. "Truth be told, I don't know what's going to happen to my son."

Colin had no idea how to respond.

"I've got me some savings, see . . ."

"You want me to invest for you?"

"Are you making another investment?"

"Any day now. Soon as the stock dips."

"You explained all that, but I didn't really understand."

"You don't need to. That's my job."

She still looked worried. "You think it would be all right with those other people, me putting my money in?"

"Celeste . . ." He found his throat constricting. The lady had seen him through so much. "Of course it's okay."

"You sure about that?"

"After everything you've done for me? I only wish I had thought to ask you yesterday."

Her face crimped with an almost-smile. "You had other things on your mind."

The receptionist chose that moment to set down her phone and announce, "Mr. Perez will see you now."

CHAPTER 20

Nine days later, Roland drove Colin to Greenville in order to pick up Celeste. Then the three of them traveled on to an upscale strip mall between Rocky Mount and Raleigh. Colin had insisted on Roland billing him for the hours. This was an attorney-client issue. Friendship had to be set aside. Roland had disliked it intensely, but in the end reluctantly agreed.

When he tried the same argument on Celeste, pay her as a consultant, she had threatened to hang up the phone.

The mall was very upscale, with sidewalks fashioned from multicolored paving stones. Integrated planters sprouted a riot of blooms. Storefronts bore signs hanging from metal poles attached to brickwork above the entrances. His father's place was a double unit, four glass windows in all.

"No use in arriving early," Roland said. He left the motor running for the AC. Ten o'clock in the morning, the heat and humidity were very intensive. "Let's run through strategy once more."

Colin only half listened to Roland and Celeste talking. His mind was already moving beyond the coming events. That morning he had made his second investment. He had decided to apply just half the total funds. This time his target was a maker of software for the burgeoning CGI industry. He thought there was every chance this asset would prove more profitable than the first. Even so, he held back money because he thought the games company stock was approaching bottom, and he wanted to be ready to ride the climb toward acquisition. His mind became captured by a single word. Diversification. It rolled around and around, like the basis for a song Billie Holiday might sing. Then he realized the two adults had turned around and were watching him. "Sorry. I was . . ."

"You weren't here, that's for certain." Celeste leaned over. "You all right?"

"I'm fine." He ran his hand over the seat's leather surface. Roland drove a Mercedes E Class. He loved the smooth ride, the elegant finish.

Celeste asked, "Colin, where is your mind?"

"Today's investment."

Roland said, "You're not the least bit worried about the coming battle?"

"I've been thinking about this for so long. . . . I'm just glad I don't have to go in there alone."

The two of them inspected him, sharing the same somber expression. Like his words had stripped away the last vestiges of their own tension. Finally, Celeste reached for her door. "Let's get this over with."

They passed through the glass doors and entered a single large room. Celeste paused just inside the entry, took in the room and the young staffers and the lone office at the back with its glass wall overlooking the chamber. Then she said, "Hmmm-mmm. Would you just get a load of this place."

Nine people staffed desks. Another six desks were empty save for ringing phones and piles of documents and colorful pamphlets. Boxes of fliers and posters lined the walls. The staff was mostly young, mostly male except for one young Latina. Colin had known a flash of very real fear entering his father's campaign headquarters, anxious that he might find Mira working there. She had become increasingly fervent about her Young Republican activities. It was driving a wedge between her and Lucas, causing them both very real pain. Colin liked them as a couple. The thought of a split, especially one over politics, both hurt him and left him feeling helpless.

He followed Celeste over to a row of padded chairs lining the right-hand wall. He seated himself and watched Roland speak with the young woman. She headed toward the glassed-in office at the back of the room. Roland hesitated, then followed her, winding his way through the desks. She tapped on the closed door, and a man standing beside Colin's father motioned for them to enter. He was a tall older gentleman in a grey pin-striped suit. He and Roland seemed to know each other. They exchanged words, Roland looked pointedly at his watch, and retreated. The three men turned and looked at Colin. Their gazes gave nothing away. Then they went back to talking among themselves.

Colin's and Celeste's chair legs were linked, meaning Celeste's bulk was mashed close to Colin's side. He did not mind. Her warmth and her strength formed the same support he had relied on the last time they had confronted his father. Together. Just like now.

Roland came back over and seated himself on Colin's other side. Wedging him in between the two adults. A human shield fashioned from strength and knowledge and trust. Roland said, "The silver fox is Grey Robinson. He's an attorney representing a number of major Republican donors. The other man I don't know. I suspect he's your father's campaign manager."

The three men in the glass-walled office continued to shoot him tight glances. Their expressions were all the same, emotionless and stony. Colin shut his eyes. He knew they assumed they held all the cards. They were the ones about to dictate terms. He would soon find out if he had taken all the necessary steps. For the moment, Colin found comfort in the simple facts that he was as prepared as he could be, and he had the support of true friends. Roland might be a more recent addition, but the man was solid. Street smart, that was the term. Colin settled his head against the cool cement wall and let his mind roam.

He had started using an online study of jazz as a way of cooling down, especially when he woke up in the middle of the night and all the daytime energies and tension loomed around his narrow bed. He loved the mathematical precision of how musicians discussed their melodies and the theory that dominated their profession. The patterns carried an entirely new language: harmonics, jazz notation, dominant sevenths, twelve bars, major and minor shifting chord lines, circle of fifths, the tonic, chords to the bar, blues harmony, propulsive energy.

"Where is that mind of yours?"

He opened his eyes to find Celeste smiling at him. "Jazz. The more I learn, the more I love it."

She examined him a long moment. "That really sets you off from most of the young people I work with."

He had no idea what she meant. "They don't like jazz?"

"I'm not talking about music. What I'm saying, it's not enough to be smart. You need a direction."

"Compass heading, you once called it."

"There you go. You take aim and you go after it. Hard as you can. You're committed." She continued to smile at him. "Knowing who you are and what you want are crucial to forming a good life. You can't imagine how fine it makes me feel knowing you're going to be all right."

Her confidence unsettled him. The fact was, Colin had no idea who he truly was. None. The question itself threatened him at a very deep level, far beneath his racing heart, utterly removed from the day's imminent threat. And as for what he wanted . . . Colin wanted to tell her how wrong she was. He had never seen farther ahead than handling the next crisis, taking the next step. Just like today. Confront his father. Make another investment. And then . . . What? He had no idea.

He wanted to correct her, beg for answers he did not have, ask how she could be so confident, when Roland spoke from their other side. "Have you told Mira and Ethan who your father is?"

He was almost glad for the reason to turn away from Celeste and his own confusion. "No."

"Probably best to wait on that. He's a major supporter of Roger Eames."

Colin nodded. "I was afraid I'd find Mira here."

"Her Young Republicans are big on the candidate, no question." Roland picked up his briefcase. "Heads up, people. We're on."

Colin looked over to find the men still clustered together watching them. He knew they were very displeased with how comfortable he appeared with Celeste and Roland. As he followed the attorney across the main room, Colin silently responded, *Tough.*

CHAPTER 21

"Come in, come in!" The lawyer Grey Robinson waved them into the rear office. "You must be Colin. Good afternoon, young man." He seemed to find nothing wrong with Colin's silence. Grey turned to Celeste and said, "And who might this be?"

"Dr. Celeste Talbot serves as the de facto guardian of Colin Eames," Roland said.

"That is not happening," his father said. "Not now, not ever."

Roland waved Celeste and Colin into seats to his right. He pulled a third chair slightly away from theirs and replied, "That remains to be seen, doesn't it."

And just like that, the lines of conflict were drawn.

Colin felt his heart rate surge, an electric response to the room's rising tension. And yet he remained somewhat removed. As if none of this could genuinely touch him.

The trio facing Colin were not defining his future. They only thought they were. And their thinking was as wrong as their assumptions over what was about to take place.

"We were so pleased to receive your request for this meeting. Weren't we, gentlemen." Grey Robinson was seated behind the massive oak desk, slightly to one side of Colin's father. The other man, who still had not been introduced, stood in the corner with his arms crossed. Removed. Isolated. Watching. He was small and unkempt and wore wrinkled trousers to what probably was a fancy suit. His shirt was marginally tucked in, the end of his belt dangling like a limp leather tongue. His gaze was a milky green and hard as a frozen pond.

Grey went on, "We had been intending to contact you ourselves. That is, if you are indeed serving as the school's attorney of record."

"I am not," Roland said.

Grey displayed a mocking and jovial surprise. Colin thought his words and gestures were far too theatrical for the room's small confines. In a courtroom, before a jury, they might work well enough. Here, Grey looked like a man out of his element. Assuming he was in total control because of who he was. An attorney representing power on the rise.

Grey said, "Excuse me, Roland. Then why on earth are you even present?"

Roland chose not to respond.

Colin's father was seated in a massive leather office chair. The wall behind him was dominated by a giant mural, the same image as on the posters decorating the front room. It showed him standing between two American flags gazing hard and intent upon the distant horizon. Overhead words were written in a script of stars and stripes: *Roger Eames for the United States Congress.*

Grey went on, "We have learned of highly disturbing issues related to students housed within the Outer Banks Academy."

"Duly noted," Roland replied calmly.

Grey took that as his signal to begin gesticulating. His voice rose in tandem with his motions. Addressing the unseen jury. "We have serious complaints that we intend to raise within the court of public opinion. Failing that, we will begin proceedings in court. Given what we have uncovered, this could go federal."

Roland waited. Then, "Are you quite done?"

"Am I . . . Don't you want to know what the charges are?"

"I have no interest whatsoever in your legal maneuverings."

"Well, you and the academy will soon enough, I assure you of that."

Roland shrugged. "Again, noted. Can we now move to the matters at hand?"

"What do you think we are doing now?"

"I have no idea."

A flush crept up from Grey's collar. "You may mock, sir. But I assure you, these charges against your group"

"Again, Counselor, I do not represent the academy. As far as we are concerned, the academy does not enter into this meeting. If you insist, I will convey your intentions. But I personally think you would be better served to alert them personally."

It was Grey's turn to go silent. Then, "You are making no sense whatsoever."

"I don't see how I can be any clearer. Whatever charges you intend to bring against the academy have nothing whatsoever to do with us or why we requested this meeting."

Roger Eames slammed one elbow on the desk and pointed at Colin. "That boy, my son, is done studying at that place."

The man standing in the corner said, "Roger."

"He's finished being fed their mess of liberal, left-leaning—"

"*Roger.*" Harder this time.

Grey said, "Perhaps I should handle this."

His father leaned back. Smoldering.

"Now then," Grey said. "The only possible way the academy can hope to avoid a lengthy and potentially damaging set of proceedings is to relinquish their hold—"

"Point of order," Roland said. "Actually, two points. First, my client is no longer a student at the academy."

The news clearly rattled the older attorney. "Your client, did you say?"

"That is correct."

"You have taken a juvenile, a preadolescent, as your pro bono client?"

"There is nothing pro bono about Colin Eames, I assure you."

"Who is paying his legal bills?"

"That is none of your concern." Roland reached into his case and drew out a single thick file. He opened the cover and handed over the first page. "What should be of immediate interest, Counselor, is the fact that my client is now a student at UNC Wilmington."

Grey made no move to accept the page. "But . . . the child is twelve years old."

"At least on that point you are correct." When no one reached forward, Roland let the page fall onto the desk. "May I proceed?"

Reluctantly Grey picked up the paper, studied it intently. The third man pushed off the rear wall and took the page from him. A flicker of those frozen eyes, then he dropped the sheet back on the desk.

Roland went on, "We are here because my client intends to enter into proceedings, in open court, to divorce his father."

The man in the corner asked, "Can they do that?"

"No," Roger growled. "They can't and they won't." He

glared across the desk at Roland. "You can dress that boy up in whatever fancy clothes you like. I'm still the one in charge."

"Respectfully, sir, that is not the case," Roland replied. "Nor has it been for the past six years."

"The very concept is *absurd*! The child is *twelve years old*!" Grey's flush now covered his entire face. "In North Carolina the minimum age for legal emancipation is . . ."

"Sixteen," Roland supplied. "That is simply the current legal standard. We intend to challenge that ruling." His gaze swiveled to the man in the corner. "All the way to the state Supreme Court if need be."

Grey looked genuinely affronted over how control had been ripped from his grasp. "This is *insane.*"

"I assure you, it is not." Roland gestured to Celeste. "My esteemed colleague, Dr. Celeste Talbot, is a senior executive with the state's Child Services. She will serve as the child's legal guardian until he reaches his maturity."

"No she won't." Roger's scarred right fist began beating time on the desk. "That boy is *my son*. I have *every right—*"

"To do what?" Celeste's rage was so intense, she did not need to raise her voice to silence the room. "Fashion this young man into a puppet to suit your political aims? Did you even hear what your son's attorney just said? Colin Eames is studying graduate-level mathematics at university."

"I want him *home.*" Roger's voice had dropped a full octave.

"You'd better get used to the idea that it's not happening," Celeste said. "Because it's *not* his home. And this child is *not* going to become your prize trophy."

"We would of course prefer to handle this quietly." Roland set a sheaf of papers on the desk separating them. "But as you will see here, the court documents have been prepared. Either you agree to this—what shall we call it, disentanglement?—or—"

The man in the corner said, "We need time to discuss—"

"There's nothing to discuss," Roger snarled.

Roland chose to ignore Colin's father. "You may have until we leave this office. If we fail to reach an agreement now, today, we meet with a senior justice at Raleigh family court in . . ."

"Two hours and ten minutes," Celeste offered.

"And then from there we travel straight to a conference with the lady we've hired to handle the boy's PR." Roland took aim at the man in the corner. "Della Lawrence. Surely you know her. Since she handled the governor's most recent campaign."

"Blow your little ship right out of the water," Celeste said. "Sink your chances of ever getting elected—"

The man in the corner said, "Wait out front while we talk."

Roger shared his attorney's crimson rage. "I want—"

The man in the corner said, "This meeting is over."

But as they rose and started for the door, Roger shouted, "We're not done here!"

"Yes, Roger, we are."

"*My son is coming home!*" His roar shook the windows and turned every head in the outer office.

"Let it go or I walk." The man's voice remained as flat and unemotional as pounded tin. "Those are your only two choices."

Nine shocked faces followed their progress across the front room, while the shouting continued on behind them. Colin felt the words strike like futile arrows. He could not even be bothered to hear what his father yelled. The man was now simply a part of his past.

When he passed through the glass doors, the sunlight struck him like a blade.

Chapter 22

When it came to informing Arnold and Sandrine and the academy, Celeste again insisted on taking the lead. Colin did not object. Despite the successful outcome with his father, the confrontation had brought back all the early vulnerabilities. Like the shadows had merely lay dormant, lurking down where he could not find them, waiting for another opportunity to rise to the surface.

It was not until they were seated in Arnold's outer office, listening to voices emanate through the thin side wall, that Colin understood. The academy had become his haven. The place where he had first found a true sense of safety. His new identity, the gifted student, the investor, all this was tied to his being protected there. Seeing his father, learning he and his team had intended to invade and attack, had threatened the first real home he had ever known. Left him looking for a small space to slip into. From where he might observe the world in safety.

Celeste sat catty-cornered from him, able to observe. "You're frightened. Why?"

"I'm afraid Arnold and Sandrine will be mad with me, you know, over how I haven't told them what's been happening."

She shifted her bulk, moving about the seat, making the legs creak under her weight, like the thought made her uncomfortable inside her own skin. "They might be. Which is why I'm here. To tell them you did the right thing."

A glimmer of light pushed through the shadows. "You really think that?"

"The only thing." She kept shifting. Back and forth, like a cat scratching itself against the wall. "I got all hot and bothered when you told me. My first reaction was, you shouldn't be the one handling this."

"It had to be me. And now you know why."

"I accept that, but I don't have to like it. Plus, everything you said, all your predictions, they need to hear from me just how right you were."

The voices chose that moment to go quiet. Arnold opened his door, smiled to them both, and said, "Why don't you come in."

It took almost forty-five minutes to lay it all out. First the investments and his group of backers, and then why they had been so important. And still were, for that matter, but from a very different perspective than before. The threat was gone. His loathing for being poor remained. Colin knew he probably should have started with the need to deflect his father's intentions. But it made more sense somehow, at a level below strategy and conscious thought, to show how he had readied himself. And then explain why.

He started with his father's second marriage. Of course, the warning signals had appeared earlier, back when his father had run for state office. But this was when it all came to a head. The new life. The structured existence defined by

Roger Eames's rising political ambitions. Wanting to create the perfect poster family. Of course he wanted the son from his first marriage back home. It had nothing to do with Colin's gifts, who his son was and what life he might want for himself, and everything to do with creating the proper image.

Colin stopped at the point when the three of them had arrived in his father's campaign office. He merely paused, like the transition from preparation to confrontation required him to start a new chapter. But Celeste saw that as her cue, and took over.

She described the meeting in such vivid detail, Colin's heart resumed its breakneck pace.

Her conclusion was presented with the same clear, unambiguous strength. "When Colin first told me what he'd been doing, and what he had planned, I was angry and I started to chew him out. But by the time we met with Roland, I began to see how he was setting these plans in motion, bringing everything together like . . ."

Arnold offered quietly, "Like a chess game."

"There you go. Like he was seeing ten moves ahead of me. Doing what had to be done."

By this point, Sandrine's elbows were resting on the table, her hands supporting her chin. She straightened and asked Arnold, "May I?"

"Be my guest."

"First and foremost, the realization I've been making here is that you are a child no longer. It's not just your brilliance. Far from it. You are making decisions with an adult's capacity to see beyond your fears and your weaknesses. We all have them. Part of maturing is gaining the confidence to respond to challenges in spite of our unfinished elements and deep-seated flaws. Which you have most certainly done in this case."

"I'll give that a big amen," Celeste said.

"So I am going to speak with you as one adult to another." She looked at Arnold, who nodded. "For the past eight weeks—"

"More like three and a half months," Arnold said.

"We only confirmed what was going on eight weeks ago, when one of the academy's largest donors came to see me. What he wanted to discuss could not be said on the phone. His company's outside attorney informed him, in strictest confidentiality, that private investigators had been hired to check on rumors regarding ill treatment of certain students."

"He specifically mentioned Sojourn House," Arnold said.

"Had to be Grey Robinson behind this," Celeste said.

"None other," Arnold replied.

"Dress that shark in a three thousand–dollar suit, he's still a shark."

"No argument there," Sandrine said. "Since then, we've heard from two other major benefactors, people whose support we rely on to keep us financially afloat."

"Tuition only covers about seventy percent of our total running costs," Arnold said. "Not to mention renovations and building new facilities."

"They were being pressed to withdraw support, at least until the disturbing reports—their words, not mine—could be fully investigated."

The two of them stopped, and waited.

Celeste said it for them. "We need Roland to make sure their attack gets stopped."

Sandrine told Colin, "I realize it is a very great deal to ask. . . ."

"No, it's not." He wanted to scream the words. Weep his rage.

"We need to contact Roland about this before he draws up the papers," Celeste said.

"You'd better call him," Colin said. The only way he could keep from shouting his fury with all his might was to sit on his hands, hunch down, tighten his entire body until it threatened to cramp. All he could think was, his days of hiding in some tight little space were over. "Do it now."

CHAPTER 23

Following the confrontation with his father, Colin's days took on a languid, summertime rhythm. He sat for his last exams at Outer Banks Academy and, ten days later, his first at UNC Wilmington. In between the two, he returned twice to Roland's law offices. The papers came back from Grey Robinson, signed by his father, forming a legal framework for Colin's freedom.

Roland had stipulated Celeste as his legal guardian. He had carefully laid out the manner in which all future meetings between father and son would take place: inside his law offices, supervised by either Colin's attorney or his guardian, and limited in both time and frequency.

Roland had also inserted a clause stating that both Grey and his client, Roger Eames, found no fault with the academy or Sojourn House whatsoever. In their opinion, the academy continued to fulfill all aspects of its duties, both to Colin and all its other students, in exemplary fashion.

His father's signature had torn the original document and

creased the final page so deeply it was visible on the six copies.

Afterward Roland had taken Colin and Celeste to lunch at the City Club of Wilmington, located in a nineteenth-century antebellum-style manor. They'd sat at the restaurant's finest table, its corner position granting them a double-aspect view of the city's historic downtown. The meal was marked mostly by all the topics they avoided. Nothing was said about Colin's father or the investments or exams or schools. They spoke with the easy familiarity of old friends, and dined on aged prime rib.

Three days later, Colin took a second long position on Legend's stock. The share price had bottomed out at just under three dollars, weighed down by Microsoft's announcement of the newly updated X Box. According to numerous online tech-journal op-ed articles, Legend's still-unreleased game would probably not be supported on the new operating system. Colin knew his investors were nervous about his intention to reacquire a stock the pundits predicted would soon crash and burn. He met with Aaron and Roland and Ethan and Mira mostly to show them a confidence that might have been lost on the phone.

The deadline for signing onto UNCW's summer classes came and went. Earlier Colin had intended to take the maximum course load. But now that liberty had started to take hold, he simply could not be bothered.

Several times each week Colin woke from nightmares, heart pounding, body bathed in sweat. The flashing images often changed, but the foundation was exactly the same. His father and attorney and campaign manager showed up at Sojourn House, usually with members of his father's old sheriff's department, always with court authorization to drag him away in chains. Often the three men grew fangs.

But once he was awake, even minutes after jerking from his nightly trauma, the quiet pace set in again. His breathing eased, his chest rose and fell more steadily, he lay there staring at the ceiling . . .

Content was too strong a word. Languid was how he described it to himself. Certainly not lazy. Just moving at a slower tempo.

For the moment, for the weeks that followed, it was enough.

That same lack of visible movement remained true for both of his new investments.

May passed with scarcely a shift. At Mira's graduation party, he feared his investors would gang up on him, pressing for a word he could not offer. Everyone was present except Celeste, even Aaron Weisfeld. But no one appeared willing to inject business or doubt into the day. Ethan and Alexi had hired a tent, one sized to cover virtually every inch of their rear yard. Which was good, because the crowd was large and the day blisteringly hot. Colin knew almost no one except the two families and Aaron. Nor did he much care. The first party he had ever attended was a delight on a multitude of levels. The band was loud and played music he had never heard before. When they took their first break, Colin walked over and asked if they played any jazz. The lead singer laughed and said, "What planet are you from?" Even this was of little importance. Colin drifted around the edges of the crowd, returning time and again to the food laid out on the trestle tables. He refused to dance, even when Mira begged. He watched the way she returned to Lucas and pouted in his direction. He offered to hold Gracie, who had grown comfortable with his presence. He watched Mira and her friends shriek their laughter, shout their happiness to the tapestry of light and shadow overhead. It was enough.

There were numerous visible changes to his world. He began to grow more comfortable leaving the academy's confines. Once or twice each week, he took an Uber back to Mayfaire's outdoor mall. Sometimes he went to the cinema.

Other times he just bought a Starbucks cocoa and sat at one of the mall tables. Studying people. Enjoying his first taste of free time.

Another significant shift came via his morning sessions at the pool. He did not go every day. He had discovered the simple pleasure of staying up late, surrounded by the slumbering and rule-bound house, and doing whatever he wanted. Sometimes he checked his calculations and the news feeds. Or he inspected his two current investments and hunted for new signs of interest. After such sessions he lay in his bed and imagined himself as an invisible predator moving stealthily through the electronic jungle. He often slept late after those midnight sessions, sometimes until noon. Those days he did not bother going to the pool. Once the public summer session began at nine, the water was too crowded, the children were too dense and active and noisy.

He never missed a weekend lesson. His progress was noted by the instructors, and in late May he was shifted to the intermediate class. It was wonderful swimming with kids his own age, sometimes older. But he missed Mira in those hours. She stayed with the youngest and the most frightened, singing her special speech, calming their hearts, introducing them to the liquid realm she loved.

The last weekend in May and twice again in June, Alexi and Ethan and their children picked him up at a quarter to six. They raced the sunrise east, then north along Highway 17 to the Hampstead Marina, which was owned and operated by a friend of Ethan's. They always arrived before the marina officially opened. Ethan unlocked the combination padlock, then they carried their piles of gear past the marina buildings and loaded them onto a boat tied up dockside. They motored into the sunrise, crossing the Cape Fear before cruising down the channel and entering the wide, open waters marking the tip end of Topsail Island. They anchored at the wonderfully named Serenity Point, and claimed what

Mira always declared was the finest spot along the Carolina coast. When Lucas pointed out their location was different every time they came, Mira threatened to cut him off. Of what, she never said. They carried over umbrella and open-sided awning and towels and coolers, anchoring the space that would remain theirs until the sun and the heat and the crowds finally drove them home. Mira and Lucas often walked north along the empty shoreline, the two of them holding hands and shooing the others away whenever they stopped for stolen kisses.

Colin spent a great deal of time seated in the water's edge, imagining his mother there beside him. He could not remember how she looked. The absence often defined the midnight void. When Lucas and Mira returned from their solitary strolls, he studied the way they moved and smiled and shared their intimate light. He was happy for them, yet ached over what he might never know.

At day's end everyone was crispy and pink despite multiple layers of sun cream, their skin tight with Atlantic salt. Mira spent the drive leaning against Lucas and humming songs he pretended not to recognize. Gracie often whimpered as she slept in her father's arms. Noah liked to travel crammed into the rear hold by himself, climbing his truck over piles of gear.

Those were the best days of all.

Colin spent an increasing amount of time with Lenny Satterly. The youth constantly surprised Colin with how little interest he took in anything beyond his languages. Lenny showed a willful blindness to the big and the small of life, the world, even himself. Only after half a dozen sessions did Colin uncover the reason. The youth was not so much in pain as living with a constant state of discomfort. Lenny's body was a burden, a trial, a poorly functioning vehicle that threatened to break down at any time.

They spent an hour or so every other evening, usually starting at the dinner table and then moving into the computer room. Lenny gave no sign he even heard the faint war sounds emanating from other computers and the constant rattle of keyboards fighting online battles, or the television in the next room. When studying, Lenny's diction became more precise, his speech so tightly concentrated each word emerged etched with a verbal laser.

Colin was often unable to follow the verbal discourses joining or distancing one language from another. But the metalinguistic calculations were clear enough, at least to him. As soon as their work shifted from words to mathematical symbols, Lenny struggled. Which only caused the youth to fight all the harder. The first time Lenny broke through his confusion and understood the meaning of an algebraic construct, how they predicted the development of certain linguistic patterns, his entire body seemed to shine with excitement. Colin recalled his own early moment, standing beside Arnold in the Child Services conference room, seeing the man trace a linear pattern that he had been unable to identify until that moment. The indescribable joy, the thrill, the illumination, it was all there again as he sat and observed Lenny almost dancing in his chair with excitement.

Two other students remained at Sojourn House through that sweltering June, a Latina girl of eleven and an Asian boy of nine. Both of them disappeared toward the end of that month, and then it was just Lenny and Colin. The home's prehistoric air-conditioning was often defeated by those hot afternoons. When he could stand it no more, Colin walked toward the highway and entered the nearest coffee shop, often bringing Lenny with him. He became fascinated by the youth, his inexhaustible hunger to learn, the longing so fierce it seemed like a barely controlled fury.

Even Mrs. Fitzgerald's rigid scheduling melted in the summer heat. She emerged from her ground-floor apartment at odd hours, usually twice each day, just to walk around the place, inspect things with her disapproving eye, and disappear. In those moments the woman seemed distracted, scarcely present.

He continued to speak with Roland every week. There was little progress with either investment, virtually none in fact. In watching the stocks, studying the news feeds, and trolling the online sites, Colin felt as though the entire entertainment industry had become trapped in the oppressive heat of that early summer. Roland showed no concern whatsoever. "So long as you're worried, we don't need to be."

"There are a couple of other opportunities," Colin fretted. "If we don't see some action soon, maybe I should shift."

"Are you being drawn by a feeling that these are stronger opportunities?"

"More like, maybe they'll move where these aren't."

"I know what Aaron would say, because I hear him telling this to his other clients," Roland replied. "Patience is a lesson you never fully acquire. You just learn to practice it with patience."

Colin was not altogether certain what the man meant, but liked hearing it just the same. "I need money for a new computer. And I'd like to get some other things. But the computer can't wait. I have some money left over from my school funds, but—"

"No, no. Don't touch the school's money. How much do you need?"

No one was taking money from the investment fund. It had not been discussed so much as become established as the norm. He knew how much he was worth, but that was just a number on the screen. Colin had tried out the words in front of the mirror that morning, and still found it coming out as a question. "Five thousand dollars?"

"Let me check. I think your file contains bank details. . . . Your account at Wells Fargo is still active?"

"Yes."

"I'll take the funds from our petty cash, have Lucretia transfer the money now, and charge it to your account."

He did not need anything like that amount. But having the money on hand, being able to reach for it any time he wanted, had suddenly become very important. "Thank you. So much."

That afternoon, as soon as the bank's online system showed the funds were in place, Colin set up his own Uber account. Together with Lenny he went down to the Mayfaire mall, parked the youth at the Starbucks, entered Circuit City, and bought the most expensive Dell they had in stock. The new full HD screen took his breath away. The processor was almost double the speed and capacity of his current computer. Four times the memory. There was no way he needed all those specs. Which made the purchase even more joyous. Colin walked back to the Starbucks, shifted over Lenny's empty cup, and set his old computer down on the table. "I want you to have this."

Lenny made no move to touch it. "Say what?"

"I bought a new one. This is yours now."

Lenny traced one bird-like finger over the surface. "Why are you doing this for me?"

Colin did not understand the question. Or how Lenny had spoken. No inflection. No joy. The youth sounded almost sad. "I just told you." When the youth remained still, Colin said, "You want me to show you how it works?"

"I know all that. What you think I do downstairs with those machines, play?" Lenny stood up, his gaze as downcast as his voice. "I want to go back now."

That evening after dinner, Colin was making another futile search of the online sites for some indication that his investments might finally begin to shift when Lenny appeared in his open doorway. Normally Colin hated having the door ajar, knowing everyone who passed could visually invade his space. But Lenny was little more than a human shadow, and the heat only added to the room's claustrophobic confines. Lenny did not knock. He did not speak. He simply stood in the doorway and waited. Colin had no idea how long the youth had been standing there before he noticed.

When Colin looked over, Lenny said, "I got something I can't figure out."

Colin followed him up the second flight and down to the corner room. It was the first time he had entered Lenny's private space. What he saw halted him in midstride. "Whoa."

"Don't you act like that." Lenny picked up the laptop and did a boneless slide onto the carpet. "Those are my buddies."

"I've never seen so much medicine."

"Yeah, well, welcome to my world."

The top of Lenny's small chest of drawers was literally covered by prescription bottles. Twenty, thirty of them, all lined up in disciplined rows. "What does it all do?"

Lenny was already working the keys. "I like to think of them as my little soldiers. They fight the good fight. They keep the bad stuff out of my life."

But when Colin joined him on the floor, Lenny's fingers stilled. He sat there, hunched over, staring at the screen. "What you did today, I never had . . . People in my world aren't nice."

Colin had no idea what to say.

"I never had somebody just give me something. And doing it like you did, no warning . . ."

"I wanted it to be a surprise," Colin said.

"Man, you shocked me right out of my skin, plopping that thing down in front of me."

"I probably should have said something."

"Naw, it was me. I should've handled it better. Said thanks.

Something." He traced one undersized finger along the side of the screen. "I've wanted one of these for as long as I can remember."

And just like that, they were pals again.

They worked together for an hour or so, but then Colin saw the kid was flagging and stood. As he started to leave he asked, "What do you want to do with this?"

Lenny stopped in the process of shutting down his system. "What do you mean?"

"When you grow up. Like, do you want to teach or—"

Lenny rose to his feet, his motions tight. "Man, do you even see the bottles over there?"

Colin found himself again trapped by all he did not understand. "Sure I do."

"Those words you just spoke, they don't belong. Not to me." Lenny shuffled over and set the laptop on the dead center of his desk. It was the only bare spot. The surface was piled with an army of books. "You're talking about a *future.* All I want, all I'm allowed to even *think* about, is having just one more *today.*"

He stood there in the doorway until he was certain the youth would not speak again or even look his way. Colin then returned downstairs, wishing there was some way he could take back the words.

CHAPTER 24

The first week in July, everything broke open. When Colin looked back, it felt as though he'd watched an online thunderstorm take shape before his eyes. The lightning, the noise, the blast of rain and wind, all that was in his head. But real just the same.

The *Wall Street Journal*'s online news feed broke the story. EA, the world's largest maker of e-games, had made a formal offer to acquire Legend.

The next day, the news was everywhere.

Thirty-six hours later, Colin's second investment became the hottest ticket in town. Two major corporations were vying to buy it outright. Bidding up the price. Two, three, four times beyond Colin's most extravagant hopes.

Colin traveled down to Roland's office by Uber. He stood there beside Lucretia's desk watching her complete the sales. Almost afraid to ask her for the final prices. Both times scarcely able to breathe after she replied. The lady was in her sixties, grey-haired and caramel-skinned and so deadpan she spoke with a drum-like cadence no matter what the news. Even when she had become another investor. Along with almost all of the other lawyers and secretaries working in Roland's firm.

After the sales were completed, Aaron walked Colin back to the elevators, patted him on the back, and said, "Enjoy your hour in the sun. Remember this moment when things don't go according to plan."

He spent the next few weeks holding to his routine. July sped into August, and the southeastern United States entered another hurricane season. Only this year North Carolina's coastal region remained locked in an unseasonable drought. Wildfires caused by lightning strikes erupted in the pine forests west of the city. Often on his dawn walks to the club, he could both smell the smoke and watch dark tendrils float in the sky overhead. Thankfully, the fires remained somewhat under control, and the city itself never came under threat.

He could feel his body gradually becoming stronger. The food, the walks, the almost daily swims, they all had an impact. He was moving easier inside his own skin. For the first time in his life, he actually enjoyed looking at himself in the mirror.

He knew his world was undergoing seismic shifts. It wasn't just the money now sitting in the burgeoning fund, or how he would be starting university as a fully matriculated student in just a few weeks. In many respects, the nightmare fears he had known as a child were with him still. All the dark shadows simply did not vanish because his father had gone silent and the investments were paying off. Colin was changing. His world was different. And yet so very much remained exactly the same as it always had been.

The second week of August, he made two more investments. A week later he added another. He continued to scour the sources, input the data, search for clues. And yet it was all done at a safer distance. Late at night, when he woke and lay staring at the ceiling, he felt as though the currents dominating his life had reached a single solitary quiet moment. But it was only a matter of time before they gripped him in another torrent of power and swept him back into the maelstrom. And throughout it all, the void at the center of his being remained the silent force it had always been.

Three days later, he went for an early dinner with Arnold and Sandrine. They took him to the Oceanic Restaurant in Wrightsville Beach, almost an hour's drive in summertime traffic. The talk was mostly about inconsequential things, though at one point they asked a number of questions about his latest investments. From that it almost seemed natural to shift over to his plans for the future. Colin found himself thinking about Lenny as he replied. On one level, he heard himself explaining how much it meant to stay at Sojourn House, have a routine, be part of something familiar. Several times during the evening, Colin felt as though Lenny had become an invisible presence there at the table. Observing the simple pleasures that had never been his to claim.

When Colin arrived back at Sojourn House, he found Lenny seated in the television room, his laptop open on the sofa beside him. "What's up?"

Lenny nodded slowly, like the question required great thought. "I've been wondering that exact same thing."

Colin walked in and pulled over a chair. "You lost me."

"You've been real nice to me." Each word was carefully spaced out. Like the individual sounds required effort. "These lessons in math, I couldn't have done them without you."

Colin had no idea what to say.

Lenny nodded, as if he approved of Colin's silence. "I've been sitting here thinking back. You know. Trying to find a time when I've been happier." The youth looked up. "What I'm wanting to say . . ."

And just like that, the light went out of Lenny's eyes.

Colin had no idea what had happened. The gentle shift, the silent transition, it left him unable to even breathe.

Lenny sighed once, and drifted over, landing on his side on the sofa. His shoulder struck the laptop, sending it tumbling to the floor.

"Lenny?"

But the child was gone.

CHAPTER 25

When Sandrine and Arnold arrived, Colin had thrown up his meal into the bushes beside the kitchen door. Grant and Mrs. Fitzgerald were out front, along with the police and the EMT wagon now holding Lenny's body.

The only time he almost lost it was when Sandrine wrapped her arms around him. Arnold kept patting his shoulder, speaking words that arrived from some vast telescopic distance. Finally, they pulled him forward and loaded him into Arnold's SUV and drove him away. Colin turned around and watched until the flashing blue and red lights were cut off by the academy entrance. They entered the flow of normal nighttime traffic. They drove to Arnold's town house. They bedded him down in the guest room. They spoke words, they offered comfort, they sheltered him the best they could.

The next morning, he woke up and lay there for hours. The sun traced its way across the floor. He must have dozed off again because the next thing he knew the sun's angle had moved westward. He rose and dressed and drifted into the living room, feeling guilty over being hungry. Notes were there on the kitchen counter, but he couldn't be bothered to read. He made a bowl of cereal and fruit, ate it standing by the front window. Then he pulled off the bedspread, carried it into the living room, lay down on the couch, and slept.

Colin attended the memorial service only because Sandrine and Arnold and Celeste ganged up on him. They did so with loving firmness. They spoke to him as friends. They pressured him into his new jacket and tie and trousers. One or another of them kept a hand on his shoulder, guiding him across the campus and into the chapel attached to the new building. The events washed over him in an arid sweep, carried by another wind pushing hard from the west, bearing the empty bitterness of a wasted life. The unfairness was an acidic dreg he took in with every breath. None of it made sense. The words people spoke to him, the caring nature of the trio who surrounded him, it was all filtered through the fog of sorrow. He heard Sandrine sniff from time to time, and watched from a distance as Celeste passed her a tissue. Colin spent most of the service wishing there was someone he could rage at. Scream his anger at all the mysteries that had stolen away his friend.

The day finally came into tight focus when Lenny's father approached him. He was a bulky man, dark and uncomfortable in a suit he probably had bought just for this occasion. His hands were big, solid, like mallets attached to wrists as thick as Colin's shins. "I heard from Lenny you been nice to my boy."

Colin spoke the first words that day. "He was incredible. I mean . . ." That was as far as he got.

Even so, the man seemed to accept the words as enough. "I never did understand what he was going on about. It meant a lot to my boy, having a friend who accepted him for who he was."

"It was more than that." Colin felt the words clog in his throat. But they had to be spoken. It was important. "He taught me so much."

"Yeah? Like what?"

Colin shrugged off the hand on his shoulder. He needed to stand alone. "I can't explain it. Not yet. But I will. I need time. I need . . ."

Once again, the man seemed to find nothing wrong with Colin's stumbling response. "I hear folks talking about a man's legacy. I don't know about things like that. Just the same, it's good to know my boy's legacy is there in you."

"I want it to be. So much."

The man started to reach out, then let his hand drop. He nodded to Colin and left the chapel, followed down the central aisle by his other three sons, all of them as large as their father.

Only then did Colin realize Mira was there.

She stood by the back row, Alexi on one side, Regina on the other.

Colin did not actually feel himself move down the aisle. One moment he was standing up front, sheltered by Arnold and Sandrine and Celeste. The next, he stood before the three of them, all in black, all of them sharing the same look. They enfolded him in three pairs of arms.

Afterward Mira insisted on walking him back to Sojourn House. For once, she remained silent, subdued. Colin dreaded having her talk about what had just happened. Chatting was Mira's way of dealing with empty minutes. Instead, she waited until they were approaching the house's front door to ask, "Do you ever think about us?"

He knew instantly what she meant. "All the time."

"I don't mean us as friends. I mean . . ."

"I know exactly, Mira. Me without my mother, you minus your twin."

"Sometimes it wakes me up at night. We haven't talked in forever, and yet you're still right there. Not in a creepy way. Just, you know . . ."

"Connected." He nodded. "You've helped me through so much. Even when you weren't around."

"I'm sorry I've been detached. This past month has become . . ."

He found an uncommon comfort in the act of finishing her thoughts. "A hard season."

"You don't know, you can't imagine, how hard." She glanced over. "Then again, maybe you can."

"Is it Lucas?"

"Can we not talk about that, please?"

"Absolutely." It actually felt good to know there were topics she was also eager to avoid. "No problem at all. I withdraw the question."

A woman's voice called her name. Mira waved at someone Colin could not be bothered to see and turned them back toward the house. She said, "During the service, I felt your sorrow in my bones."

"Some day I'll be able to tell you what it meant seeing you here."

"You don't ever need to. Not for me, anyway."

"How did you know?"

"Celeste called. She seems really nice."

"She is. That and more."

She breathed in the sorrel-scented air. "It's strange."

"What?"

"I told Regina first. Then she came over. And we told Mom." She shook her head. "Mom and I, we're so incredibly close, but I needed Regina there. When she walked in, I just started bawling. I didn't know the guy, your friend. I wasn't crying for him. It was just . . ."

"You felt for me." Colin wiped his eyes.

When they reached the front steps, Mira held him for the second time that day. "Connected."

Chapter 26

Two weeks after Lenny's memorial service, Mrs. Fitzgerald retired. She left in a silent hurry, saying farewell to no one save Sandrine, and that was delivered with all the formality of a military salute. If Sandrine and Arnold and other members of the faculty were upset over her abrupt departure, Colin could not detect it. Instead, he had the distinct impression they were all quietly satisfied to close that particular chapter and start another.

That last week in August a new head of Sojourn House was named. Consuela Dupree was a cheerful, rotund woman with eyes that found delight in everything she saw. The difference between her and Mrs. Fitzgerald could not have been greater.

Consuela had three young children of her own. There was no mention of her moving into Sojourn House. Instead, two mornings after the announcement, Arnold and Sandrine led him into the ground-floor apartment and said, "What do you think?"

Colin continued to feel partly disconnected from the

world. So many things appeared abruptly, without warning. Almost in tandem with the way he had felt about adults in his early years. "About what?"

"About what, the man says." Arnold swept his arm around. "Moving in. What do you think?"

The words seemed impossible to join into a coherent thought. "I don't understand."

Sandrine tugged on his arm, pulling him over to the sofa lining the side wall. Brown and leather and punctuated with tight brass tacks. Colin had never seen anyone sit there. It proved to be as uncomfortable as it looked.

"You cannot imagine the impact you had on Lenny. We were all so worried about him. He never seemed to communicate with anyone unless it was about his studies. He was not just withdrawn. He lived inside a shell, he never . . ."

Colin watched as Sandrine came within a hairsbreadth of breaking down. He saw Arnold seat himself on the sofa's arm next to her. Wrap her in his arms. And hold her until she managed to regain control. It felt strange and yet immensely gratifying to know he was not the only one who ached, who struggled every time he thought of the absent youth.

When her lips uncrimped and her tremors ceased, she straightened and swiped at her eyes and tried her best to smile. "Sorry."

"For what?"

She liked that enough to reach for his hand. "Have you ever heard the word *prefect*?"

"Somewhere."

"It's fallen out of fashion. But in times past, a prefect was an older student who held a position of responsibility within a house or dorm. They served as a bridge between the students and the faculty."

"A lot of the students here are older than me."

"In years, yes. That's true. But I'm not sure that will matter."

"Everyone here knows you're studying at uni," Arnold pointed out. "That sort of thing might erase the age issue."

Sandrine said, "Plus, where we really need your help is with the younger students."

"I don't know if I can. Or if I'd be any good."

"It's a huge transition, I know. Will you give it a try?"

"If you think . . . Okay, I guess."

"Excellent." She rose to her feet and offered an over-bright smile. "I assume you won't mind if we do a bit of re-modeling."

They were still working on the apartment when school began. Colin remained upstairs in his room, though the confines had never felt more restrictive. Mira had started at UVA while Lucas was now at Georgetown. Colin's communications with his dearest friend had become limited to brief phone chats and text messages. She was both overwhelmed and thrilled. Her relationship with Lucas was going through another difficult patch, and she often complained about feeling as though they were separated by a pair of bipolar worlds. Which made no sense, of course, but Colin knew what she meant and liked how she was trying to include him in this ongoing trauma. Her world was defined by a roller coaster of conflicting emotions. He wanted to be part of that.

Three weeks into the new term, his grandmother died. Roger Eames sent official notification that he wanted Colin to attend the service. Celeste brought the news. He was so very grateful she had not brought Arnold or Sandrine along. She more than anyone else understood just how conflicted he felt.

The next day, he folded clothes into his backpack, being careful to include things he could not afford to forget, like matching socks and hairbrush and belt and tie. He walked down the road to the club, listening to the birdsong and feeling a faint brush of coolness, a whisper of a different season ahead. He swam his twenty laps, five hundred meters being his new normal. Careful, steady strokes. Ten laps crawl, five backstroke, five breast. He was by far the youngest of the club's regular morning swimmers. The adults knew him now, some even greeting him by name. Afterward he showered and donned his formal gear, then stopped by the coffee shop for a smoothie and a banana. Colin was standing under the front awning when Celeste pulled up.

The service was held in the Rocky Mount Memorial Park's chapel. Celeste spent much of the drive laying out precise instructions regarding Colin's behavior. She spoke in a stern manner, as if expecting him to protest. In fact, Colin was almost soothed by the clear line of action. It framed a way he could move through this experience in safety. He hoped.

As the dark-suited congregants gathered, Colin entered the chapel. Celeste followed at a discreet distance. Now that they were here, neither felt any need to speak. A man he did not recognize handed him a heavily embossed page, almost like a menu card. Beneath a dark banner was his grandmother's name and the dates of her birth and death. Colin walked up the central aisle to where his father and new family were seated on the front left row.

On one hand, the physical sensations that accompanied him were taken from the multitude of nightmares where his father played a major role. His heart raced, his body felt clammy, the chapel's frigid air could not stop him from sweating. And yet Colin viewed it all from a safe distance, as if the legal structure defining his life had become a physical barrier.

He stopped on the altar rail's other side and offered Roger Eames his hand. His father rose and towered over Colin. Roger's hand felt carved from stone. There was no warmth to his grip, nor his gaze. Roger Eames eyed his son with brutal coldness.

Despite how the contact had left Colin trembling, he did as Celeste instructed and worked his way down the row. Shaking hands with Roger's second wife, then the two sons. Finding the same frigid hostility in all their gazes. And something else. Roger's new family all shared a tight uncertainty, as if they could not identify who this person truly was, the kid who had gained the power to defy Roger Eames.

By the time Colin took position on the front aisle's left corner, the chapel was almost full, everyone dressed in what he could only assume was politically correct attire. Colin's only contact with his grandmother had been during her stay in hospital. The minister spoke words he could not be bothered to hear. Twice Colin thought he saw his father start to lean forward and glare in his direction, then stop.

Colin found himself recalling an event from his childhood. They were returning from a backyard barbecue at the home of a Rocky Mount police officer. The family lived a few blocks from their own home, and the two of them had walked. There had been a lot of laughter and easy talk among the gathered officers, some gentle joshing, a lot of drinking. As he and his father had returned home, his father's footsteps had become slightly off cadence from the alcohol. Suddenly his father had waved at the vague distance and declared, "You got no idea what we face out there."

All Colin could see was the stately orderliness of their Rocky Mount neighborhood. But suddenly Colin felt as though he could see danger radiating far in the distance, strong as summer heat. He had no idea what to say, so he remained silent.

"Take one step into the county's bad areas, you'd get your wake-up call. Believe you me." He stumbled over a ridge in the sidewalk, righted himself, said, "Bad as bad can be."

They walked on another half block, when abruptly his father wheeled about and stared down at his son. "You're always so quiet. You're the quietest kid . . . Just like your mother was. Did you hear a word I just said?"

"I heard everything, Daddy. And I remember."

Roger Eames weaved slightly, like a boxer preparing to ward off blows. "Why can't you *speak*?"

Colin said the first thing that came into his head. "Sometimes when you come home, I think the shadows are trying to come in with you."

Another fractional weave, one foot to the other and back again. "I can't let that happen."

Colin could almost read what his father wanted to hear, written in the chalk-blue sky beyond his father's head. "Thank you for keeping us safe, Daddy."

As Colin sat in the chapel, he wondered how it might have been for a different son. A boy who shared his father's attitudes and perspective on life. A son born to confront, to fight, who wanted to grow up and cross the line and enter the state's dark zones. He had never felt any need to blame his father. The only rage he had ever felt toward Roger Eames had come when the man's desire for control, his need to do battle with anyone who opposed him, had hurt others. Never Colin. He sat there and wondered if the reason for this was because he had always sensed that it was at least partly his fault. For never being the son his father desired.

Soon as the service ended, Colin rose and left. After the chapel's crypt-like frigidity, the hot sunlight felt good on his head and shoulders.

Celeste asked, "You want to attend the gravesite service?"

For what, he wanted to ask. But the thought felt disrespectful. So all he said was, "I'm ready to go now."

In the weeks that followed, a coffin began to litter his dreams. The distance was often so vast he could not actually see the casket. But the vacuum that had carried him through the meaningless ritual was stronger now, deep as the unseen currents of his life. They enveloped him and dragged him forward. Up ahead loomed his own empty grave.

He always woke up gasping from those dreams, terrified he had become another student whose scream shattered the night. But Grant never appeared at his door, so Colin had to assume his terrors had all remained trapped inside.

The renovations to the downstairs apartment dragged on. Problems appeared, deep-set issues that required rewiring one entire side of the house. Then they discovered major plumbing leaks. For weeks the house echoed to the sounds of hammering and power tools. Dust gathered in all the downstairs rooms, despite the builders' best attempts to shield their work. Camila fretted and fumed and added daily mopping of all the downstairs floors to the students' chores. Colin despised the sense of being trapped yet again inside emotions and forces over which he had no control.

The last week in September, he took his troubles to Celeste.

They tried to meet or speak by phone every six weeks or so. The day and time changed according to her schedule. She wanted him to have this chance to release, away from the school, in an environment he knew was safe. That day, Celeste was back in the Wilmington Child Development Center for meetings. Colin journeyed in a state of high unease, as if his skin was uncomfortable with containing the tumult and conflicting energies.

Once he started talking about the nightmares and his turbulent emotions, he wondered at why it had taken him so long. The confession did not come easy, however. He stumbled, he stopped, he struggled with both hands grasping at the empty space before his face. When he went silent, his only consolation came from the sense that Celeste understood.

She took her time responding, a few breaths through tight lips, almost but not quite whistling. She turned her chair slightly, so as to study the sunlight dappling the office's side window. Then, "We're moving into some very deep territory. So I want you to understand going in, you might not grasp everything I'm saying. This isn't like your next algebraic formula, you're not building on things you've come to terms with. This is new."

"I understand." And he did. She was not just speaking words. He could almost see her laying out a course, guiding him through this new portion of his life's map.

"Many people go through their entire lives without ever getting a clear fix on what you call your inner void. But the truth is, very many of us are defined by this specific issue. This is especially true with young people. All these connections that are coming up through social media, the young people I'm seeing, they're totally in sync with these new apps and what they mean and what they can do. They're *connected.* They talk and they share online all the time. But when they come to me, you know what I hear them saying? I go to meetings with my associates from all over the nation, you know what we talk about? It's the same thing everywhere I go."

She paused, and then spoke the next three words very slowly. Like each was a complete sentence. "They . . . feel . . . lonely. Disconnected. Some are genuinely frightened by how empty their worlds feel."

Another pause, then her speech resumed its normal rapid cadence. "Their contact with the outside world is limited to what they can put down in a dozen words, a single thought. Depth is something they find in the wrong end of the swimming pool. As a result, their yearnings for a deeper experience, for true and lasting love, become lost to the torrent of *now*. Do you understand what I'm saying?"

Colin nodded, but he wasn't sure Celeste even noticed. She continued to inspect the sunlit glass as she went on, "For so many young people, they don't know who they are, where they're going, not even what they want to do with tomorrow. Forget next week or with their own future lives. Those sort of questions frighten them. They have let themselves be defined by whatever is hot in these new mediums. This shapes how they view love, the partner they're seeking, what will make them happy and fulfilled. All too often they come to me after getting exactly what they think they want, and it turns out to be just an awful experience. They come face-to-face with just how alone they truly are. And they're terrified."

She planted her elbows on her knees. Getting in close enough for Colin to see the dark flecks in her gaze. "Your problem, what you're facing, is both the same and it's different. The same, in that you've been sheltered in an artificial environment for going on seven years. It's allowed you to develop, but it's also kept you from developing. You see where I'm headed?"

There was no reason why her words should cause his heart to hammer in his chest, hard as a bird frantically trying to escape. None whatsoever. He nodded.

"The difference is, you're *aware.* You recognize this deep inner longing for love and relationship and family. You're doing what you can to maintain control of your life. Even when all these events strike you hard."

He licked dry lips. "What do I do?"

"That's not for me to tell you. That's what you have to discover for yourself. What I can say is this. Your age, your situation, it's crying out for you to find your identity. Who are you, Colin Eames? What do you stand for? You understand what I'm saying?"

"Sort of."

She looked up at her bookshelf, frowned, and shook her head. "I could give you something to read, but you're already living inside your books, maybe too much. What you need to do is keep on being aware. Develop a keener sense of observing yourself. And something more. Start to see others and their needs as equally valid."

"They want me to be the house prefect."

"There you go. That's a good place to begin right there."

"I don't even know what it means."

"Yes you do. But the idea of treating these other kids as important makes you uncomfortable. You want to be the guy on the lonely pedestal. Am I right?"

"No . . . That's not . . ."

When he couldn't finish his protest, she looked satisfied. "Identity. That's the word you need to be studying. This is the first key to true and lasting love."

Colin left the session feeling both vastly uncomfortable and utterly dissatisfied. As if he had expected she would offer one thing, and then had been forced to accept something of lesser value. A feeble alternative to a clear compass heading. Even thinking about what she'd said and the word she'd repeated, *identity*, left him prickly inside his own skin.

Even so, the nightmares ended. And they did not return.

CHAPTER 27

That autumn Colin followed the election because his father was running. The experience was unpleasant in the extreme. Not really because of the vitriol, nor how the Obama and Romney campaigns dominated so much of his news feeds and online worlds. There was simply so much he could not understand. The anger in people's voices and faces, the rigid stances they took, and the way they reacted with the poison of vipers to any opinion expressed by the other side. All because of a name, a word, a passing comment. Such days carried remnants of earlier times, being confronted with adult behavior he could not understand. Everyone seemed to have taken a side. Celeste, Arnold, Roland, Lucas, Mira, Ethan, Alexi, Regina, Sandrine. Everyone but him.

He stayed up on election night and watched his father be declared North Carolina's newest United States congressman, representing the first district.

Obama remained in the White House. Signs dotting the streets disappeared. The constant barrage of television and online ads vanished. Gradually the news about his father diminished, until it became just another vague murmur, a shadow mostly residing in Washington, D.C.

The changes instituted by Mrs. Fitzgerald's replacement gradually infiltrated their world. Initially the Sojourn House students drifted about, as if they were afraid the former head might jump out of her office, scaring them back into her rigid version of life. Mrs. Dupree did not say anything. Nor did she institute any major new rules. But little by little the atmosphere within the house began to relax. Then at dinner one night, a girl laughed out loud. The entire room went quiet, all of the students wide-eyed and wondering. Gradually smiles bloomed everywhere.

Colin still wasn't sure what it meant to be a house prefect. Even so, he met with the other students, exploring what the word might signify. He felt hugely uncomfortable, as if he were being called to play a false role, like he lied with every word. Then early in October, he finally hit upon an idea that seemed to work. At least with some of the students.

The concepts Celeste had discussed that last meeting continued to resonate. Especially that term she used. *Identity.* He was no closer to understanding what it meant for him personally. But as he looked at the other students, really looked, he thought he saw the same absence. They might not know the word, or even be aware of what wasn't there.

It felt very strange at first, using what did not exist as the link to forging an intimacy. But he could see it working. Some of the younger ones came and lingered in his doorway before lights out. Speaking about nothing important. Yet clearly liking the fact that he was there and available. Afterward he found himself thinking back to his own first transformative moment, when Arnold had ignited in him that thrill. Because of the missing isosceles triangle.

The longer he followed this pattern, the more confident he became. Let the adults have the answers. Let them talk in straightforward terms. Shaping the confusion of life into something that made at least a little sense. Speak about end results and stability and patterns and next steps. That was not his job. He was there to show them it was okay to be confused. And frightened. And hurting. And lonely. He had been forced to name the shadows, just like them. He might be a step or two farther along the path. But he was still struggling. Just like them. What he could tell them was, he had identified the questions. Who he was. And where he was going. What true love might someday mean. He never spoke about any of that outright. Instead, he let it shape his responses.

The farther they moved into the new school year, the more certain he became that it worked.

His thirteenth birthday came and went with scarcely a whisper. Celeste wanted to take him out, Arnold mentioned it as well, but both seemed to find nothing strange about him saying he had other plans. To celebrate, he swam, then took an Uber to the mall, saw a film, ate a meal in the food court, went home. Wished himself a happy birthday standing in front of the mirror. Because it was.

Celeste's work at the Wilmington Child Development Center had entered a new phase. She had her own office now, and was down at least a couple of days every week. Colin waited until her visit the first week in December to describe his work as a prefect. When he finished, she remained silent, studying him. Then, "You started on this when?"

"After we last talked. Sort of. It took a while to shape the idea."

"Why am I only hearing about this now?"

"At first, I didn't know what I was doing. I couldn't even name it."

"You were operating from gut instinct."

"Pretty much."

"After that?"

He shrugged. "I needed to know if it was actually going somewhere. With the students, I mean. Not me."

"You had inserted yourself into an experiment of your own making."

"Did I do wrong?"

"Did . . . Colin, you are a wonder." She pulled out her phone and set it on the low table beside her chair. "You mind if I write this up?"

"Why should I mind? Write it up for what?"

"A journal. I'm naming you as coauthor." She touched the screen. "All right. I'm recording now. From the top. Go."

An hour and a half later, as he was leaving the room, Celeste called him back. "Young man," she said, leaning heavy on the words, "it is good to know those students can come to you when their world gets shaken."

Chapter 28

Mondays, Wednesdays, and Fridays were given over to university classes and studies. Colin did away with the previous term's haphazard manner. He was there to learn, the opportunity was a gift, he needed to be responsible. . . . All the adult arguments finally began to make sense. Colin found himself often thinking of Lenny on those days. Especially when he took time to do almost nothing. Sitting under a tree in one of the university quads, wandering through the library stacks, lingering in a student café, listening to the talk swirl about him, pretending to be busy working a problem. All the things Lenny had yearned for. Colin often lifted his cup to the memory of his departed friend.

Tuesdays, Thursdays, and Saturdays started with a long, hard swim, then were given over to the growing fund. He continued to make new investments, closing off positions whenever his analysis reached the critical juncture.

Arnold and Sandrine had invested some of their retirement savings. Through them, the college endowment inserted what they called a modest amount. All of Roland's partners and most of the firm's support staff were involved. Ditto for the firm where Ethan worked. A number of Mira's and Lucas's friends at school were putting in every dime they could scrape together. Counting on him.

Just after Thanksgiving, Colin's personal take passed the million-dollar mark.

He didn't tell anyone. He assumed Roland and Aaron both knew, though neither said a word. After that summer's five thousand–dollar cash injection, Colin had taken nothing more. He spent money on clothes, Uber, the occasional meal, the coffee shops, cinema. Otherwise, the numbers alongside his name meant very little. Symbols on a screen. For Colin, the most important reward came from having gotten this concept very right. The pressure was still there, the tension highest just before he called Lucretia and gave new instructions. But alongside the constant sense of walking the financial tightrope, Colin also felt a growing calm. He knew he was good at this.

Then the second week in December, everything changed.

Chapter 29

The opportunity sprang out of nowhere, and at the ideal moment. The previous week they had closed two of their three open positions. The cash just sat there in the fund's accounts, a frightening sum if he allowed himself to think of it as anything more than symbols. Elements required to put the next step into motion. The *Journal* spoke of the December doldrums, almost as if the world could be forgiven for taking a month off.

Then rumors appeared on the three professional chat rooms he had come to consider his best conduits for initial alerts. For the first time ever, all three registered the news on the exact same night. An LA-based music company had built itself into a regional powerhouse, comprising four semiautonomous divisions: a distribution company, a top-of-the-line recording studio, a concert organizer, and a quasi-independent group handling backlists and music rights. But five dismal quarters in a row had wreaked havoc with their cash reserves. The stock had tanked, and their major investors were pushing for an executive-level overhaul. Before it was too late.

The news sources all reported the same thing: Two different global powers were considering an outright purchase. Interest in acquiring the group was driven by the strength of their backlist and good reports about two new signings.

Colin gave it a day. The calculations almost completed themselves. The upside was stratospheric. He searched the major feeds and discovered a paragraph in the business section of the *LA Times*'s online business news. He feared he had left it too late.

There was nothing else on the horizon. Not even a hint of motion anywhere, at least until the new year.

Colin called Lucretia and committed all the cash they had on hand. Seventy-seven percent of the fund's holdings.

Christmas came and went in a series of events and friends and families and celebrations. For the first time in his life, Colin found himself fielding invitations. Arnold and Sandrine, Celeste and her extended family, Mira and Alexi and Ethan, Roland and Regina. He ate to the point of feeling genuine pain when he lay down at night. On three separate occasions he drove with friends through Historic Wilmington and walked the upscale streets, gawking at the lights and the window displays and the people. He tasted spiked eggnog and whiskey sours for the first time, and loathed them both. It was a wondrous, magical period. He was sorry to see it end, just fade away on the first of January, descending into silence and a sort of bemused contentment on many faces.

Through it all, he kept having these niggling doubts. Tight whispers that reminded him of the unseen fears he had carried throughout his early years. The shadows that loomed behind unopened doors, the silent threat his father brought into the house on bad days. The uncertainty, the absence of control. All of it came and went in great swirling eddies that sometimes attacked with such force the entire world came to a screeching halt. And then it was gone again. Vanished. The world restarted, the laughter and happy chatter resumed, he was once again surrounded by people who cared.

For the first time in months, Colin took to running his calculations every night, and sometimes again the next morning. Inputting whatever new data he could find, which wasn't much. Even during the week between Christmas and New Year's, the unease would not let up. He assumed it came from the size of this investment. After all, this was the largest position his fund had ever taken.

Nine days into the new year, the builders were gone and the cleaners finished. Arnold and Sandrine led him through the downstairs apartment. Colin had never been farther than the front office, which was now transformed. The heavy dark furniture, the uncomfortable sofa, the yellowed wallpaper, gone. In its place was a bright and airy room with a simple pale wash on the walls and ceilings, and matching beige carpet and sash drapes. Even the two windows had been replaced. He had never noticed the view until that moment. Always before his focus had been exclusively on the woman seated behind the massive oak desk. Which was gone as well, replaced by an IKEA-designed work table of pale wood with bright blue metal legs. The office also served duty as his parlor, and now contained bookshelves and new sofa and comfy chair and flat-screen TV. The kitchenette had all new appliances, the small dining table stationed against the opposite wall. And downstairs a bedroom, as bright and cheerful as a windowless room could possibly be. Single bed of pale wood, matching dresser and cupboard, new bathroom. Colin walked from room to room in a daze.

That night Colin filled his plate with the others, then carried his dinner into the apartment and ate alone. He doubted he would do this very much, unless work demanded it. The time together in the dining hall was too important. But to-night was special. The silence, the space, the newness and clean lines, the solitude . . . He stopped several times just to breathe in the pleasure.

At precisely one-fifteen that morning, he awoke from a nightmare he could not remember. The clock on the bedside table seemed not to show the time, but rather to shout in pale blue luminosity that he had left it all too late.

CHAPTER 30

Colin raced upstairs, flung open his laptop, and went back to the very first notes he had made about the investment. Perhaps it was the new apartment, the shift from one existence to another. Whatever the reason, the instant he started reviewing his initial calculations, he saw.

His hands were shaking so bad he misdialed four times. Roland and Regina were visiting her parents. But thankfully, Lucas was still at home over the winter break, and answered with a sullen, "Who is this?"

"It's Colin. I need Aaron's cell and his home number."

"Colin . . . Do you know what time it is?"

"Lucas, listen to me. This is life or death. Can you get it?"

Lucas was fully awake now. "Well, sure, I guess. Hang on, I need to boot up Dad's . . . No, I know, Mom has it. . . ." His voice trailed off as he dropped the phone to his side. There was the sound of footsteps thumping down stairs, then the rustle of pages, and, "You got a pen?"

* * *

When Aaron Weisfeld's cell went to voice mail and then so did his home number, Colin thought he was going to have to stop and vomit before he could continue. But the nausea passed after a moment, and he dialed again. This time, the attorney answered with, "This had better be good."

"Sir, Mr. Weisfeld, it's Colin. We have an emergency."

"Colin? Son, it's a quarter to two. . . . Is that the actual time?"

The man sounded more than simply disoriented. His words carried a feeble note, as if the shock of being woken fully revealed his age and fragility. Colin said, "It's a scam. All of it. If we wait until tomorrow, it might be too late."

"Slow down, Colin. Wait, wait, let me sit. . . . All right. Tell me again what has you so worked up."

"I should have seen it before. Maybe I did. But I never thought, it didn't occur to me until now."

"Long breath. Slow the tempo." Gradually Aaron's voice took on the crisp, precise cadence he showed in the office. "From the beginning, now."

But Colin didn't even make it halfway through the initial intel that formed the foundation for his investment before Aaron shared his urgency. "We've been set up."

Colin huffed a tight sob of relief. Just having this venerable legal warhorse share his fears made it all both much better and far, far worse.

Aaron went on, "I'll call Lucretia, tell her to meet us—"

"No. Wait. How did they know?"

"Sorry, I don't follow . . ."

"Someone had to tell them how I identify the targets. How many people know this? You, me, Roland, Ethan . . ."

"Maybe they found out on their own."

"And the timing," Colin persisted. "We were cash rich. Three positions closed. Almost eighty percent of our total capital just sitting there."

Aaron's voice tightened further. "Meet me at the office. I'm leaving now."

When Colin's Uber pulled up in front of the office building, the security guard already had the door open. He greeted Colin with, "All these years, I never seen the old man move that fast. Must be some major case you got going on."

He led Colin to the bank of elevators and used the passkey to send him up. When Colin emerged, Aaron was standing by Lucretia's desk. He said into the phone, "Yes, Levi, I'm still holding." To Colin he said, "I'm on the line with a trader I use occasionally for off-hour deals."

Lucretia's central computer screen was already loaded with their current market positions. Soon as Colin took in the size and scope of their current deal, he felt another wave of nausea.

Aaron said, "If we move forward today, how much of a hit are we talking about?" He listened, frowned, said, "Hold a moment, Levi." He covered the mouthpiece. "We're in the slowest market period, which means there will be very few buyers—"

"We can't wait." Colin felt as though he screamed the words. What came out was flat, toneless. Inside it was as loud as thunder.

"He thinks it could be as much as twenty, even thirty percent."

"Compared to losing everything? This is a choice?"

Aaron started to ask if he was certain. Colin could see the doubt in the older man's gaze. He had all the reasons there, lined up like bullets in a gun. But in the end Aaron merely uncovered the phone and said, "Sell it all, Levi. Yes. Regardless. You're recording? Good. Cover our position as soon as you possibly can."

CHAPTER 31

By six-thirty all the partners except Roland had gathered. He and Regina were on speaker, driving back from Charlotte. The seven men and four women made a tousled, weary, worried bunch. Lucas was there as well. Only Lucretia was absent. An e-mail had popped up on Aaron's screen the instant he'd entered the office portal: Lucretia's brother was critically ill, she had snagged a last-minute seat to Caracas, please count this against her annual vacation, end of story.

At seven-thirty Mira arrived with Ethan, both of them bearing coffee and hot egg-and-cheese bagels from the diner across the street. Colin started to call Celeste, then decided there was no reason to give her another reason for early morning concerns. He sat behind Lucretia's computer, as deaf and blind to the swirling tension as he could possibly remain. Lucretia's trio of screens were hooked into all the major news feeds. Colin kept the off-market activity on the left screen. The early morning financial sources could be programmed to shoot up alerts, similar to the running electronic ribbon that surrounded most trading floors. That occupied the right-hand screen.

On the central monitor, Colin hunted.

At a quarter past eight, he found what he had been seeking.

When he looked up, it felt as though he was suddenly brought to full wakefulness. He had become so deep inside the fund's records he had lost track of what was going on around him. Two different arguments gripped the room. One was over the timing, whether they should take things at a more gradual pace. Levi had apparently called twice, alerting them to buys that had covered less than half of their total position. And already the prices were down twelve percent from the previous day's close. The second argument was whether they should be doing this at all. Colin realized he needed to use the bathroom. As he crossed the main room he listened to the angry voices and the strident urgency, his opponents almost shouting that it wasn't too late. When he returned, he stopped by the side wall and said, "There's something you need to know."

The angriest voices paid him no mind whatsoever. Colin waited. He viewed the room from a far distance, sheltered now by the conviction that he had gotten it right. It was Mira who first noticed the change. She nudged her father, and together they gradually silenced the room.

Colin waited until the last angry voice went silent. Then he announced, "Lucretia has erased her involvement."

Aaron was the first to comprehend. "That's not possible!"

Ethan came next. "Son, are you certain?"

"Our records show her not having invested anything."

"Of course she does." Aaron started for Lucretia's computer.

"Not that one," Colin said. "Use another."

Aaron veered toward the next desk. "I know for certain she invested every cent. . . ."

"Check the fund accounts," Colin said.

Ethan stepped over beside the older man. Aaron was so small the accountant could lean over him and insert his face directly alongside the attorney's. Aaron snapped, "Do you *mind*?"

Ethan straightened. "She's not listed among current investors."

One of Roland's other partners snapped, "That doesn't mean a thing."

Aaron's fingers flew over the keyboard. "She's *never* been listed."

His partner who had been protesting the loudest went pale. "We both know that's not true."

"I'm looking at the initial investors. A month later. Sixty days." Aaron appeared to have aged a dozen years in minutes. "Her name is nowhere in the accounts."

The partner spoke more uncertainly this time, "Maybe you got it wrong. Maybe she just said she put her money in."

Colin said, "There's more."

When all eyes were on him, he said, "She covered her tracks well. All her involvement was erased from the firm's duplicate records. But I kept a third set. A separate cloud account."

The partner demanded, "Is that legal?"

Ethan asked, "Did you actually say that?"

"Let him finish," Aaron snapped.

"Those records show she withdrew all her funds and erased her involvement at seven-fifteen on the morning of New Year's Day."

Aaron passed a trembling hand over his face. "I counted her as a friend."

People came and went. Time seemed to reluctantly proceed forward, one stubborn tick at a time. Aaron continued to field calls from Levi. He made notes on a yellow legal pad and reported the sales as they came. Colin did not pay much attention. He couldn't. The events crowded in now. The closeness of how they had come to losing it all. Going long on such a large portion of their holdings meant they could potentially have been held liable for a huge amount more than was actually invested. . . . His limbs grew so weak he sank into a chair he did not see and sat there, trembling. All these people, and those who were not present, they had counted on him. They had *trusted* him. And he had led them right to the brink of ruin.

Finally, at twenty minutes past nine, as the support staff clustered in the firm's foyer, confused and uncertain, Aaron took yet another call. He listened, thanked Levi, and cut the connection. "It's done. Our position has been fully covered."

The same quarrelsome partner asked, "How much did we lose?"

Despite the interrupted night, the strain, the man's age, Aaron went through an instantaneous transformation. "Shame on you. You heartless oaf. You lost *nothing*!"

"I just meant—"

Aaron seemed to grow in size, and in that moment Colin saw the man who dominated courtrooms with his power. "Oh, we all know fully well what you *meant.*" He pointed to where Colin sat. "Now get down on your knees, crawl to that young man, and beg forgiveness for all the trouble you have given him and all the rest of us."

"It was his investment—"

"Exactly! His investments have brought us one immense return after another!" Aaron stabbed the air between them. "Apologize to him. Then slink into your office and check your records. See just how much you made off the back of this young man. Then come back and apologize again!"

The gathering broke up then. Colin accepted a few handshakes, though most refused to meet his eye. Mira embraced him. He felt almost nothing.

When the room cleared, Colin followed Aaron and Ethan into the older man's office and said, "I want to close the fund."

CHAPTER 32

Through the days that followed, each event felt like another nail hammered into Colin's previous ambitions. He became redrawn at some visceral level. So many friends and strangers misplacing their confidence in him. Because he had this gift. And he had entered into the entire process trusting as blindly as they had. Why? Because he was still a child.

Four days after they pulled out, their target company declared bankruptcy.

The following day, when Aaron was able to search beyond the official court records, they learned the group had a second legal representative. Not the one named in the court proceedings. Another one. Hidden by way of representing the company president, and not the corporation itself.

Grey Robinson.

Three days later, on a Monday, Roland and Aaron insisted on taking Colin downtown to the City Club for lunch. Colin had managed to sleep uninterrupted through the previous night, a first since discovering the deception. This was his fourth visit to the place, twice before with

Roland and once with Aaron. He had almost become accustomed to people staring, to comments following him across the room. Only today he added a mental echo of his own to the whispers. Saying how he should have seen this coming.

After ordering, Aaron started in on plans to lodge criminal complaints against Lucretia. He was in the middle of explaining the difficulties involved, because the lady remained in her home country of Venezuela and the extradition treaty was a mess, when Colin broke in with, "I don't want to talk about that."

Aaron settled back, his head only a few inches higher than Colin's when seated. "Very well."

"I don't want to know anything more about that. Ever."

Roland asked, "You would prefer we not press charges?"

"She broke the law," Aaron pointed out. "A number of them."

He had wrestled over that. "What you do as lawyers is your business."

Aaron asked, "Will you testify? That is, assuming we can formulate the case."

He nodded, not so much in agreement as in confirmation that he had thought about this as well. "I was a part of this from the beginning. Just like her. If you call on me, I will testify."

Aaron waited as the meals were placed before them and Colin's iced tea was replenished. "Going after Grey Robinson is next to impossible."

"No matter how guilty he might be," Roland agreed.

"His fingerprints are all over this matter," Aaron went on. "But proving this in a court of law will be difficult in the extreme."

"He will have covered his tracks," Roland said.

Colin used his fork to clear the air between them. "Let's eat."

The food was excellent, and he was famished. He had not finished a meal in over a week. Afterward he lined his utensils on the empty plate and said, "Grey Robinson wasn't behind this."

Roland's protest was so mild, Colin had the sense he was approaching the same conclusion. "You can't know anything for certain."

"I don't need evidence. I know. It's that simple."

Aaron's response surprised him. The attorney nodded slowly, his eyes lidded now. The wise and battle-hardened veteran studying the terrain. "Off the record?"

"Absolutely."

"What I say, it goes no further."

"I understand."

"Then I agree with you. Grey is a legal snake of the first order. But to willfully break the law, even if he was certain of his ability to avoid detection, this puts his entire career at risk."

Roland started to speak, but in the end he merely sighed. Pushed his plate to one side. Sighed again.

"I've been doing some research of my own. Your father's campaign manager is one Matthew Alexander. He is known as a gutter fighter. A strategist who will do anything at all, whatever it takes, to bring his client victory."

Roland protested, "He didn't need to do anything like this to win."

"This was not about winning," Aaron said. "Or rather, not about winning *this election.*"

Roland offered a quiet *ahh.* A vocal sigh over he knew what was coming.

Aaron turned to Colin. "Alexander sees your father as a winner after his own heart. Your father wanted . . ."

Colin said the word for him. "Revenge."

Roland protested, "But why?"

"Because I stopped him from taking over my life. I took away his power of control."

Aaron's chin rose a notch. "This is important to your father, having control?"

"It's vital. It's the code he lived by as a sheriff. It's how he survived. At least, that's what he always claimed."

"Then I can probably track out what took place," Aaron said. "Your father threatened Alexander with dismissal. 'Do this or I find another manager for my next campaign.' And the one after that. And so forth."

"Your father is being mentioned as North Carolina's next senator," Roland said.

"There you go. Your father demanded, Alexander went to work. Contacting major donors. Working his connections. Uncovering . . ."

Once again, Colin saw the need to speak the word for him. "Lucretia."

"What bribe they offered, the terms, I cannot imagine. . . ." Aaron waved it aside. "And here we are. Enjoying a fine lunch. Celebrating the fact that it did not all end in disaster." He lifted his water glass in a toast. "Because of you, young man. I know you see this as a terrible mistake."

"Because it was."

"On the contrary. You saved us from losing everything." Aaron sipped his water, the sunlight casting liquid prisms over the starched tablecloth. "Consider this your first trial by fire."

CHAPTER 33

The week before Easter, his share minus taxes appeared in Colin's account. All of it.

Roland was almost apologetic when he called. "Aaron and I discussed it. There may be issues with the authorities, having so much money show up in the account of a minor. If anything arises, you refer them to me. Aaron and I will handle it."

Colin stared at the numbers on his online account page. Trying to digest its full meaning. "What should I do?"

"Several things. Speak with the branch manager. Set up an investment account. Park all but your petty cash there." Roland hesitated, then added, "I feel a bit foolish, advising you on matters of finance."

"This isn't the same," Colin replied. "This isn't investment. This is *money.*"

"Indeed it is. Well then. I would suggest we insert me as cosignatory on the investment account. Or Aaron, whoever—"

"You. Definitely."

"I am honored. Very well, just a moment." There was the sound of rustling pages. "How does two o'clock Thursday afternoon sound?"

Colin was very nervous going into the meeting. He had met several of the bank managers during his visits. They and the tellers, men and women alike, seemed to enjoy finding reasons to stop by, speak with the child who always appeared on his own, always kept several thousand dollars in his account, always managed his affairs without adult supervision. He thought their cheery greetings carried the false gaiety of clowns.

Mateo Garcia was something else entirely.

He carried himself with the balanced ease of an aging boxer. In that regard, he was very much like Colin's father. But from the very first moment, he treated Colin with an almost courtly grace. There was no hint of derision or doubt to his greeting. He shook Colin's hand and ushered them into his office, stood by the edge of his desk until they were seated, offered them coffee, drew over a chair on their side of his desk, ignored the stares that followed their motions through the interior glass wall, kept Colin at the center of his attention.

Even so, once the formalities were out of the way and all documents signed, Colin sensed a reversion to type. The experienced funds manager doing his best not to talk down to his newest and youngest client. All the brochures were stacked up there on his desk, ready to be laid out in a colorful array. Explaining why Colin had been right to come here, correct in trusting this man and Wells Fargo with his money—

"I don't want any of these funds invested anywhere," Colin said.

Even now, when his carefully prepared spiel was shattered, Garcia maintained his composure. "Excuse me?"

"You can put them into money market funds only. Make no investment that will delay movement of funds when I'm ready."

"When *you* are ready."

"Correct. And another thing. I've been studying your investment strategies, at least what I've found online. In the future, I may decide to grant permission for you to take certain steps. But nothing you do, no fund you choose, may charge an up-front commission."

The older gentleman responded by turning his caramel-colored gaze toward Roland. "That would severely restrict the number of options available to us."

"It might be a good idea if you took notes," Roland said mildly. "I am here to bear witness to my client's wishes."

"Your *client.*"

"Did nothing I said on the phone break through your expectations?"

"Of course, Roland. Don't talk silly. But—"

"Everything you see there in this young man's account, the entire sum, is due to his calculations. His actions. He started with *nothing*. Do you understand what I'm saying? *Nothing.*"

"That's not possible."

Roland nodded. "Finally, we are on the same page. Nothing about what has happened over the past year is possible. Starting with how we met. A young man, little more than a child, asking to borrow money. Then impressing me and my partners to the point where we trusted him with our own funds. Granting him a fund manager's commission. Standing by and watching as he made one absurd investment decision after another. Wanting time and again to tell him he was wrong to do what he did. And yet, our investments continued to rise until . . ."

"Yes? Until what?"

When Roland remained silent, Colin said, "I was duped. I almost lost everything."

"Because of criminal activities," Roland said. "Nothing about this was your—"

"It was all my fault. If I hadn't been such a child—"

"Stop with that nonsense."

"If I hadn't been so blind," Colin insisted. Releasing the shadows and the guilt. "If I hadn't been so certain that I knew everything. That I could trust my calculations in every situation. That I could trust the market."

"Blind is the absolute last word I would ever use to describe you," Roland said mildly.

"And what happened. I came within four days of watching the account sink to zero. End up owing money I didn't have. Needing to choose between bankruptcy and seeing everyone—"

"Colin, these accusations are simply—"

"Everyone who *trusted* me. Everyone who *relied* on me. Everyone who gave me their *savings*." He panted softly, standing at the end of a nightmarish race, fleeing shadows which threatened to catch up every time he fell asleep. "Everybody in the fund going into debt. Because of me. Being a child."

Roland watched him with unblinking solemnity. "Nineteen members of my law firm. Eleven accountants and their support staff. Trustees for the academy. Professionals at the business of investment. Every single one of them also blind, if you insist upon using that terrible word."

He leaned forward, closing the distance between them, drawing so near Colin could smell the heavily sugared coffee on Roland's breath. "And then what happened. Right in the nick of time, this so-called blind child caught sight of what we had all missed. A person we had known and trusted for almost ten years was perpetuating an act of criminal fraud.

Not against you, Colin. Against us all. Do you hear what I'm saying? *You. Saved. Us.*"

Roland stayed like that. Inches from Colin's face. Driving home the message with a silence so intense he forced his way through Colin's painful guilt. Not healing the rift. But at least offering a hint of solace.

Finally, Garcia broke the silence by saying, "So. No up-front commission on any future investment. Anything else I should be made aware of?"

Through the long super-heated spring and summer, into the cooler autumn months. Winter came and proceeded smoothly into yet another spring. Almost abruptly, he turned fourteen. More seasons, pushed and crammed and segmented by studies and exams and new responsibilities.

The next seismic change struck the week before his fifteenth birthday.

Fremdt suggested it was time to find a thesis topic.

It took him a long moment to understand what the professor was talking about. When he remained silent, Fremdt unleashed his trademark ire. "What, you think I will let you coast here forever?"

"I'm not coasting."

"I see you in class. Bored and idle and mooning over the pretty girls twice your age."

"I don't moon."

"You're not *struggling*." He gripped the air between them with ham-sized fists. "I want to see you *sweat.*"

Colin had no idea how to respond.

"There, you see?" Fremdt dropped his hands and his gaze to the papers littering his desk. "I give you until the summer. Either you find something worth struggling over, or I find it for you. I tell the dean you begin graduate studies next fall."

Colin remained where he was. "But I won't graduate for another eighteen months."

"You think you are the first person who is ready before the university system says?" Fremdt did not bother to look up. "You keep earning credits. You do both degrees together. Now go. It's time I make other students sweat."

It was during his birthday visit to the barber that Colin was introduced to his next passion. The diminutive hairdresser's name was Angelo, and he revealed himself to be a true fanatic when it came to vinyl. "I can't believe you've never heard the difference."

"I don't even know what you're talking about."

"Well, this is too important to discuss in pieces." Angelo seemed almost angry, the way he snapped the towel off Colin, then brushed him down with harsh drumbeats timed to his words. "And too complex to handle in dribs and drabs."

The younger barber, the man who had cut Colin's hair that second time months and centuries ago, said, "You best run while you still can."

Angelo demanded, "Remind me why I don't fire you."

"'Cause you know I'm the voice of reason here." The younger man made a shooing motion to Colin. "Fast as you can. Out the door. Don't never look back."

Angelo led Colin up to the front. "We close at seven. You want, get back here after all these heretics have gone home."

Colin was not certain what he was going to do, nor could he say how he felt about Angelo's invitation. He ate a solitary dinner at the mall's Italian restaurant, bought a ticket to the film he'd spent two weeks looking forward to seeing. But as he passed through the cinema's lobby, he veered around and went back to the circular booth where the cinema manager observed the evening crowd. He handed the woman his ticket and said, "Something's come up. I need to change this for another night."

Colin wasn't certain how he felt about this next step, meeting a man he really didn't know behind the closed doors of a business after hours. When he knocked on the shop's glass doors and Angelo peered out at him, he realized the barber felt exactly the same. Instantly his unease vanished. He waited while Angelo relocked the door, then followed him past the empty leather chairs into a back office. Angelo pointed him to a leather office chair positioned directly in front of a stereo system that climbed a series of steel and glass shelves. "Sit there."

Angelo left the office and returned with one of the chairs meant to hold waiting customers. "I wasn't sure you'd show up."

"Neither was I."

Angelo seemed to like that. He cut on the system, made numerous adjustments, then said, "Ever heard the work of Keith Jarrett?"

"No."

"Good. I want to start with someone you don't know." He started to punch a button, then said, "We're going to use piano because it best illustrates what I'm going to show you. This is a first-class digital recording. Ready?"

"Yes."

He pressed the button, then seated himself. "This is from *The Cellar Door Sessions*, recorded with Miles Davis in 1970."

Colin felt the music wash over him, invading his space in a manner that headphones did not allow. It rose up in solid yet quiet waves, filling the room. When the cut ended, he breathed a quiet, "Wow."

"Save your wows. Now listen to this." Angelo lifted the cover to a turntable, started the motor, set the needle in place, adjusted the amp, and settled back. "Same track."

When the music ended and Angelo lifted the needle, Colin

just sat there. Trying to come to terms with what he had just heard.

Apparently Angelo found what he desired in Colin's stunned expression. He stepped around the desk and returned with a cigar and ashtray. Another trip, this time to bring out a bottle and cut-crystal glass. "I take it you're not interested in single malt."

"No."

"Cigar?"

"Yuck."

"Nix on the cigar. There's cold Coke in the fridge up front."

"I don't . . . No, thank you."

"Do I need to show you any more examples of the differences?"

"No." Colin pointed to the turntable. "I want more of that."

"Stick with Jarrett?"

"Absolutely."

From that point, the evening took on a timeless feel, at least for Colin. Between cuts, Angelo explained the key differences dividing digital from analog. He used terms like warmth, richness, and depth. He drew graphs in the air between himself and the system, showing how digital recordings by definition cut segments from the music's vibratory patterns. How as a result, the digital recording did not capture the complete sound wave.

Each set of comments was limited to only a few sentences. As if the real reason for their time together was the music. Only the music. Then another track was played. Another album slipped from the cardboard sleeve and set on the turntable. As the music started, Angelo settled back, relit his cigar, sipped from his replenished glass. If the barber was in any way affected by the whiskey, he gave no sign.

Angelo returned time and again to his personal favorite album, *The Survivors' Suite*, recorded under the guiding hand of Manfred Eicher, the producer behind the young ECM label. Colin personally preferred the orchestral arrangements Jarrett put together under the Impulse label. When he said so, Angelo simply replied, "This young man is seriously addicted to swing." He switched albums and turned the volume up to where the music vibrated in Colin's chest.

It was almost eleven when Angelo led him back to the front of the store. Colin found himself reluctant to step into the almost empty mall and release himself from the magic. He stood there by the entrance and said, "The name on your equipment. Bowers and Wilkins."

Angelo nodded approval. "Some people like to mix and match. I prefer a system built to fit together. Or so it seems to me."

"I like that idea. Very much."

"So remember it, tuck it away for when you're rich and famous." Angelo offered his hand. "Young man, it's been a pleasure."

Colin thanked him, wishing there was something stronger he could say. He walked the silent corridor, phoned for an Uber, and carried the scent of Angelo's cigar out into the night.

CHAPTER 34

The next morning, Colin was waiting outside the salon when Angelo arrived at half past ten. Colin offered him a plastic shopping bag. "I got you these."

The man made no move to accept. "You didn't need—"

"The salesman said the Blue Note reissues will soon be making waves. He played me cuts from the Grant Green album. Their system isn't nearly as good as yours. Plus the store was noisy."

"Which is why I don't bother with analog out front. Why risk messing up a good thing?" He took the bag, looked inside, said, "You got me . . ."

"Their latest five albums."

"Colin, no. It's too much."

"Yesterday was my birthday. What you did, it's the best gift I ever received." He was already backing way, keeping Angelo from giving back the bag. "The salesman said you can exchange any you don't want."

He hurried away, forcing himself not to run, feeling as though he was fleeing in embarrassment. When he reached the mall's main avenue, he glanced back to find Angelo still standing there, watching him. Colin waved and turned the corner, wondering if this was something adults learned. How to fit together words of gratitude that wouldn't leave him feeling so inadequate.

Colin spent Christmas Day with Sandrine and Arnold. Mira's family were on a West Virginia ski holiday. Roland's were visiting his parents. Sandrine and Arnold lived in a lovely town house overlooking the Landfall golf course's northern perimeter. The day warmed to where they could open the balcony doors. Colin gave Arnold a set of drivers the pro shop manager said he had been toying with for months. Sandrine's main hobby away from school was cooking; she received a set of Swiss Victorinox kitchen knives and a Sabatier Maison knife stand. It was the first time he had shopped for others, focusing on what they would want, ignoring the cost. Their response touched him deeply.

He waited until the Christmas rush was over, then took an Uber to the Audio Advice specialty music store on Orleander. He told himself on the way over there was no reason to be nervous. He was not required to buy anything. If they wanted to treat him like a child, fine, he'd take his business elsewhere. Even so, when he entered the store his hands were sweating. He wanted this to be a unique event. Something that genuinely marked his entry into a new universe.

He drifted around for a while, until a skinny man in his twenties walked over and said, "You looking for something in particular?"

"Yes. I'm interested in a system."

"A system. Well. You've come to the right place." He wore rumpled jeans and a chalk-blue shirt and a goatee. "That's what we specialize in. Systems."

Colin started to walk out. He knew the man saw a child.

He had debated coming with Arnold for that reason. But this was different from things in the past. This was . . .

"I'm very serious. I know what I want. The question is, are you willing to help me." He knew he spoke overloud. He could see other people glancing his way. But he couldn't help it. "This is important."

Something sparked in the man's intelligent eyes. "Sure. I get that. Buying a system is a big deal."

"I'm focusing on jazz. Analog. The turntable will be the primary . . ." He hesitated. "What do I call it?"

"Conduit works as good as anything. Or source." The guy studied him. "How old are you?"

"Fifteen."

"Do you need a parent or guardian to help?"

"No. It's just me." Colin showed his debit card. "I can pay."

"And you're serious. And it's important." The guy grinned. "I bet you're not interested in a set of ten thousand–dollar speakers tall as you are either."

"Not now, not ever."

"That's about the only kind of kid client we get. A child of somebody rich, they come in here looking for something that will blow out the house windows. Impress their buddies."

"I don't have buddies like that."

"And you're not after show."

He pocketed his card. "And I've earned the money myself."

"At fifteen, no less." The salesman appeared to be enjoying himself now. "You do realize we're talking about *serious* money."

Colin found himself relaxing. "Yes. And that's exactly what I'm looking for. A serious system."

"You don't strike me as Wilmington's first kid drug dealer."

"I've made investments."

"At fifteen."

"You've already said that."

"Yeah, well, some things bear repeating. You know what you're after?"

Colin released a tight breath. "I want the best small system you have for hearing analog jazz. The only one I've actually heard was Bowers and Wilkins. I liked the sound a lot."

"That makes two of us." He pointed to the smoked glass covering the rear wall. "Why don't we retire to our soundproof room and make some noise."

Colin settled on a full Bowers & Wilkins system for everything except the turntable. The salesman's name was Liam, and by that point the morning's commission almost had him dancing in place. Colin liked the way he handled the albums, a practiced motion that treated them like the gems they were. When it came to a turntable, he accepted Liam's urging and bought the Sonos Pro-Ject with a Sumiko Songbird cartridge. Colin then added glass and steel shelves and matching speaker stands. They finished by walking down the two rows of analog jazz albums, Liam offering suggestions that showed his passion went far beyond the coming payment.

When Colin set the five albums he'd selected as starters on the counter—two of Benny Goodman, two of Billie Holiday, and one of Keith Jarrett—the salesman said, "The man knows his music."

"Not even a little bit," Colin replied, warmed by how he was now seen. The *man*. He hoped it was not just because of the money he spent. He didn't think so. "But I want to learn."

Liam watched him sign the receipt, checked the signature, said, "We can arrange the technician to set you up sometime next week."

"Tuesday and Thursday and Saturday all work," Colin replied. "Classes start next week. The other days are out."

"Where do you go to school?"

"UNCW."

"Get out."

"But I live at Outer Banks Academy. That's where I studied before."

"Outer Banks Academy, that's what, a school?"

"Sort of." Colin watched him slip the albums into a bag. "Thanks a lot. This has been fun."

CHAPTER 35

Two weeks into the winter term, Colin purchased a Trek FX hybrid bike with flat-bar handles and Shimano drivetrain and disc brakes. With Roland's assistance, he also attended a series of driver's ed tutorials with a private instructor. Once he had his official DMV learner's permit, he joined Roland and Celeste at family court so his attorney could request a special dispensation allowing Colin to obtain a full driver's license seven months early. The judge clearly knew both Roland and Celeste, and in Colin's mind had already accepted the reasoning as valid. Just the same, the procedure took over an hour, and the judge insisted on Colin taking the stand.

Sitting the driver's test and obtaining his full license only happened because Roland pulled strings and then escorted him to the after-hours exam, which was handled personally by the DMV's manager.

The following Saturday, Mira took him car shopping.

She and Lucas were back to take part in a family wedding. Her gaiety over spending a weekend with her beau seemed forced to Colin, but he knew better than to ask questions. What she wanted him to know, she would tell him. And apparently Mira didn't want him to know anything at all.

During her months away Colin thought she had matured in numerous subtle ways. Her gaze seemed deeper, her mannerisms more womanly. Colin thought she was growing into the most beautiful lady he had ever seen, and said so.

Even her response to this was different. "You know what they say about beauty being only skin deep."

"Not with you," he replied. "Not ever."

She stopped for a light and gazed at him. "You are still my second best friend."

But the words threatened tears. He could see the effort required to crimp her face tight, blink fiercely, and move through the green light. Colin watched them pass their destination and ventured, "You've gone too far."

"No, I haven't."

"Mira, the dealership is vanishing in your rearview mirror."

"Oh, pooh." She was recovered now, and smiling. "You don't want some boring old Buick."

"Mira . . ." He watched her pull into the Porsche dealership on New Center Drive. "What are we doing here?"

"What you said, silly." She did not rise from her Volkswagen so much as bound. "Buying you some wheels."

It was so nice seeing her resume the joyful near-dance that had defined their early times together. A cluster of salesmen inside the glass-fronted showroom watched her skip over to a cobalt blue Macan GTS, where she announced, "Colin Eames, meet the new love of your life."

"Mira, no."

"Why? Don't you absolutely love this?"

"For you, maybe. For me, never. Not in a million years."

"How did you possibly age into a boring old fuddy-duddy while I was away?"

The fact that two salesmen were approaching made his

face flame. "Let's review this. You're suggesting I buy a . . . how much is it, anyway?"

She pretended to squint at the sticker. "A lot."

"What do you think would happen if I get stopped by a police officer, with a one-of-a-kind court-issued specialty license, driving this?"

She waved that aside. "With this car, you'll outrun them, silly."

"Mira, please, no. Let's go, okay?"

She pouted the entire way back to the Buick dealership, then slouched against the side door. "I'll just wait out here and mope, thank you very much."

They had exactly what Colin wanted. He knew because he had searched their website, then phoned three days earlier and put down a cash reserve on this very car. The Encore was the smallest version of the car Celeste had been driving all those eons ago. It was silver with faux pale-doeskin interior and a modest 1.4-liter four-cylinder engine. Colin thought it was perfect. Mira declared it ideal for her aged grandmother and then complained when she was drawn inside because the purchase required her direct involvement. The salespeople wanted her confirmation that the buyer's court-issued license was indeed valid, and the insurance documents he had already obtained through Roland's office were not bogus.

Mira followed him back to the academy, beeping her horn and waving one arm out the window at how slow he took the streets. She then joined him and slouched down far enough to keep anyone she might know from ever seeing her in what she had already named a snoozefest on wheels. They ate Italian at one of the Mayfaire restaurant's outdoor tables and talked about nothing of importance. For the return journey Mira flipped her sweater over her head, knotted it under her chin, and declared that only a babushka would be happy the way Colin drove.

It was the happiest outing he had experienced in a very long time.

Three weeks later, Colin entered the UNCW academic dean's office. "Professor Fremdt said you wanted to see me?"

"Come sit down." But Dean Sykes didn't wait for him to settle into the chair to demand, "What's this about your wanting to audit music classes at Chapel Hill?"

"I need a better understanding of structure."

"You mean music theory."

"I guess."

"Where are you going with this?"

Fremdt had asked him the same thing. "I'm not sure yet."

"Are you interested in composing?"

"No. Definitely not." When the dean sat there observing him with that crystal grey gaze of hers, he went on, "I've done a little studying on my own. The Cartesian system of graphs was used to represent music before it was introduced into geometry. There are a lot of possible areas of overlap."

"Math applied to music."

"More like calculus. Logic systems and their relationship to harmonics." Colin had struggled the same way in his discussion with Fremdt. "Sorry. I'm just getting started. I don't have anything completely formulated yet."

She inspected handwritten notes on her desk. "He also mentioned your wanting to attend their graduate-level classes in software design."

Colin nodded. "Looking at how artificial intelligence systems might be applied to musical structures."

Dean Sykes's smile did not actually reach her lips. But it was clearly there just the same. "I see. Or rather, I understand enough."

"Is something funny?"

She lined up her pen in parallel to the page holding her notes. "In a way. Professor Fremdt called me because he wanted to be certain you were assigned to him as a doctoral candidate. Now that I've heard your proposal, I can well understand Fremdt's sense of urgency."

"I'm nowhere near ready to present a thesis proposal."

"Young man, it may interest you to know that previously I served as assistant academic dean at Chapel Hill. I have interviewed any number of would-be grad students whose thesis concepts were less well formulated." She leaned back, steepled her fingers. "Here's what we're going to do. I will speak with my former associates in Chapel Hill. You will of course need to be interviewed. . . . How will you travel?"

"I have a driver's license. And a car." When Dean Sykes frowned over his records, he added, "The court made an exception."

"So you have been planning on this step for some time."

"Hoping, more like."

The news seemed to please her. "In that case, I will make the necessary introductions at their schools for music and software engineering— "

"Can you please not tell them what I want to do?"

She looked up, her gaze tightening to laser intensity. "Something tells me you are far more advanced in your aims than you let on."

Colin decided not to respond.

"I see. Very well. Fremdt will remain your supervisor. Be forewarned; as you continue, Chapel Hill may insist you be counted among their own graduate students. But for the moment we will adjust your records to show you are now working toward two degrees simultaneously. And I hereby offer a provisional approval to your multidisciplinary thesis." Another flash of ferocious intensity. "We are granting you a highly unusual level of autonomy, Mr. Eames. Not to mention bending any number of rules. Do not let us down."

* * *

That winter and spring passed in a series of overlapping experiences. Colin held to his morning swims, at least twice each week, sometimes three, rarely four. He grew taller, but not by much, and held to a slender build that most resembled his mother's. He would never develop his father's bullish strength. But he could feel his body growing stronger and fitter. Every time he needed to buy new clothes to suit his changing body, Colin took it as a minor triumph.

His monthly chats with Celeste were often little more than perfunctory hellos. He spoke occasionally with Mira, but she seemed perpetually distracted. Stressed by matters she did not want to discuss. She claimed to be busy with a project and too overwhelmed to see him, even talk for long on the phone. Roland became involved in a major court case, and they only managed a few rushed phone calls. Finally, one Saturday in late May Colin found Regina sunning herself at the pool and asked what was going on.

But the woman gave Colin a Latina's version of a sphinx. "There are times," she replied, "when a mother is obliged to say nothing. Mostly because that's the best description of what she knows for certain. Nothing."

"Where is Lucas?"

"That is part of the nothing I'm not going to talk about." Regina smiled. "See how easy that is?"

"I don't like being shut out like this."

She laughed. "*Mi querido chico,* you and I have that much in common."

The drive to and from Chapel Hill formed an unexpected pleasure. He left before dawn on Tuesday and came back Thursday after his final class. Through the student office Colin found what the owner called a studio but in truth was a large bedroom with a makeshift kitchenette in one corner. The prewar house stood two blocks off Franklin, the center of student life. The nights he spent in Chapel Hill felt like stolen glimpses of a new phase. He did not want to call it adulthood. He had no idea what the word meant. Only that it unsettled and appealed in equal measure.

The studies required for his new directions threatened to overwhelm him. The software engineering course was a near-constant grind. He made progress simply by focusing on the math, the formula, and temporarily setting aside all the issues needed a more detailed study.

UNC Chapel Hill was totally different from the Wilmington campus. For one thing, it was huge. Over thirty-five thousand students were enrolled. The level of classwork, the intelligence of his fellow students, the demands made by his professors, everything about the place was several grades above what he had experienced thus far.

The music theory class was so difficult he feared for a time that he might even fail the course.

Even so, by the end of the term he began to see a way ahead. Not a clear compass heading. Not by any means. But there was at least a glimmer of light, a reward for four months of dark slogging.

Fremdt wanted him to stay on for summer classes. "Econometrics," he barked. "Econometrics is the ticket. You want to see your math applied, yes? So study how it works with money and how money rules the people out there." He waved his hand at the sunlit window. "See if you can make smart interpretations of all their foolishness."

Colin knew his professor disapproved of him moving away from pure maths. Even so, there was a certain appeal to the man's suggestion. "Maybe next year."

"No, no, not with econometrics. You can't see the depths of this when you mix it with other elements."

"That's just it, you see. I already feel like I'm just skimming the surface in music theory. And maybe the software courses as well."

That stilled the big man. "You received an A in both."

"I gave back what the teacher expected. That's not enough. I need to see where this is going. I need to *understand.*" He shrugged. "That's as clear as I know how to make it."

Fremdt examined him a long moment. "So. This summer, you do what, laze by the pool? Count the clouds? A new drug of choice, perhaps. Or maybe there is a woman."

Colin felt his face burn. His body was going through changes that at times threatened to overwhelm him. Alien urges that had nothing to do with his mind. He wasn't ready to talk about them. Especially not with Fremdt. "I'm going back over the course materials. Really study them. See what directions open up."

"Software design and music theory. Together."

"And the problems you gave me in calculus. They're not together yet. But maybe they will be."

Eight days later, a new Sojourn House resident entered Colin's life.

Sofia Hernandez lost her mother at birth and her father at nine, the same year she entered Outer Banks Academy. She had an uncle, but nothing was said about him except that Sofia would be spending the summer in residence. She and Consuela had formed an immediate bond, which was very good, because that spring Sofia had begun having problems with her eyes.

All through the last of May and into early June, Colin watched the two of them go off to numerous doctors' appointments. Then Consuela's youngest came down with chickenpox, and out of desperation she asked Colin if he would help out. "The girl is an angel, and the situation is terrible."

"Of course I'll help."

"She has another appointment at the UNC Greenville

hospital tomorrow at three." Consuela's child began wailing in the background, accelerating her speech. "Make note of the miles. The school will repay use of your car. Take her to lunch. Anything she wants. Keep the receipt."

Sofia's passion was history. She was a silent child and spent the ride over and back and the time in the waiting room reading on her tablet. Colin had no idea how to start a conversation. They had shared several dinners together, at least in the sense that their two bodies had occupied the dining room. But Sofia had rarely looked up from her tablet, and even then he wasn't sure she had actually seen him. She was not impolite, merely uninterested. But he had no problem with silence.

Three days later, there was another doctor, this one at New Hanover Regional, the main Wilmington hospital. The visit lasted so long they missed dinner. Colin asked if she wanted to grab something in the hospital cafeteria before they left. Sofia responded by looking at him. Really looking.

Colin said, "What?"

"Could we go to a Mexican restaurant I know north of the city?"

"If that's what you like, sure, I guess."

"It's on 17, up toward Hampstead. Guelaguetza Oaxaca. My father used to take me."

Colin had no real interest in spicy food, but he didn't complain, because already Sofia was emerging from her normal withdrawn state. She turned off her tablet and watched the road, the buildings, people, the gathering night. The restaurant was a simple place in a local strip mall. The exterior wall was painted with purple Day-Glow cacti wearing bright orange sombreros. Sofia ordered in rapid-fire Spanish, then told Colin, "The chef is from Guadalajara. He says his specialty is torta ahogado."

Colin told the man behind the counter, "I'll have what she's having."

The night was so mild they ate at a picnic table set beneath a neighboring oak. The food was fantastic.

Midway through the meal, Sofia said, "You're at university, yes?"

"Right. UNCW."

"But you also go to Chapel Hill every week, yes? Why do you stay at Sojourn House?"

He shrugged. "Nowhere else to go, really."

"Your family . . ."

"Is it okay if we don't talk about them?"

"Sure." She bent back over her meal. "I don't like my family either." Another bite, then, "What do you study?"

"Right now, I'm struggling. Trying to tie together some different subjects. The school calls it interdisciplinary."

"That must be nice."

"It doesn't feel that way now. Maybe someday. If I can make sense of it all." He risked asking, "What's the matter with your eyes?"

"I have dysplastic nevus."

"I don't know—"

"They're like freckles. On my retinas. They're growing." She pushed her plate away. "The doctors are worried because that's a sign of worse things. Choroidal nevus. And melanoma."

"I'm so sorry."

She nodded. "If it's the one thing, I'll probably go blind. If it's the other, they have to take out my eyes."

He struggled then. Trying to find room for breath. And the news. And the look in that young face.

This time, he was the one who needed the silence. It took him all the way back to the campus, and inside Sojourn House, before he could manage, "Whatever you need. Day or night. I'm here for you."

She climbed three stairs, then turned back. Her eyes held a

most remarkable darkness, and a depth too great for her young years. "Nights after the hospital. They are so very hard."

"I could come read to you, if you like. I mean . . ."

She did not smile. Not really. But the look warmed him just the same. "That would be so nice."

Thirty minutes later, he knocked on her door. "Come in."

She was tucked away in a bed identical to the one he had occupied for over seven years. Only with her the bed seemed vast. Colin left the door open and pulled the room's lone chair over close to her bed. "What should I read?"

She indicated the tablet on her bedside table. "It's already drawn up."

He turned it on, read the title page, " 'The Silk Road: A New History of the World.' "

"It's wonderful," she told him. "The writer, he looks at history as if the center of the world was Asia. Not the west."

Colin had to smile. "So you don't want to hear a story about a princess trapped in a tower with her teddy bear."

She snuggled deeper, watching him. "Read."

And so it began.

Two, sometimes three nights each week, he entered her room and read. Grant stopped by a few times, just checking through the open door, then retreating. Consuela occasionally stayed on after dinner and sat with them as well. Holding Sofia's hand, pretending the history fascinated her like it did the child.

The first week of July, it all came to a head. He and Consuela both accompanied Sofia to New Hanover Regional that day. When the doctor summoned them into the conference room, they kept firm hold of Sofia's hands. The light-panel covering almost the entire side wall held a dozen images of her eyes. The doctor stood at the far end, as if wanting to distance himself from their tension. He announced, "Benign."

Colin felt as though he had forgotten how to breathe.

Consuela asked, "You're sure?"

"I, my colleagues here and at Greenville University Medical. We agree. The tests all indicate the same thing." He tapped one eye, then the other, moving down the line. "Here and here and here. All of them. Dysplastic nevus. Freckles. No malignancies." He seemed unable to accept the news himself. "What is more, the growth of these freckles has slowed to almost nothing. Young lady, you are beyond fortunate."

Sofia flung herself into Consuela's arms. And wept.

Colin asked, "So, she's done? We can go?"

"We need to monitor the nevus, make sure they do not extend so far as to mar her sight." He found it easier to study the images. "At this stage, the mind will overcome these blocks in her retinas, just like it does for the point where the optic nerve connects. But if she begins to notice any deterioration, or cloudiness . . ."

They celebrated with another Guadalajara feast. One so joyful not even the occasional tear could mar the event.

Through the rest of that summer, every now and then a small hand would knock on his door. And he would climb the stairs and enter the narrow room. And read a young girl to sleep.

CHAPTER 36

The next week Colin went in for his regular haircut, and Angelo invited him back for another evening session. He had scarcely settled into his seat when there was a knock on the outside door.

"Stay right there." Angelo left in a cloud of cigar smoke, and returned with a sleek African American gentleman, dapper in starched striped shirt and vest and trousers to a gaberdine suit. Pearl and gold cuff links. Diamond pinkie ring. Hair that shone in the overhead light. "Colin, meet Jaden Barrett. Another jazz addict."

"How do, Colin. How do."

Colin wasn't sure how he felt, having an interloper join them. "Nice to meet you."

"Jaden and I play poker once or twice each month. We and his missus all like the horses."

"Try and make it to Charlottesville for the Foxfield, Camden for the Colonial," Jaden told him. "We take in the Derby or Preakness every year or so."

"Get out to Vegas now and then." Angelo pulled in another chair. "Take the big one, Jaden. Make yourself comfortable."

He settled into Angelo's office chair. "You like to gamble, Colin?"

He hesitated, then settled on a simple, "No."

Angelo held the cigar box open to Jaden. "Other than he's got a fine ear, I don't know hardly anything about this kid."

Jaden cast a practiced eye over Colin's clothes. "Man's getting his money from somewhere. You got family, young man?"

"I . . . No. Not really."

"Seems to me, either you do or you don't." He accepted a glass of the single malt, breathed the fumes, nodded approval. "You don't want me asking questions, say the word. Man's got a right to keep his secrets. We'll just hold ourselves to the music."

Colin took his time answering. There was something in the man's easy manner, he knew it was mostly show, that down deep probably lurked a risk, a threat. But not to him. He knew it was abductive reasoning on a minimum of data. But he liked and trusted Angelo. And Angelo trusted this newcomer. So . . .

"I've started a couple of times to talk. But these sessions, they mean so much, I didn't want to disturb anything."

"These *sessions*, the man says." Jaden nodded. "The music is important to him, just like you said."

Angelo remained standing beside his desk. "Why would talking about yourself mess with our sessions?"

"My life, it's not normal."

Jaden actually chuckled. He looked at Angelo, said, "I came for the music, I'm staying for the show. Come sit yourself down, old friend. Let's hear what the man has to say for himself."

Twenty minutes later, they had still not started with the music.

Jaden was well into his second glass. Taking it in small draughts, savoring it and Angelo's cigar with the same sense of easy pleasure as he did Colin's story. "Let me make sure I got this straight. You moved into that genius school at . . ."

"I was six."

"And you started UNC Wilmington at . . ."

"Twelve."

"Where you studied . . ."

"Calculus. Other stuff."

"Math stuff."

"Until last year. Then I started attending classes at Chapel Hill in music theory and software engineering."

"And because of what you've learned from Angelo here, you're working on . . ."

"A mathematical foundation for harmonics and musical development. That will probably become my graduate thesis."

"*Graduate* work, now. At fifteen." Jaden nudged his friend. "You're trying to find a way to teach a computer to make jazz, is that what you're saying?"

"No." Just the same, Jaden's words teased out another flicker of that distant light. "Well, no . . . I don't know what I'm after. It's been a struggle."

"Can't imagine why." He glanced over. "Can you, old friend?"

"You guys lost me a long while back. I'm lucky if the cash register balances out at the end of my day."

A few more puffs on the cigar, then, "You ever heard of Bart Howard?"

"No."

"Bart and my daddy were friends. My daddy, he played clarinet and tenor sax with a number of bands. Bart was retired when they met, my daddy was still climbing the career ladder. But sometimes those things matter a lot less than people like to think. Bart was a songwriter and composer, mostly swing and bossa nova and cabaret, but he put his hand to a lot of different sounds."

Angelo said, "He wrote almost half of that Johnny Mathis album we played last time you were here."

"He also wrote 'Fly Me to the Moon,'" Jaden said. "Kaye Ballard was the first to record it. Then Frank Sinatra, using an arrangement by Quincy Jones. The song went on to become Sinatra's signature sound. Peggy Lee, Joe Harnell, Julie London, Paul Anka, they all recorded it. My daddy once asked Bart about writing that song. Know what he said? 'I spent forty years getting ready, so I could write it in twenty minutes.'"

"I don't want to wait forty years," Colin replied. "Not for anything."

"You're a man in a hurry, sure enough. But sometimes you get where you're aiming when the time is right. Not when you want." Jaden tapped his cigar on the ashtray. "My advice to you, young man, is enjoy the ride. Now enough of this talk. I don't know about you, but I came here to hear some good music."

"Before we start, there's one more thing." Angelo lifted a printed sheet off his desk. "Just got off the computer before you showed up. Fifth of August. Mark your calendar. Third row center."

"So where's mine?"

Angelo pulled the page away from Jaden's outstretched hand. "Soon as I see your two hundred and fifty bucks."

As Jaden reached for his billfold, he told Colin, "We're joining Chick Corea at the Live Oak Bank Pavilion."

He felt his heart surge. "Can I come?" He caught Angelo's hesitation and added, "I can pay my way."

Angelo said, "I'd be happy to have you join us, but that's a lot of money, especially for someone your—"

"I've made almost eight hundred thousand dollars. It's just sitting in a money market account."

He felt Jaden's chair begin to make little jerking motions, and realized the man was laughing.

Angelo said, "Run that news item past us again."

"Naw, we know all we need to for the moment. Get back on your computer and see if there's another ticket. Once that's done, we got all night to hear how the *man* here made his fortune."

It was well after midnight when they finally called it quits. Jaden offered to drop Colin at the academy, claimed it was almost on his way home. Jaden's ride was a slate grey BMW 740i, and their talk was about Corea and his music. When Jaden pulled into the academy's semicircular drive, he cut the motor and said, "You do that gentleman a world of good."

"He's been great, introducing me to jazz."

"Angelo lost his wife to cancer, oh, must be close to a dozen years ago. They couldn't have kids. Since then he's spent too much time on his own. My wife and I tried and tried to get him to go out, see lady friends who'd love to share his autumn years. He always says the same thing. Once you know heaven, it's hard to come down to earth."

"I can't imagine what that must be like," Colin said.

The space between them was flavored by cigars and whiskey and the echoes of good music. Jaden asked, "You didn't have much of a home life?"

"My mother died when I was four. My father . . . I don't like talking about him."

Jaden's only response was to puff out his cheeks, blow softly, then, "You need to find yourself a role model. People who can show you the other side of the coin. What it means to love. Be fulfilled by a good relationship."

Colin thought of Arnold and Sandrine. Roland and Regina. Ethan and Alexi. Even Mira and Lucas, on their good days. "I have that."

"So the next time the shadows start gnawing at your nights, you take a good long look at what they have. What keeps them alive and in love and in sync."

It was the first time Colin had ever heard an adult talk about shadows like that. "Thanks for letting me come to the concert. It means a lot."

Jaden's teeth flashed in the night. "Little man, Arnold and I, we wouldn't have it any other way."

CHAPTER 37

When he told Celeste about it several nights later, she laughed out loud. "You spent the evening listening to music with Jaden Barrett? If that don't beat all."

"Who is he?"

"Jaden Barrett is one of the highest paid divorce lawyers in the Southeast. He clocks out at over a thousand dollars an hour." She chuckled. "I wonder who he billed that time to."

"I thought . . ."

"What?"

"All they talked about was poker and horses. And jazz. I thought maybe he was a bookie. Or a professional gambler. Something."

"He'd probably agree with the gambling element."

"How do you know him?"

"You ever heard the term *pro bono*? Barrett's served as pro bono attorney on a few child-custody cases I've brought to him. And some other things we don't need to mention in polite company. He's one of the good guys. When he wants to be."

Colin had no idea how to respond.

"I imagine your barber friend grew concerned about this young kid who pops in for late night jazz sessions. Well dressed, groomed to the max, getting all fit and tan with his swimming—"

"Stop with all that."

"What, stop. It's the truth. So Angelo mentions you to his poker buddy, and the buddy says, maybe I should give this kid a look." She chuckled again. "I'll give Jaden a call, tell him you're another good guy. Did you tell him about your investments?"

"It sort of came out."

This time she laughed out loud. "Man, I wish I had been a fly on that wall."

"We're going to a concert together. Fifth of August. At the Live Oak Bank Pavilion." The stream of frustrating days ahead seemed endless. "At least I've got something to look forward to."

"Colin, what's the matter?"

"Nothing."

"Don't you give me that. Is it just your studies?"

"There's no 'just' to that mess."

"Is that all it is? If not, you know you can tell me—"

"I'm lonely." The words tasted hot as lava in his mouth. He felt ashamed for having even spoken. Just the same, there were more pushing, pressing to emerge. "I don't have any friends my age."

Celeste gave that a respectful beat, then said, "I've been half expecting this. Maybe I should have brought it up before now. You are in a difficult position. Every teenage passage is awful. Don't get me wrong, but yours is . . ."

"I know. Special."

"I don't like using that word. I was going to say, particularly stressful. And loneliness is a big issue. Other than your physical state, you are not an adolescent. You can't relate to other fifteen-year-olds except as a prefect. As their superior. Which you are. Not like, you're better than them."

"I know what you mean."

"And because of your age, the people you're drawn to see you as somewhat beneath their notice. I mean, socially. Which leaves you bereft. I hate having to talk to you like this, but it's the truth."

Just having it out, being understood, helped more than he could ever have imagined. "What do I do?"

"You're going to hate hearing this. I know I would. But the answer is, give it another year."

"No way."

"You'll be taller, you can practice claiming to be older than you are. But until then, well, a lot of the time it's going to feel like you're holding your breath."

Nine days later, the second Wednesday in July, Colin traveled to the bank by himself. The investment manager, Mateo Garcia, was exactly the same, courteous and cordial and grave all at once. He even seemed to be wearing the same slate grey suit. "Roland called me this morning after the two of you spoke. He wished to stress how important it is that I pay the most careful attention to what you have to say."

Colin was vastly relieved to hear they had spoken. Roland had been tied up with a court case for months. It was the first conversation they'd had since March. "He told me I could trust you."

"To do what, exactly? Roland didn't say."

"I want to take a long position on a stock." Colin had mentally practiced what he wanted to say all morning. Now the words formed an orderly row in his head. "If you feel like it's necessary to give me advice, okay, but I'm really not interested."

Mateo leaned back in his seat. "I see."

"It's important that all my instructions are carried out immediately. The same day. The same hour, if possible."

He made a note on a sheet of paper. "Go on."

"Most important of all, I need to make sure that what I tell you doesn't go anywhere else. No one hears of this. No one else acts on it."

"These investments, they're not based on insider knowledge."

"No. They're not."

"Because I am required to alert the authorities if there is even a hint of illegality."

"I have developed an algorithmic system of tracking stocks," Colin said.

"The funds in your account . . ."

"All came from this system."

"And you are concerned that the, let's call them opponents, might catch wind of your reentering the market."

"Exactly."

"I have known Roland for over twenty years. And never have I heard him speak so highly of a young man." Mateo nodded thoughtfully. "Very well, I will supply you with my private contact details. You may reach me day or night. And I give you my word, what we do here will go no further."

Colin took a long breath. He had the sensation of standing on the high-dive platform, his toes gripping the edge. He dove. "So let's get started."

He told Arnold and Sandrine the following Sunday afternoon. They grilled steaks on their balcony, Celeste joining them as she had a couple of times before. Just the four of them. Easy in each other's company, old friends.

When he finished relating his decisions, and the meeting with Mateo, Arnold declared, "I want in."

Sandrine tched. "I assume there is a request imbedded in that command of yours."

"It wasn't a command," Arnold replied. Smiling now. "More like a poor starving high school teacher down on bended knee."

Sandrine said, "There are so many things wrong with that statement I don't even know where to begin."

Colin said, "I'm not taking money. From anyone."

Arnold made a face. "There go my hopes of ever buying you that yacht you've been wanting."

"I never asked you for a boat," Sandrine replied. "Not to mention how I almost got seasick standing on the Wrightsville pier in that storm last year."

Colin went on, "The risk is too big. The thought of losing other people's savings gives me nightmares."

Celeste was the one who said, "I understand."

"So do I," Sandrine said. When Arnold did not speak, she elbowed him. Harder. "Tell him."

"Can I complain a little longer?"

"No."

Arnold heaved a mock sigh. "Okay, all right. But a guy can dream."

She nudged him again, only she was smiling now. "You don't watch out, you'll be dreaming on the sofa tonight."

"Another thing," Colin said. "It's time I start paying my own way. With the university. And my room and board. Everything. Actually, it's past time."

Arnold shook his head. "Not a good idea."

"Why not? I thought your donor, the CEO, would be delighted."

Sandrine replied, "It's a trust, Colin. The trust makes these decisions. We assume the lady herself knows. But we can't say for certain."

"The trust has committed to covering the cost of your education," Arnold agreed. "Accept it and move on."

When he looked ready to argue, Celeste said, "Wait until you're done, then donate to the trust."

"Now there's an idea," Sandrine said.

"Or directly to the school," Arnold said.

"I don't feel comfortable with that," Sandrine said. "It might seem like we've been pestering him for money."

Colin watched the argument flow back and forth, all three of the adults involved now. Talking about the most ethical way for him to remain involved with the academy. A future link that would last. Without damaging the personal side of their relationship.

Friends.

CHAPTER 38

It felt better than good, having a daily reason to ride the market's roller coaster. It took Colin's mind momentarily off the ongoing struggle with his studies. He had almost forgotten how much he enjoyed formulating his algorithms, keeping tabs on all the news feeds, inserting the raw data into his foundational structure, watching the computer generate a predicted outcome. He held himself to the one investment. A quarter of his total savings. The stock became trapped inside the summer doldrums for what seemed like forever. Even so, he remained content.

Another portion of those summer nights was given over to cartoons. Sort of.

He upgraded his television, hooked it to his sound system, took subscriptions to the paid channels, and watched every CGI animated feature from the previous six years. The Pixar projects in particular he found fascinating on a multitude of levels. Liam, the salesman who had helped Colin select his sound system and now introduced him to the latest jazz albums, turned out to be an online game freak. Colin bought all the games Liam recommended. Playing them proved only mildly entertaining. He never fully engaged with the imagined worlds, especially those created as battle zones. But the concepts *behind* the games he found fascinating. He joined several online chat rooms dedicated to the games' software designers. He became comfortable with their terminology and specialized methods: real-time rendering, immersive scene building, complex imagery, virtual reality, using stacked computer power backed up with cloud access to accelerate the creative process, building a rendering farm, twenty-four frames per second and what that meant on the engineering front. He especially loved the concept of interactive imagery, which relied on the gamer's choices to fully develop both scenic structure and point of view. The need for speed, both online access and the gamers' computing power.

He went to bed most nights almost happy.

Later that month, Colin returned from his morning swim to find Sofia Hernandez seated on the house's front steps. Beside her was an Asian girl. Because of her diminutive stature Colin first thought she was a child Sofia's age.

"Hi, Colin. This is Tiana."

The way the girl studied him, Colin realized with a start she was a teen. And despite her size, quite possibly older than he was. "Hi."

Tiana tilted her head, allowing a dark and silken river of hair to flow over one shoulder. "I'm waiting."

With that gesture, Colin realized she was also beautiful. "Excuse me?"

"The way Sofia talks about you, I want to watch you walk on water."

Sofia said, "Tiana studies history with me."

"Correction. I race to catch up. Which I hate."

"No she doesn't. Tiana starts at Duke in January."

"Congratulations."

Tiana surveyed his form: sandals and gym shorts and stained T-shirt and towel draped over his backpack. "Sofia also said you dressed so nice. No water walking, no elegant attire. How utterly disappointing."

"No it's not," Sofia said. To Colin, "She's been wanting to meet you since forever."

"Nice thought, terrible syntax."

Sofia leaned back. Happy. "Tiana is Hawaiian. Which is so cool."

"I know what you're thinking," Tiana said. "It's a long way to commute. Wow. So funny. And original."

Sofia said, "She lives with her aunt and uncle. They're nice, too."

"Actually . . ." He felt compelled to speak. But could only come up with, "Nothing."

"You have nothing to say, or nothing in your head?"

"Both."

"Wow. Is that the math nothing or the Zen nothing?"

"It's the I'm-not-even-going-to-try-and-keep-up-with-you nothing."

"I suppose we can give that an E for feeble effort." She bounded to her feet. "Colin, you may walk with me."

They went off campus the following afternoon, and then again two days later, and the day after that. And the next. Each time they made it a threesome. Colin actually enjoyed the jaunts with Sofia. She was gradually leaving the shadows behind, becoming an effusive girl with a magnetic smile. She and Tiana chattered away, allowing him to float contentedly, like a benevolent patron. He served as driver and let Sofia choose the films and afterward the two ladies argued over food. Their selections were limited to restaurants serving Mexican or Asian Pacific, which Sofia pretended to moan over, and then ate everything.

* * *

Finally, when he could stand it no longer, Colin phoned Mira.

He couldn't take this to Celeste. Why, he had no idea. But Mira was different. He needed to speak with her so badly he felt a leaden ache in his chest when the call went to voice mail. He asked her to call him back as soon as she had a chance. Then he went outside and paced. Around the quad. Again. He phoned once more. This time all he said was, "Please, Mira. Now. Please."

She called him twenty minutes later. "You can't complain about me being out of touch. You can't ask me about . . . anything." The last word emerged with a great explosion of breath.

"Mira, remember when you met me at Lenny's funeral?"

"Of course I remember." Her voice was flat as pounded tin. "How could I ever forget such a thing."

"When we walked afterward, I was terrified you'd ask me something. Anything that might force me to let go of everything I was struggling to hold back. But you knew, didn't you?" He gave that a beat. When she remained silent, he went on, "Remember what you talked to me about?"

"The internal vacuum." She almost whispered the words. "You losing your mom. Me, my twin."

"Understanding each other. Being connected in a way that makes no sense. And it helped me, Mira. So much."

"Is that why you called?"

"No. Well, yes. Sort of." He took a very hard breath. Expelled it with the words, "I've met a girl."

A silence, then, "What?"

"Her name is Tiana." Just putting the name out there in the atmosphere shot an electric zing through his heart. "I really, really like her."

"Does she like you?"

"I don't . . . I think so. Maybe. Yes."

"Well, Colin, this is great. Isn't it?"

"I guess so."

"You guess? What is there to guess about?"

"I'm so scared, Mira. I have no idea what to do or even to say around her. We've been out, I don't know, six times, counting our walks. And it's always been with Sofia."

"Who?"

"A girl here at Sojourn House. She introduced us."

Mira actually laughed. "You've been taking along a chaperone?"

"Sort of."

"Colin, honey, why?"

"I told you. I don't know what to say. How to act. Anything."

"Sweetie, here's a little news flash." Her voice shed a hundred thousand tons. The Mira of old emerged, almost musical in the way she continued, "If she has put up with six, count 'em six, chaperoned dates with you, the lady is hooked."

"You don't know that."

"Oh, yeah. I know." She paused for a chuckle. "Is she hot?"

"She's really pretty. Chinese Hawaiian pretty. She's also older than me. She'll be seventeen the first week in October."

Mira laughed again. "She's hanging out with you and the chaperone, six dates in . . . how long have you known her?"

"Three weeks almost."

"Colin, that lady is so totally into you it's not funny. Actually, it's hilarious. But you know what I mean."

"What do I *do*?"

"That's simple. Ask her out. Unchaperoned. See how it flies."

"What if I mess it up?" He rubbed the hand not holding his phone up and down his pant leg. Trying to erase the fear sweat that beaded everywhere. "What if I . . ."

"What if you fall in love."

He nodded. Unable to speak. Hating that it was out there in the open. And loving it.

"Colin, honey, that's what life is all about. Taking risks." Her voice fractured then. "Sometimes it doesn't work out, and there's nothing you can do about it. And when that happens, *if* it happens . . ."

"What?"

She sniffed. "I have to go. But do it, Colin. Now. Ask her out. And call me when you're done. I want to know everything."

So they had a date. The same as with Sofia, and totally different. Colin held to the same routine because at least that much he knew she would enjoy. He drove them to the Cineplex. They took in a film he couldn't remember a thing about two minutes after they left the cinema. He drove to Nori Asian Fusion on Market. She chatted with the same rapid-fire ease as when Sofia was present. There were no awkward pauses because Tiana did not allow them.

Fun.

Colin called Mira the instant he walked through the apartment door. Voice mail. He didn't want to leave a message, but on the third try he did just that. Thanked her. Said it went great. Thanked her again.

Mira never called him back.

The following week, Tiana announced, "My aunt and uncle want to meet you."

Colin had no experience with either dates or their parents, so he said, "Okay."

"Just like that, okay, the man says. Like he didn't avoid being alone with me for years."

"We just met."

"Whatever. They are inviting you to dinner on Saturday."

"Sure . . . Wait, that's the fifth of August."

"And once again the math genius is correct."

"I can't. I'm . . . I have plans."

She did not grow angry. Her face simply went blank. Like a wax mask. "You have another date."

"No, well, sort of. Not like you're thinking."

"How do you know what I'm thinking?"

"I'm going to a concert. With two friends. Chick Corea is playing at the Live Oak Bank Pavilion. I'd love to invite you, but it's been sold out for weeks."

"And these friends are . . ."

"Two guys, Tiana. One of them introduced me to jazz."

A flicker of life returned. "You like jazz?"

"*Like* isn't strong enough. It's a drug I take through my ears."

She almost smiled. "Then you and my uncle may actually have something to talk about. Then come before the concert. They need to understand you're as old as I claim."

"Tiana . . . I'm fifteen until September."

"And I'll turn seventeen three weeks later. Which is all they keep saying. They need to understand your years don't matter nearly as much as they think. Because you're already the most mature person I've ever met."

"Tiana, that's the nicest thing anyone has ever said about me."

"Well, it's true."

Colin decided now was the time to confess. "I've never been on a date before."

"Never?"

"Not with anyone. Now is when you tell me I'm doing great so far."

Tiana's elfin spirit returned. "A couple more nights without Mademoiselle Sofia, you might get a passing grade."

The Saturday finally came. A day of firsts. Colin's first concert. His first time in the Live Oak Bank Pavilion. His first sunset in the midst of live jazz.

His first kiss.

He made the afternoon a sort-of formal event. He could tell Tiana was disappointed with his plans and how excited he had remained all that week. She had visited his apartment twice, dropping in, or so she claimed, her tone idly curious. He had spent the week studying Chick Corea's music, preparing for the concert as best he could, not certain how it would actually be. Even with her there in his rooms, he could not completely let go of the wonder. Being treated as just another jazz enthusiast. Age no longer of any real importance. For that one night. Of course, Tiana felt his frisson of excitement. Her silent jealousy was almost beautiful. The second time she visited, on concert Saturday, she announced she was going back to Hawaii, her uncle had decided to take a last-minute holiday, they had snagged seats, they were leaving the next day. And here he was, so thrilled by everything that did not include her. Colin did his best to say how sorry he was, he would miss her, but even this sudden absence could not invade his anticipation. Tiana was clearly disappointed when the news did not make her the sole focus of his attention.

So he invited her to lunch. A spur of the moment thing. She settled on the Tomiko-San restaurant on Eastwood Road. He knew Tiana expected him to balk at the menu's prices, and showed confusion over his happy acceptance of everything she chose.

Which granted him the chance to say, "I know you don't like how I won't tell you about myself."

"Not at all," she sniffed. "I've always preferred my men to hold a bit of mystery. It adds . . ." She saw his face fall. "What?"

"I don't like being put in line with all your other men."

The restaurant was only about half full, the midafternoon crowd containing three birthday groups who filled the space with their clamor. The waitress had given them a side booth, large enough for six. Tiana slipped from the other bench and said, "Slide over."

When she was seated beside him, she said, "I was wrong. I meant it as a joke and it came out wrong. I apologize."

And just like that, everything was fine. So good, in fact, he told her about himself. It was the first time he had ever spoken with such ease. He talked through the entire meal. His only hard moment came when he described making those first crucial investments under the time pressure imposed by his father. United States Congressman Roger Eames. Tiana listened with wide-eyed solemnity, asking nothing, her only motions to eat and wave away the waitress whenever she approached.

When he finished, she rewarded him with a kiss. Her lips were spiced with the meal's flavors, chili and garlic and clove and her own special essence.

She pulled back, and he sat there with his eyes closed. Thinking that he would remember this moment for the rest of his life.

Colin followed her directions to a nice home on a big lot in Forest Hills. Their lunch had left him with little time to spare, but she still insisted he come in and meet them. At that point, Colin's ability to refuse her anything had evaporated. The house was large and modest at the same time, a quiet declaration of wealth and conservative values. Colin found himself thinking how his father would probably love the place. The couple fit their home, and were clearly concerned with this young man following Tiana inside. He spent a few moments going through the motions, then excused himself. Tiana followed him as far as the front stoop, where she kissed him again. Colin could feel the elders' gazes tracking him back to the car, keeping his feet from floating entirely free of the earth.

He took 74 west and made good time. Colin arrived well before the concert was scheduled to start. He spent a few moments strolling through the surrounding parkland, watching the people enjoying their fancy packed meals and iced buckets of wine. Beyond the open-air pavilion, the northeast arm of Cape Fear River sparkled in the afternoon light. When it was time, he joined the early throngs entering the stadium. A gentle breeze drifted through the hills forming a backdrop to the stage. Colin marveled at his internal state. The confusion and silent upheaval that had formed an almost constant presence was gone. In its place was a happy calm, a state so alien he could scarcely accept it as real, much less apply a name.

Angelo and Jaden arrived twenty minutes later. He exchanged greetings, nodded to their chatter, but the important thing, at least during that incredible moment, was how they treated him as one of them. A member of the clan. Colin related how he had spent the week. Studying the musician's history, his current album, the other musicians playing tonight. They showed no surprise whatsoever. Instead, it seemed to confirm what they already knew.

The band's method of introduction was both unique and spectacular. One by one the four senior band members stepped onto the stage and performed a solo. Frank Gambale on guitar. Jean-Luc Ponty on violin. Eric Marienthal on sax. Brian Blade on drums. Finally, the man himself stepped onto the stage. The applause was thunderous.

During their sixth song, it happened.

And it began with the memory of Tiana's kiss.

Colin found himself inspecting the internal void, the empty point at the center of his heart, and doing so without the customary pain. Instead, he breathed around it with an element of new comfort, a sensation so alien he had trouble accepting it as real. A number of others began gathering in that same space, people who cared for him and accepted him for who and what he was. Friends and now Tiana. Colin struggled to put a name to what he felt, and finally accepted the simple fact that he was becoming a man.

The band had played several cuts from their new album, *Lineage*. Corea then switched gears, and played a song from his earlier days with Stanley Clarke and their band Return to Forever. Soon as the first bar sounded, the crowd erupted. Colin felt a chill course through his entire body. The thrill of being surrounded by people so viscerally connected to him, the evening, the music . . . Amazing.

Midway through the song, Colin watched as his life's diverse fragments all flowed together. The conflict and resistance and effort that had defined the months . . .

Gone.

He listened to the music with a new intensity. The fact that some newly awakened portion of his brain now sang in harmony only heightened his ability to *hear*.

Each of these incredibly talented musicians, they played *in tandem*. They flowed *together*. And as a result, the music took on new power. It became greater. It formed . . .

Colin did not consciously organize his thoughts. They simply flowed, as clear and precise as the band members.

The mathematical exactness of jazz. The algorithmic principles. The cartoons. The music theory. The software engineering. The . . .

He listened to the music, while inwardly he shaped his own.

By the time the melody ended, he knew what he was going to do.

CHAPTER 39

It seemed to Colin as though an entirely new universe opened before him. Time and again he was reminded of the history surrounding the Hubble telescope, how astronomers responded to those first clear images. Flummoxed and thrilled in equal measure. Which was precisely how he felt.

The days swam by. He was vaguely aware of outside activities. Tiana and he spoke most afternoons, brief snippets of conversations, or so they felt to him afterward. She had contracted a virus of some sort and was not coming back with the others. She refused to go into details, and Colin did not press. Their shared moments were treasured breaks from the drama unfolding in his head. Gradually it enveloped even his apartment. The only way he could keep track of things was to create a wall graph, which grew to dominate the entire living room, and finally trailed its way around all the kitchen walls and then into the downstairs bedroom. It was like watching an octopus take over his home. A great beast of the deep unfolding its tentacles, writhing and hunting in mathematical splendor. Colin found it glorious and exhausting.

The upcoming presidential election formed a noisy backdrop that grew increasingly strident with every passing week. His father's face began to show up on the nightly news, Donald Trump's champion in North Carolina's coastal regions. Roger Eames both ran for reelection and extolled the man whose cause he had taken as his own.

Colin did his best to ignore it all. And failed.

The work on his new project grew tendrils against his will, binding him to people and society and today. He observed fracture lines growing along political leanings, first in what he read, then revealing themselves in far too many adult conversations. Ethan and Alexi's political stand grew increasingly rigid. Roland and Regina changed churches, a transition both refused to discuss. From Mira he heard almost nothing.

Gradually he became more confident riding his bike. Colin took to leaving his apartment soon after dawn, while the world and roads were still quiet. He loved discovering new routes, places, people. He found a riverside café frequented by cyclists, and from them heard about the River to Sea Bikeway, and how it connected to bikes-only paths extending throughout the city. On cloudless days he began leaving the academy before daybreak and riding east across the causeway, then north along Lumina, fourteen miles each way, halting at an empty public beach access where he sat in the cool sand and watched the day take hold. Seated there before the sapphire sea, listening to the music of breaking waves, Colin often thought he understood why his mother had remained so still, and returned home so content. Those days often held the season's only real sense of progress.

The last Friday in August, Tiana revealed she had a chest

infection. "They won't let me come back. The doctors are saying October. Maybe. At the earliest."

The previous week she had confessed to asthma. Bad enough to have hospitalized her several times as an infant. Colin replied, "You have to get well before you travel."

"But school!" She almost wailed, then had to stop and cough. "Term! Exams!" She hit another high note with, "Duke!"

"Your parents are right. You can't come now." He was studying the paper octopus when it struck him. "I have an idea."

When he finished telling her, Tiana rewarded him with silence, then, "Sofia insisted you were a knight in shining armor. Now I'm beginning to think she was right."

The week before term started, Colin hit a wall.

He invited Arnold over, carried by some vague hope that explaining what he was trying to accomplish might unplug things. Arnold and Sandrine had just returned from a month-long vacation in the High Sierras. Colin's suntanned adviser was thunderstruck by what he found upon entering. "Great heavens above!"

"This is nothing. You should see downstairs."

Arnold did a slow sweep of the walls. "What are you doing?"

"Nothing. What I'm *trying* to do, that's as far as I've gotten."

His two windows were now framed with the latest attempt at algorithms. "What are you trying, then?"

But the concept sounded so absurd, he could not draw out the words. So lame. All he said was, "I thought I had an idea to tie everything together. Maybe I was wrong."

"No." Arnold stepped back. "Physicists have been struggling with a unified field theory for over a generation. It doesn't mean they're wrong to try."

Colin reflected on that night at the concert. "I thought I was so close."

"Maybe you are." He studied his younger friend. "Walk away. That's the ticket. Leave it behind. Go do something fun."

"Fun. I remember hearing that word somewhere." He changed the subject then, and explained what he had in mind in regard to helping Tiana. Using his position as prefect to serve as Tiana's examiner. Take the exams to the lady, set up the time schedule according to school rules . . .

Arnold barely let him finish. "It's great. No, better than that. What's the word I'm looking for?"

"Stuck? Frozen in place? Screaming with frustration?"

"Look at the funny man. Seriously, Sandrine has spoken several times with Tiana's parents. They all agree she should not return yet. Between the diabetes and the chest infection . . ." Arnold caught sight of his expression. "You didn't know?"

"Only about her chest thing. She is super secretive."

"Something else you have in common. Word of advice. Let her tell you when she's ready. But yes, the lady has some health issues. And her parents want to keep her away for the semester. Which would hold her back from graduating and entering Duke. Until now." Arnold nodded. "You should come over, watch Sandrine do back flips. Tiana is one of her favorites."

Colin took to walking upstairs in the middle of the night when he woke and could not go back to sleep. Tracing the cardboard tentacles, looking for the missing elements that might draw him closer to his aims. Some mornings, as dawn painted faint grey strokes on his east-facing windows, Colin began to see the calculations and words and concepts take on an entirely different form. Like lines of color and tension, binding and struggling and writhing in something that might actually become beautiful, someday, when the frustration was not so overwhelming. As the mornings strengthened, almost mocking his weary state, he felt increasingly convinced that he was on the right track. At the deep level of bone and sinew and subconscious actions, he thought it was only a matter of time. And work. And many more mornings like this.

On the approach to the new academic year, Colin made an appointment to see Fremdt and Dean Sykes together. He struggled through an attempt to explain both the problem and his intended goal, but neither seemed to mind. They both gave their approval to his auditing the classes he had already taken for credit. Effectively losing the semester, and yet granting him the space to hear the lessons a second time, and continue searching for those hidden links. Colin left the meeting uncertain they actually understood, but grateful for the confidence they continued to show in his abilities.

And then, the third week of September, two days after his birthday, Mira called.

Their communications had grown so strained, and so one-sided, Colin had stopped phoning. He could not remember the last time they spoke. Nine weeks? Eleven? He demanded, "Why haven't you been in touch?"

"Same reason I didn't come home this summer. I've been hiding. Mostly."

"From what?"

Mira changed the subject with, "How have you been?"

"Struggling so hard I almost stopped missing you."

"That sounds serious."

"It is. Was. How are you, Mira?"

"Struggling, too. Can you come? I don't want to venture south. If I drive down, my folks . . ."

He understood. "When was the last time you saw your family?"

"I actually can't remember. Two months? Fifteen years?"

"I'm happy to drive up. How does tomorrow sound?"

"I didn't mean you had to drop everything."

"Mira, dropping everything would be a pleasure. Especially if it means seeing you again."

Her tone lightened immensely. "Tomorrow would be great."

And just like that, the silence and the distance were gone.

The trip on I-95 from Wilmington to Charlottesville took five hours. Colin broke it into manageable segments, stopping for coffee and a meal and another coffee, timing it so he missed Richmond's afternoon rush hour, then stopping at a Red Roof Inn long before dusk. The journey proved to be a mental elixir, drawing him ever farther from the intensity and frustration and barriers. Granting him a much-needed opportunity to view his objectives from a distance. Over dinner at the neighboring Denny's, Colin liked studying the book holding his notations. In reality most of his attention remained on the cardboard octopus back in his apartment. From such a distance as now, he could see the gaps more clearly. Realize the points where the smooth flow became bumpy, then halted altogether. By the time he returned to his motel room, Colin felt as though the answers to his questions had become a trifle clearer.

Mira met him at an off-campus coffee shop. It shared an upscale strip mall with the restaurant where she worked three nights each week. Mira did not look good. She had lost weight. Her beautiful raven hair hung limply down her back, like it had become defeated by whatever shadows she now carried. "I look awful, I know."

"What's wrong?"

"I thought I could just say it. You know, finally get it out after all this . . ." She took a ragged breath. "Lucas took an internship in Washington this summer."

He had no idea what to say. But she clearly expected

something, almost seemed to need it. So he tried, "That's a long time to be apart."

"He's been working as an aide to Nancy Pelosi." Her eyes filled with tears. "He's graduating early and taking a year off before law school so he can join her staff."

"In Washington?"

"Washington, San Francisco . . ." She examined him through a glaze of tears. "You really don't understand, do you?"

"Mira . . . I guess not."

"It's *Pelosi.*"

The way she spoke that name, the anger and loathing emblazoned on her features, almost frightened him.

Colin had the sudden impression of seeing Regina standing there, just behind Mira's chair. Roland's wife observed them from a safe distance, showing Colin the same timeless concern as when he had asked what was going on. He knew whatever he said might inflame Mira's tumult. Which was the last thing he wanted.

As if guided by Regina's silent wisdom, he reached across the table and took Mira's hand. "I've missed you."

"Did you hear what I just said?"

"Of course I did." He kept his voice as calm as possible. Almost flat. "So much of what is good in my life has come from meeting you. This incredibly beautiful girl who just plonked down beside me at the pool and started talking."

She sniffed. "I don't plonk. I never plonk."

"Everything has been so natural with you ever since. Your family have just pulled me in. The investments, the way my life has been shaped because of them. And you. Especially you."

She wiped her eyes. "They miss you almost more than me. Not quite. But close."

"I miss them too. Mira, no, I don't understand. I don't need to understand." He gave that a beat, then added, "Whatever you need, however I can help, I'm here."

From that point, her words came out in tight snippets. He

sensed she used the public place as a way of maintaining at least some control. He heard how she and Lucas had spent over a year arguing over his political direction. How Lucas had become increasingly involved in the current election. How he wanted to make this his life's work. How it reached the point where they simply could not discuss it any more. Not and stay together. Which they couldn't. Not if Lucas insisted . . .

"Of course," Colin said, when in truth he had no idea why these two people, so much in love and so right for each other, could not see their way past politics.

When she was done, he rose and walked her back to the boundary of her pristine campus. They hugged, and she thanked him, and he left more confused and uncertain than when he had arrived. As he drove away and rejoined the highway south, for the first time in what felt like months, he did not think of anything except his hurting friend.

Four nights later, two-thirty in the morning, Colin woke from a dream so terrifying he had no choice but call her. Soon as Mira answered, he started in. "Mira, I'm sorry. I know this isn't . . . I had to call."

"Colin?"

"I've had the worst dream. It wasn't just a dream, it was . . ."

"Colin, wait, I can't . . . All right. Tell me what's wrong."

"I dreamed about my mother."

There was a long pause. Somewhere in the distance, a police siren wailed. A chopper drummed softly from far overhead. When Mira came back on the line, every vestige of sleep was gone. "Has this happened before?"

"Not ever."

"Do you want to tell me about it?"

He didn't. The memory still scalded. But he needed to. "She called to me. Soon as I heard her voice, I knew who she was. She said . . ." A shuddering breath. "She said I owed her. I carried a lifetime debt. There was something I needed to do for her. I had to do it."

"Did she say what that was?"

"Live." Saying the word again relaunched his heart rate.

"Just that one word?"

"Yes. Then I woke up. Screamed my way out of bed, more like."

"Your mother told you that you had to live. That was the debt you owed her."

"Yes."

"Did you actually see her?"

"A shadow. Sort of a silhouette. But I knew it was her. Instantly. Almost before I heard her speak. I knew."

"Colin, if that had been me, if that had been . . ."

He spoke her brother's name for her. "Bacha."

"I would be skinless. I mean . . ."

"I know what you mean."

"I would have jumped right out of my skin and gone screaming into the night."

"That is how I feel. Exactly."

"Live," Mira said. "Wow. I'm sure glad I don't need to sleep anymore."

"I'm sorry to have called."

"No. You don't get to apologize." She breathed the word. *Live*. "What do you think it means?"

"I was hoping you could tell me."

A long pause, then, "What's the name of that wise woman who's helped you through the hard times?"

"Celeste Talbot."

"Maybe you should tell her about this."

"That's a great idea. I will."

"Only not just yet. You don't need all three of us to go into heebie-jeebie overdrive at three in the morning."

"No. I'll wait until tomorrow. Two doses of heebie-jeebies is enough for one night."

"Is that a smile I hear?"

"Not even close."

"Yeah, it is. You can't fool me."

"Good night, Mira. And thank you. So much. I've missed you."

"Go smile yourself back into bed. And, Colin . . ."

"What?"

She whispered the word again. Drawing it out low and deep, her version of a Boris Karloff moment. Almost laughing as she did so.

"Live."

The next morning, Colin hired an online research firm to identify his mother's maiden name and locate her burial place. If he had gained anything from the dream, it was a sense of having left this visit far too long.

The firm's response did not make for easy reading, as they included the formal burial announcement, which stated that Brenda Everett was survived by her loving parents and three sisters. No mention of either her husband or her son.

He might as well never have been born.

The following week, as Colin cycled back from the pool, a single solitary thread of an idea wove its way into the early morning air. He spent the rest of that day and much of the night following along, seeing just how far he could take it. And the answer was, quite far indeed.

Nine days later, Colin drove the hour north on Highway 17 to Jacksonville. He was extremely reluctant to break from his work. He worried that the visit might erase his growing sense of having finally found what he had been looking for. The grand theory of everything, or at least the concept that might drive all of the various fragments together. But this was the anniversary of his mother's death.

He parked at the boundary of the Mill Avenue Historic District and bought a bouquet from a neighborhood florist. The Everett family cemetery fronted onto Ward Avenue. The surrounding wrought iron fence had recently been painted, and an NC historic site placard explained that the family had settled its Jacksonville farm before the American Revolution. The quarter-acre property and its several dozen gravestones were sheltered by the two largest live oaks Colin had ever seen.

His mother's name was carved into a polished slab of granite the color of a winter sky. Just the name and dates. No benediction, no regret.

Colin stood surrounded by birdsong and a soft rush of wind through the overhead branches and the murmur of traffic. He found himself wondering what toll this loss had taken on his father. He suspected Roger Eames had carried the slow-burning internal fire since his own childhood. The main difference now was, Roger Eames had a purpose that fit his character. In any case, his father had loved this woman, and together they had granted him the gift of life. Colin lay his bouquet upon the grave and stepped back.

After a time he walked back to where the car waited, leaving her surrounded by the family who had no interest in whether he lived, or who he was becoming. Colin was both sad and fractured. And glad he had come.

But as he started to drive away, an idea struck. Colin cut off the motor and drew up Google maps on his phone. The nearest ocean access to Rocky Mount was Atlantic Beach. Colin knew instinctively this was not where his father would have taken them. His clearest memory from those shared moments was how empty the shoreline was, how few people, how the only sounds were the waves and the gulls.

He walked back to the same florist and bought a second bouquet, then drove east. Colin took the Emerald Isle bridge, then turned south, past the Islander Hotel and the Emerald

Isle Country Club, and parked in the lot fronting a sign that read simply, 'The Point'. He stripped off his shoes and socks and crossed the dunes, carrying the bouquet. The beach was almost empty, the sand soft and sparkling in the late afternoon sunlight. He stood there a long moment, surrounded by all that was no more. After a time, he lay the bouquet in the sand, on a spot he thought his mother might have loved.

Chapter 40

The third week in October, Colin ordered Mateo to cover his position in the market. The stock had not yet reached its zenith. But he knew it was time to clear the decks. There was no room for anything else now.

Later that same day, he took down the octopus.

It had become such a fixture in his home and life, the act carried an emotional impact, like he was wrenching at something deep. Even so, the sheets and his myriad calculations needed to come down. Now that he knew what was required, all he could see there on the walls were the absent elements. The portions that had remained incomplete. The calculations that were still just a bit off. Misguided, because he had not been sure where he was going. Now that he knew, it was easier to work from the flow behind his eyes. The power was gathering and muscling into proper shape. As a result, his cardboard designs belonged to a different era. Even so, removing the hand drawn sheets, being careful not to let the tape scar the paint, left his chest feeling hollow.

When he was done, he called Tiana.

They spoke almost every day, one or the other calling, sometimes connecting for a video chat, but often preferring to focus exclusively on voices, on words. Soon as Tiana spoke, she was there with him. In the room, an amorphous bundle of energy and grace, surrounding him with the island's spice. As if he listened to her voice and became partly transported the five thousand miles west. Away from the lingering doubts, the work that lay ahead, the day. He did not speak about what was happening. He had not yet told her anything. Mostly he listened. She was the one who needed a friend, an outlet, someone not chained to her room in Kailua, a neighborhood on Oahu that she both loved and loathed. She talked about her tutorials and the assignments that shaped her semester away. She talked about her parents and two older brothers, how their love and concern often threatened to stifle. How she was taking longer walks each day, and had started swimming again. Only by chance had he learned the family pool was a full twenty-five meters and framed by palms and blooming frangipani. Her family owned land, developed real estate, was all she had told him. Bored beyond reach by the mere mention. Or perhaps simply not wanting to allow that portion of her life to invade their space. Something he certainly understood. As he sat on the sofa and listened to her talk, staring at the tattered stack of posters on the table in front of him. Fifty-one pages in all.

Tiana ended their conversation the same way as always. "You're still coming? You haven't forgotten?"

"December the sixteenth. My flight is booked."

"That's years away. Come sooner." When he did not respond, she pressed, "Come now."

"I have classes too, remember?"

"Oh, pooh. You're their golden boy. You can get away with murder, much less a few lost days."

"More than a few."

"You don't miss me even a little bit."

"You're right. It's not a little bit. It's so much the numbers don't exist." He was smiling now, glad for the chance to look beyond the coming days. "And you know what happens when I arrive."

"You hold me and don't let go."

"I have been appointed your examiner—"

"Oh. That."

"And December the eighteenth, you sit down at your desk and I monitor you—"

"I love it when you talk nasty."

"And again on December the nineteenth."

"And then I get to show you my world."

"I can't wait."

"Then come *now.*"

"Good-bye, Tiana. Study hard. Stay well."

"You are such a strict prefect."

"I'm *your* prefect."

"And don't you forget it."

Colin needed another eight days to reach the point where he knew it was time to go public. The work was not done. Not by a mile. But just the same, he needed to start putting things in motion. He arranged to meet Roland and Aaron the next day. Downtown Wilmington, City Club, lunch, his treat. He wanted to discuss this out of their office, reduce their risk of being drawn away by some other pressing need. He hoped they would give them a table by the window, from where they could hopefully catch a glimpse of what Colin intended.

That evening he went for a walk. The air was cooled by a strong northerly wind, a presage of the season to come. The stars created a silver wash overhead. The surrounding port city's energy seemed incredibly intense, such that he only made it a hundred meters down the sidewalk before returning to the academy's main quad. He walked two circles, safe here, able to focus all his intent upon what was about to happen.

But when he returned inside, Roger Eames invaded his sheltered cove.

As Colin walked the central corridor, his father's voice reached out from the television room. Gripping Colin, hauling him into where he had no choice but to look. There he was, Roger Eames, standing by a podium decorated with over a dozen microphones, the sleeves to his dress shirt rolled up to reveal his muscular forearms. He gripped the podium. And he raged.

The sound of rasping anger took Colin straight back. Mentally he became the small child tucked away in the corner, waiting for the moment to flee upstairs, escaping the man's barely controlled wrath. Colin could not fully comprehend the words. Just like his worst childhood moments, watching his father take down the half-gallon of Maker's Mark and sit at the kitchen table and vent. Because that was precisely what he did now. He glared out over the crowd. And he vented.

Twice the camera pulled back, revealing the candidate his father was introducing, then sweeping over the audience. The crowd was massive. The arena stretched out in every direction, a dozen tiers of screaming people rising *behind* the stage. And so many of the faces shared his father's rage.

Colin had done his best to avoid even glancing at the rising tide of election fervor. He had refused to allow even a shred of his attention to be dragged away from the work at hand. What he saw now assaulted him like a physical blow. He could not fully take it all in. His father was not merely addressing this enormous crowd. He gave voice to their own fury. Each time he stopped, they waved a sea of posters: DRAIN THE SWAMP. LOCK HER UP. TRUMP FOR PRESIDENT.

MAKE AMERICA GREAT AGAIN. The printed words and the shrill cries and the ecstatic rage implanted on the sea of faces, they assaulted him.

His father looked straight at the camera and said something about the man who was going to change the way Washington did business, the next president of the United States. . . .

Colin forced himself to turn and walk unsteadily from the room.

Chapter 41

When he arrived at City Club the next day, Colin still bore the remnants of his father's invading force. Instead of launching into the topic at hand, he found himself trying to describe what it was like being assaulted as much by the crowd's reaction as seeing his father raging at the podium.

"Roger Eames has become one of Donald Trump's champions," Aaron said. "I must say the two seem made for each other."

"It is exactly what I saw." The crowd's excitement and fervor and anger reverberated through him and the room both. "I don't understand it."

"So many feel the same way." Roland was as somber as Colin had ever seen. "If Trump wins—"

"God forbid," Aaron said.

"If he does, and I think there is a very real likelihood that he will—"

"The polls say otherwise," Aaron said.

"The polls, the polls. I see so many people taking comfort from the polls," Roland replied. "And you know what I say to them? You are not looking at these crowds. The way they stand in line for hours, waiting for a chance to be in the same room with this man."

Aaron turned and looked out the window. Old Town Wilmington moved to a quiet and stately pace. The wind remained strong, the day reluctant to warm up despite the midday sun.

Roland went on, "And who are the people taking these polls? Do they come from among Trump's supporters? Hardly. They are young, multiracial, intelligent. They are from a different strata of society. A different *universe*."

Aaron sighed and remained silent.

"These pollsters, they claim to interview a diverse population. But do they ask what these people think of the pollsters themselves? Of course not. And what happens? The people who are being asked, the ones who know what these young intelligentsia think of their candidate? They lie. That's what. They lie."

"You don't know that," Aaron said, worried now.

"You wait. Two and a half weeks from now, we'll see how much I know."

Aaron shook his head. "I did not come to lunch for you to feed me nightmares."

"You wait," Roland repeated. "We may soon be talking a four-year nightmare."

Their conversation only heightened the clarity of Colin's recollection. "The way the crowd reacted. It scared me."

"It frightens me as well," Roland agreed.

Colin related the conversation from his last meeting with Mira, the schism between her and Lucas. "The way she said that congresswoman's name. Pelosi. Like it was poison."

Aaron asked, "Ethan and his family are pro-Trump?"

"I have avoided asking," Roland replied. "But I think, probably." He shook his head. "Lucas is heartbroken."

Colin asked, "Their relationship is over?"

"I fear so." He continued shaking his head. "They've been close since kindergarten. Now this."

"But *why*?"

"Ask a hundred people, get a hundred different reasons," Roland replied.

Colin knew he had to push that aside. "There's something important we need to discuss."

Roland attempted a smile. "More important than who will become our next president?"

"Business," Colin replied. "It can't wait."

The table's atmosphere brightened before he was more than a couple of sentences into his pitch. That was how he had viewed this lunch. He was pitching an idea and a vision both. He liked how they responded, the excitement his concept generated. It made the entire project seem more real, actually something he might achieve. He relished the way they drew him in, filling him with their enthusiasm as they ate and talked and planned.

For a moment at least, a single brief interlude there in the antebellum house in historic Wilmington, Colin found himself able to step away from the old shadows. And talk about a future he might actually claim as his own.

Finally, at long last, on the eighth of November, he was ready.

There was an exquisite sense of scaling new heights as he entered Dean Sykes's office with Roland and Aaron. Colin did not even try to tell himself it was just another meeting, a minuscule step along the way. For the first time, he felt as though the summit was visible. Far in the distance, along a rocky path with a steep climb up ahead. But the fact that he could catch the smallest glimpse, name his objective, gave him chills.

The receptionist apologized that Dr. Sykes was running a few minutes late. She ushered them into the conference room and asked if they wanted coffee. When the door closed, Aaron told Colin, "My esteemed partner should not even be here."

"Nonsense," Roland replied. "I have every right."

"Tell him to leave," Aaron said. "He will only muddy the waters."

"I am trapped inside the case of the century," Roland said, studying a pair of shoji screens adorning the side wall, displaying a lake and a fisherman casting a net. "I need a break. Court is adjourned for the day. The halls of justice are too burdened with election day fever to get any work done."

"Hardly a proper reason for him invading my legal space," Aaron said. He thunked his briefcase on the table, popped the catches, and drew out a pair of files. "As your legal adviser, I must insist you kick out the interloper while there's still time."

Colin swiveled his chair in tight quarter-circles, infected by the same excitement as the attorneys. "The appointment with Electronic Arts is set?"

"Ten o'clock tomorrow," Roland said.

Aaron looked horrified. "Don't you *dare* suggest you intend to show up there as well."

"Can't," Roland said. "Depositions."

Aaron gave a mock sigh of relief. "Remind me to send the judge flowers."

Colin asked, "And the patents? The incorporation?"

"Everything will be in place by close of business today, or heads will roll among my firm's junior staff," Aaron assured him.

The dean knocked and entered, wearing what Colin thought was the same silver-grey outfit as the first time they had met. The only change was a string of pearls one shade darker than her jacket. "What is this?"

"Aaron Weisfeld and Roland Perez," Aaron said. "Attorneys representing our client, Colin Eames. A pleasure, Dr. Sykes."

Her crystal gaze shifted from one to the next as she seated herself. "And the reason for this meeting is . . ."

"Our client has begun work on a new process, one with unique ramifications. We need to clarify his situation in regard to the university."

"I don't follow."

"He is a student. He is in the process of developing something with, how shall I put it . . ."

"Far-reaching potential," Roland offered from Colin's other side.

"Quite so. Because he is matriculated here, we thought it best to advise you of this situation in advance of our moving forward."

Colin endured another moment of the woman's laser-tight gaze. Strong as his father's, but even here in this room with its gathering tension, there was no threat. No danger. The only emotion he felt was . . .

Exhilaration.

The dean rose to her feet. "Just one moment."

Dr. Sykes left the room. They waited. Five minutes later, the receptionist returned to ask a second time if they wanted coffee, water, anything. Five more minutes became ten, then fifteen. Aaron answered e-mails and texts on his phone. Roland received a call and slipped to the room's far corner. Colin took out his leather-bound notebook and studied his notes. The last five pages contained a list of everything he needed to have in place before tomorrow's meeting. He had gone over the points so often he read them in his sleep. Those dreams always ended the same, with him discovering a sixth page filled with everything he had forgotten to do. Colin never slept after that dream. He flipped the notebook's pages back to the algorithms that formed his breakthrough. His project felt alive, as if he held something pulsing in his hands. Each shift of the page caused another silent bolt of power to course through him.

When Sykes finally returned, she was accompanied by a technician who managed to cross the room without glancing up from his texting. "Okay, they're ready in Chapel Hill. Where are the controls?"

"On the credenza's top shelf, last time I checked."

The techie slid open the shoji screens, revealing a wall-size monitor. He fiddled with the console until it came to life, revealing an African American man with the rumpled air of a professor facing severe time pressure. He eyed the trio seated at the table's far end as Sykes said, "This is Dr. Lassiter, dean of Chapel Hill's law school." She took the same chair as before, then said, "You may proceed."

"As I was saying, my esteemed colleague has developed a new process—"

"Based upon his studies here at UNC Wilmington and Chapel Hill," Sykes interjected.

"Partly, madam. That is most certainly *partly* the case. Which is why we are meeting."

Lassiter spoke for the first time. "What is the nature of the student's invention?"

Roland said, "Nothing has been said about an invention."

He used his chin as a pointer. "Aaron Weisfeld I know. You are?"

Aaron replied, "Roland Perez has been serving as my client's principal attorney for a number of years."

Lassiter switched his angry gaze to Colin. "How old are you?"

"That is beside the point," Roland replied.

"Our client turned sixteen in September," Aaron replied.

"And he has been a student with us since . . ."

Sykes replied, "Three years and counting."

Colin said, "Actually I took my first classes when I was still twelve."

Lassiter blinked but did not respond.

Aaron went on, "We are here simply to clarify one point, and then we will take no more of your valuable time."

"And that is?"

"The University of North Carolina system holds no claim to anything my client has developed," Aaron said. "Now or at any point in the future."

Sykes said, "That is an extremely complicated issue."

"Only if you choose to make it so," Aaron replied.

Roland said, "You have students graduate from here and go on to make their marks in any number of disciplines. Do you seek to retain a segment of their future earnings?"

"This is different in the extreme," Sykes said.

"How so?"

"Colin Eames has been researching and designing this project while still a student," Lassiter said.

"Again, Counselor, there are any number of precedents to counter that argument."

"He used university labs—"

"Correction. All his work on this specific project was accomplished off campus."

"No labs," Colin said. "Not ever."

Roland added, "In any case, our client has signed no agreement regarding ownership of research he might have conducted while here."

"It is implied," Lassiter said.

"Courts of law frown upon implied ownership," Aaron countered. "Again, the precedents go back years."

"Decades," Roland agreed.

"We need time to discuss the implications," Lassiter said.

Aaron nodded. "Very well. In that case, my client hereby resigns from the university."

Sykes blanched. She asked Colin, "You would just walk away?"

Roland answered for him. "Only if you force him to do so."

Sykes continued to glare at Colin. "You feel no loyalty toward the institution that has granted you so much?"

"On the contrary," Roland said. "Our client has established a trust. One that will act in conjunction with the group that has financed his time here. If his project proves as successful as we anticipate, ten percent of all earnings from this project will go toward future scholarships."

Sykes leaned back. Lifted her gaze to the ceiling. Then, "Give us a moment."

"Most certainly." Aaron opened his file, drew out several sets of documents. "In case you might find this helpful, we have drawn up the agreement covering today's conversation."

CHAPTER 42

It was midafternoon by the time they left. Both men were late for other appointments, so Colin drove back to the academy. He did his best to ignore the lines standing outside polling stations, the myriad of placards planted along the sidewalks, the people who waved posters overhead and shouted at passing cars. His father's name repeatedly appeared, seeking to break through and invade.

There were even placards planted in front of the academy's entrance, and more than a dozen stuck in the quad's lawn, some for Hillary, others Trump. Colin fled inside, locked his apartment door for the first time in forever, turned on his stereo, and tried to lose himself in jazz. But for once not even Keith Jarrett was welcome. The music formed a discordant echo, a refrain that did not fit with the day. Colin left the house, and to his relief saw a groundskeeper pulling up the placards and carrying them away.

He paced.

When it was time for dinner, Colin re-entered and filled a plate. One of the student computers blared early East Coast returns; they were supposed to be blanked out until polls closed. But this was Sojourn House, which meant one of the students had managed to circumvent the blocks. He retreated back into his apartment, locked the door, and ate because his body needed food. He might as well have dined on sawdust.

Mira's phone went straight to voice mail; she had warned him she would be unreachable for days, perhaps centuries, if the bad guys won. Only half joking when she said it. Tiana was off doing something important with her family. She had probably tried to tell him what it was, but just then Colin could not remember. He left the house and did another circuit of the main quad, then called Celeste. "I know you're watching the returns and I don't want to disturb."

"That's the perfect way to describe my current state of mind," she replied. "Disturbed."

"Are people always so angry around election time? I can't remember. Or maybe I just blanked it out."

"No, this is definitely different."

"I don't get it. I mean, Trump—"

"It's not the man himself. Well, it is. But he's only one small part of a much bigger picture."

"I don't understand."

There was a long pause. Then, "Hang on a second."

He heard the background television go quiet. When she returned he said, "If you want to stay watching the returns—"

"They'll be going on for hours yet. It's good to step away." A chair squeaked as she eased her way down. "You remember back a while, you and I talked about something when you were hurting."

He nodded to the gathering night. "Identity."

"There you go. I may be seeing society at large through the lens of my adolescent patients. But I don't think so. You want to hear my take?"

"I love it when you talk with me like this. Like we're two adults."

"Because that's exactly what we are. All right. Here goes, for what it's worth. I think our nation at large is facing the same identity crisis. Change is striking people fast and hard, coming from all sides. Challenging the way they see themselves and their position within society. Changing the very fabric of their culture. What they see on the news, how the world is becoming too complex to understand, it makes them wonder if they even belong."

Colin settled on a bench facing across the quad toward the entrance. Headlights flashed through the curved archway, tight glimpses of the world beyond his haven. "They're angry."

"Anger and fear and confusion make for a potent mix. It drives people to extremes, both on the left and the right. They look for people with answers. *Simple* answers. Black or white. Friend or enemy." She went quiet for a time, then, "You still there?"

"Listening. Thinking."

"People watch these returns, they wait to see whether their candidate won. That's all they're after. What they're not seeing is why the other side is treating them like they're the enemy. And that is the threat. The real outcome of an identity crisis on a national scale."

"I've heard my father use that word. Enemy. I try to avoid listening. But for the past couple of weeks he's been everywhere."

"He's become Trump's man around here, no question. But that's not the point. Well, it may be for you. But not for society at large. You see?"

"He represents them."

"He expresses their anger. He binds them together on a perilous level."

Hearing her speak with such clarity finally released him

from the day's tension. He realized he was exhausted. So tired he did not know if he could stand. "I'd better go."

But Celeste did not seem to hear him. "It's not about this election. Not really. Whether their man wins tonight is not the real issue. I'm not saying it isn't important, because it is. But even if he loses and Hillary wins, this crisis is not going away. People don't see that yet. But they will. They'd better. Because if they don't . . ."

He listened to the night for a time, then, "What?"

"I've said enough. More than, I expect."

"Tell me."

"Another time. You go get some rest." She tried for a brighter tone, and failed. "And good luck tomorrow. I'll be thinking about you."

CHAPTER 43

The next morning Colin left his apartment at half past seven. His appointment in the Research Triangle Park was not scheduled to begin until eleven, and Aaron had warned him that senior executives at Electronic Arts were notorious for running late. But Colin had insisted the conference room be reserved for a full hour before the meeting was officially scheduled. He had no problem with waiting.

As he made his way through the slow and sullen traffic south of Raleigh, he felt as though he had been aiming for this since the day he entered the academy. Whatever happened, however the meeting went, today marked the start of a new life chapter.

He stopped for a late breakfast at the RTP's Metro Diner, and at a quarter to ten he turned in to the Electronic Arts' Research Triangle campus.

EA's headquarters were located in Redland, California. But after the acquisition that fueled Colin's first investment foray, EA began growing its North Carolina operations to include the new-games division and R&D. The company resided in a series of glass and steel structures that reflected the autumn sun like copper crowns. When Colin entered the main lobby, Liam rose from his seat by the rear wall. Colin greeted the technician with, "Thanks so much for helping out."

"Hey, you're offering me serious bucks to spend a vacation day inside every gamer's idea of Mecca." Liam glanced around, tugging on his goatee. "I should probably pay you."

"You have the equipment?"

"In the van. I brought extras of everything, just in case."

"Then you've already earned your keep." Colin started toward the reception desk. "Let me see if they're ready for us to set up."

Liam had also brought a flatbed cart, which meant they were able to transfer everything in just two trips. Once Colin had finished deciding on the positioning, he slipped over to the exterior windows and flipped through his notes for today's meeting. He did not read so much as check off a mental list of what needed to be covered. The building overlooked a broad swath of old-growth forest just beginning to show off its autumn finery.

Liam interrupted his musings with, "Ready to test."

But as Colin turned around, he became trapped by what he saw there in the interior windows.

The conference room's glass wall overlooked the largest office space he had ever seen. The ceiling was well over twenty feet high and showed exposed beams painted like a springtime forest. There had to be a hundred people working and milling about the central space. More. Some of the employees showed a triumphant glee. They traded high-fives, they shouted their laughter.

And overlaid upon this tableau was his reflection.

He had grown another couple of inches, and the swimming and cycling had resulted in a defined musculature. His new outfit, purchased for this occasion, consisted of a midnight blue silk-and-cotton knit shirt and matching gabardine trousers.

But that was not what captured his attention.

The majority of those employees did their best to ignore the exultant Trump supporters. One man gesticulated in anger, his face creased by very real pain, while a large group stood or sat around him, watching in genuine sorrow.

They were hurting. And they were afraid.

Liam stepped up beside him. "Looks like the winning team are in the minority out there."

Colin nodded, but that was not what he was thinking. He knew that feeling. He understood what it meant to feel threatened by the outside world. To have their sense of control and perspective stripped away. Shattering their vision of today, and even worse, their hope for a certain kind of tomorrow.

Only these were adults.

Those who shone with the triumph of an unexpected win effectively ignored everyone else. Colin could almost see the divide growing between these two groups. As for those whose candidate had lost, Colin ached for them. They had assumed their childhood vulnerability was behind them. They had assumed their adult world was going to follow the course they desired. But the previous day's election had proved them wrong.

Liam said, "Shame you've got to go on today."

Colin turned away. "It is what it is."

He had found his means of bonding. The same as with the frightened Sojourn House children. He did not have answers. His birthright counted him among those on the winning side. But he personally stood with the others. He understood their fear, their helpless anger.

It was not the method he might have preferred, forging a bond through sharing a divided world. But it would have to do.

Chapter 44

Aaron arrived just as Liam completed the final adjustments. He offered Colin a glum greeting, accepted the introduction to Liam, seated himself, sighed, and began texting. Ten minutes later, the EA team gradually entered and slumped into chairs and worked their phones. There was no chatter. Even the victorious staffer was silent. Only one person bothered to greet Colin at all.

Five minutes passed, then Chad Helms arrived. The former CEO of Legend Inc. was now head of EA's Research Triangle divisions. Chad was accompanied by the only EA team member wearing a suit, a narrow-faced man in his forties with square-rimmed glasses. "Hello, Aaron."

"Morning, Jerry." To Colin, "Jerry Lieberman, EA's head of legal."

The in-house attorney nodded to Colin. "Shame about the day."

"Can't be helped." This from Chad. He waved his hand at the others. "You wanted our top gamers. Okay, we're here. Now what?"

Colin rose, but instead of heading for the front of the

room he made his way slowly around the table, introducing himself, taking in each of their names. Five men, two women, all in their twenties, all fiercely intelligent, all skeptical, but at least by the time he finished their attention was fully on him.

Colin began, "The announcement of every new EA game generates huge excitement. EA has become the trademark brand for fully immersive experiences. Gamers do not simply play an EA game. They *become* it. They *identify* with their online avatar. The evidence backing this claim is clear enough. Last year, EA sold just over fifty million dollars' worth of personalized merchandise. Seventy dollars for a T-shirt, ninety for a plastic avatar, all bearing the weaponry and name of the individual user. A brilliant move, by the way."

The in-house attorney asked Chad, "Is that public knowledge?"

"Probably not," Chad replied. "Doesn't matter. Go on."

"I say it's time to expand this identity issue," Colin went on. "Take it to the next level. With music."

Liam was seated on a stool in the rear corner, headphones around his neck, with two portable tables in front of him supporting the control gear. At a nod from Colin, he switched on the massive flat-screen monitor they had positioned at the front of the room. There was a similar screen imbedded into the wall. But Colin had decided on this move so as to maintain full control of his pitch.

He stepped to one side and said, "This is a proprietary system I have developed."

"The patents are now in place," Aaron confirmed.

"This is a two-part algorithm for game music. It is totally new. There is nothing like it anywhere. As most or all of you know, formulas like this are called interactive or parallel algorithms, because they restructure results based upon incoming data. If we ever manage to create fully independent and free-thinking computers, these interactive algorithms will most likely form the design basis."

Colin fit his hands around the top two-thirds of the screen. "This is the foundational structure. It and all the primary data remain in the EA central computer." He shifted down to the bottom third. "This secondary algorithm is inserted into the player's own system. The result—"

"Hang on a second." Chad Helms leaned forward. "You're that kid."

Jerry from Legal said, "Who?"

"Sure, I heard rumors about you." To the others, "Some Wilmington kid caught wind of the Legend buyout a week before the rest of the market."

"They weren't rumors," Aaron said. "And it wasn't a week. It was a month and a half."

Troy, the senior techie said, "I always thought those stories were bogus."

"Far from it," Aaron said. "Not only did he set up a long position on Legend stock in advance of the first press notice, he did it twice."

And just like that, they were with him.

Colin said, "You licensed Legend's original hit, *Barsoom*, to UNC's software engineering department. So that's what we're using for today's demonstration." This time, Liam beat him to it, throwing up the game's logo before Colin looked his way. "If you'll open the laptops in front of you, and please select your avatars. We are going to play level seven."

"My absolute favorite." Troy again. "I grew up wanting to move permanently to level seven."

Everyone except Jerry showed glimmers of genuine excitement, even Chad. The in-house attorney asked, "Do I have to play?"

"Absolutely not." Troy again. "Same goes for you, Aaron. Can't allow Legal to slow us down."

Aaron said, "And here I was, all ready to go battle hot."

"That's not even a term," Chad said. "I'm head wizard, and nobody gets to complain even a little bit."

When they were all named and suited and armored and weaponed, Colin halted them with, "Before we start, you need a heads-up on what is about to happen. Each of you have now become a musical instrument. The melody I've chosen is a fusion jazz number from Steve Winwood's latest album called *Mozambique*. I'm using this without proper licensing. This is for today's trial run only. This song works because it follows a number of very distinct musical patterns, with unique solo opportunities for each instrument. Which means in this demonstration, each of you can stand out."

Troy asked, "How?"

"By taking the lead in a battle."

Two of the other gamers leaned back, breathed in unison, "Oh. Wow."

Chad asked, "What?"

One of the women said, "This. Is. Totally. Wild."

"If it works," Troy said.

Chad said, "As your boss, I am demanding that somebody bring me up to speed."

Colin said, "Even before the player arrives, his or her musical signature will announce their appearance. As they enter into the next arena, the tempo will heighten, and the team's structure will determine the music's complexity, arrangement, and solos. If or when an avatar dies, their instrument vanishes from the melody."

Troy asked, "And the opposition?"

"If you confront a different team, there will be discord between the opposing groups. When one team triumphs, this is reflected in the music. If your team faces game-based opposition, which happens here in level seven, the enemy forms new percussion instruments."

"Enough talk," Chad said. "Players, weapons hot."

Colin gave them half an hour. Long enough for the entire interior window to become jammed with faces. Long enough for the door to be flung open and several dozen more employees to pry themselves into the room. Long enough for the eight players to scream as loud as the music, which was very loud indeed. Liam's four speakers, set in the room's corners, caused the walls to shiver. Colin had only prepared the one song. It ran through five times. He doubted any of them noticed.

Gradually Colin took a mental step away from the excitement, the thrill of getting this right, and observed the faces now lining the interior windows. The hostility and fear and friction and divide were gone now, at least temporarily. He studied the excited employees, saw the electric thrill of being on the cutting edge of something new, and wondered what it might feel like. To heal wounds of a more permanent nature.

If only.

At a sign to Liam, the room went quiet, the screens blank. Colin waited through a very noisy protest, even from Chad. When they were all watching him once again, he said, "Now imagine this with your own proprietary music."

Aaron said, "You sign the bands. You arrange the music. You own *everything*."

"You set up a different type of music for each of the game's levels," Colin said.

"Classical, jazz, rock, electronic, rap, entirely your decision," Aaron said.

Colin and Aaron had not worked on any sort of tag team, but now that it was happening, Colin found it almost natural. "The groups put out albums based on the game's music. Timed to your new game's global release."

"You have the rights to create arena events," Aaron said. "Open up the ticket sales to online gamers before the general public."

"The higher their game status, the sooner they can buy, the closer to the stage they sit."

"You're taking the idea of music ownership and control to a totally new level," Aaron said.

Chad looked around the table. "I'd say we're definitely interested."

"We have *got* to have this," Troy said.

"This adds a totally new dimension." This from the senior lady.

"I've got chills," said one of the guys plastered to the interior wall. "And I didn't even play."

"Dibs on the next go," said another onlooker.

Chad's attorney leaned forward so as to find Aaron. "We are talking proprietary? Exclusive ownership?"

"We *might* be," Aaron replied. "Given the proper incentives."

Chad rapped the table. "All right, team. Session's over. Time for numbers. Grinding of teeth. Shouting of voices. Wrestling of contracts."

"Boring." Troy rose, walked over, offered Colin his hand. "When I came in this morning, I thought I was looking at the end of the world."

"Not even close," Colin replied. "But I'm glad I could brighten your day."

CHAPTER 45

An hour later, as they were packing up the room, Liam told him, "Excuse me for bluntness, but I want in."

Colin did not pretend to misunderstand. His body felt weightless with fatigue, a gentle torpor that added its own sweet music to pushing the trolley back toward the elevator. A number of people in the huge central room stopped what they were doing and waved. As the elevator doors closed, Colin saw smiles.

He turned to Liam and said, "I was hoping you might feel that way."

"Why didn't you say something?"

"I wanted to see how it went today."

"From my corner seat, I'd say it went exceedingly well."

Colin nodded agreement. Aaron was still upstairs. The two attorneys had moved to the lawyer's office to discuss details. But as it stood, EA was taking an exclusive interest in Colin's project, with an eye to also buying Lyric Incorporated, Colin's newly formed company. They were offering stock and a percentage of both the new game's purchase price and online monthly rental charges. The details of this were now in Aaron's hands. But whatever the outcome, as long as the product performed as shown, the deal was as good as done.

Colin said, "You're sure you want to go with a start-up?"

"And give up my future career in retail management? Absolutely."

The elevator doors opened and they pushed the trolley through the lobby. Once they were outdoors, Colin said, "I have no idea what shape this will all take. But if it's possible, you're in."

He helped load the equipment, waved Liam's van away, then entered his own car and left the campus. The two-hour drive back to Wilmington proved the perfect elixir. Tiana would be waiting for his call. But first he needed to try to come to terms with what had just taken place.

All that work. All those months and years of study. Of *trying*.

On a whim, he passed through Wilmington and took Salisbury Street all the way to Wrightsville Beach. He parked in the East Greensboro Street beach access lot and used the restroom to change into swim trunks, sweatshirt, and slaps. Middle of a November weekday afternoon, with a northeasterly wind blowing, he had the beach almost to himself. He walked away from the Johnnie Mercers Fishing Pier, face into the wind, going nowhere, breathing deep. Free.

He found himself studying a trio of smaller oceanfront homes and wondered if he might buy one, settle within walking distance of the place his mother had loved. The feeling was oddly mixed, as if such thoughts were invasive.

The EA software team were two months from completing work on their new game's raw foundational software, perhaps longer. Colin could not start work until that happened. He would spend the weeks writing up his thesis and . . .

He spun about and walked swiftly back to the car, doing his best to push the tomorrows away.

When he was back behind the wheel, he took out his phone and called Tiana.

She answered with, "How did it go?"

"It's done."

"What do you mean, done? Done, as in they liked it?"

"Done, as in they're buying exclusive rights. They want me on board as well."

"But you're still coming, yes?"

"Of course."

"I mean, it's great that you're now the game world's latest kazillionaire. But it's not official until we celebrate."

"I'm leaving tomorrow."

That silenced her. "What?"

He had only just decided. "I want to get away. Can I come?"

"Colin, of course . . ." She sighed. "I hate to do this, especially now."

"What?"

"My parents are raising a stink. They think I'm too young, they think *you're* too young, they want me to wait until after college and fall in love with a good little Chinese Hawaiian. . . ."

"They don't want me to stay with you."

"For a few days, I could force them, you know, with battle axes and heavy armor. But is that what we want?"

"No."

"I'm so very, very sorry."

"For what? They're your parents. Do you still want me to come?"

She breathed long, soft, and replied, "More than you can ever imagine."

"Oh, I can imagine a lot. Believe me. More than a lot."

"What are we going to do?"

"Nothing's changed. I'm still coming."

"Tomorrow? Really?"

"If I can get a ticket. What's the nicest hotel close to you?"

A pause, then, "The Kahala. But it's super expensive."

"You just said it yourself. I'm about to become super rich. Will you call them and book me a room?"

She laughed, a sound like silver bells. "For how long?"

"Tell them . . . through the new year."

"Colin . . . that's six weeks!"

"Call them now, okay?" He fished in his pocket. "Here's my card number. Do you have a pen?"

Another chiming of those silver bells. "You're serious!"

"You were the one who said we needed to celebrate. I'll call you as soon as I've booked a ticket." Now he was the one to laugh. "I hope I don't freak out or something. I've never flown before."

"You're kidding."

"No, Tiana. This is a season of firsts."

"I can't believe you've never been on a plane!"

"I've never been anywhere."

Until now.